DEATH OF A
SWAGMAN

ARTHUR W. UPFIELD

DEATH OF A SWAGMAN

A Scribner Crime Classic

COLLIER BOOKS
MACMILLAN PUBLISHING COMPANY
NEW YORK

Collier Books
Macmillan Publishing Company
866 Third Avenue, New York, NY 10022
Collier Macmillan Canada, Inc.

ISBN 0-684-17482-0

First Scribner Crime Classic/Collier Edition 1986

10 9 8 7 6

Printed in the United States of America

Contents

DEATH OF A
SWAGMAN

I. Merino and Rose Marie

No GANGS of yellow men carrying earth and rubble in baskets, no human chains of men and women, and even children, carrying stones in their lacerated arms, built these Walls of China. No Emperor Ch'in Shih Huang Ti directed over a million men to raise this extraordinary barrier lying athwart the bushlands in the southwest corner of the state of New South Wales, Australia. The colour of the country is reddish-brown, and upon this reddish-brown land the soft fingers of the wind built a wall of snow-white sand some twelve miles long, three quarters of a mile wide, and several hundred feet high. No one knows when the wind laboured so mightily to build the barrier, and no one knows who named it the Walls of China.

On the morning of October twelfth, in an isolated hut lying within the sunrise shadow of the Walls of China, the body of a stockman named George Kendall was found in circumstances plainly indicating the act of homicide. Following the discovery, Detective Sergeant Redman arrived at Merino, a township three miles westward of the hut and the Walls of China. With him in the car were an official photographer and a fingerprint expert. They were driven to the police station in the view of the excited inhabitants, and in the course of the investigations questioned and cross-questioned all and sundry, took pictures of the scene of the crime, and reproduced fingerprints left on objects within the hut.

The arrival of Detective Inspector Bonaparte, alias Bony to his friends, was in marked contrast. His interest had been captured by the statements and documents compiled by Detective Sergeant Redman, and he drifted into Merino six weeks later in the guise of a stockman seeking a job. At the only hotel he drank a couple of deep-nosers with the licensee, then parked himself on the bench on the hotel veranda and proceeded to smoke his atrociously made cigarettes.

Merino is not markedly dissimilar to any one of a dozen townships in the western half of New South Wales. Its houses, its shops and government buildings are all constructed with wood, iron, and tin, the only effort to beautify the place having been the planting of pepper trees along the borders of the one formed street. Some eighty people only, including children, were living in Merino when Bony visited the place to look into the death of George Kendall.

What had induced the early settlers to found this township puzzled even Bony, who was interested in such matters. Its site was on the eastern slope of a vast land swell. The track from Mildura came over the broad summit and down the gentle slope for more than a mile, to pass the two large dams which supplied the township with water and the windmill which provided water for travelling stock. Then it continued for another mile until it reached the western and upper end of the main street. Passing through the township, it flowed gently down the slope for two miles, where it turned sharply to the north as though aware that it could never flow up and over the great rampart of snow-white sand known as the Walls of China.

The hotel was the first abode to welcome the traveller from Mildura. From its veranda Bony was able to gaze down the street, between the twin lines of pepper trees, and to view the huge range of sand humped and peaked in snowy whiteness in this land of red-brown earth.

Opposite the hotel stood the corrugated iron garage owned, as announced by red lettering on a white board above the open front, by an Alfred Jason who also was a wheelwright and a funeral director. His house stood next to the garage and farther back from the street, and then came the compound in which was the police station, the stables and the small lockup, and a small building which had done service as the morgue. Still lower down the street could be seen the fronts of shops and, on Bony's side, the school and the church.

Business was stagnant during any afternoon before five o'clock. It would seem that no one drank at the hotel bar during this period of stagnation, for Bony had the hotel bench to himself save for the flies and a town dog. Now and then he did see within the garage one and sometimes two men, and could hear their labours with hammer and drill on iron. The afternoon was warm, and he had walked far this day, so he composed his body full length along the bench, his swag for a headrest, and fell asleep before deciding whether to make himself known to the senior police officer or to work incognito on what he was sure was going to be an interesting investigation.

He was awakened by a hard voice asking:

"What's your name?"

Like that of his maternal progenitors, Bony's mind became fully active the instant he awoke, but he opened only one eye to observe a uniformed policeman looking down at him with disapproval writ plainly on his large, weather-tinted face.

"Hey! You! What's your name?"

"Robert Burns," replied Bony languidly, before yawning. "Go away."

The request to depart was less irritating than the yawn to the policeman, who ranked as sergeant. The irritation was excusable, because Sergeant Marshall had never become accustomed to being yawned at by stockmen who slept during daylight hours on benches outside licensed premises. Like most big men when angry, he spoke softly, saying:

"Ho! Good as any other name, I suppose. Where d'you come from?"

Bony did not alter his recumbent position, but he closed the open eye and said with extreme boredom in his voice:

"Way down in Texas."

The sergeant waxed sarcastic.

"Is that so?" he purred. "And where do you think you will be going to?"

To which Bony replied with a lilt:

"To my Little Grey Home in the West."

"So . . . so . . . so!"

The front of Bony's shirt was gathered into a huge fist and he was lifted bodily to his feet. The sergeant's bulk dwarfed him. The sergeant's face was faintly purple. There was acid in his voice.

"As an American friend of mine used to say: 'You've said a

mouthful, bo.' I will even accompany you to your Little Grey Home in the West. Better bring your swag along. You might find it cold tonight."

Bony wanted to laugh, but refrained.

With the upper part of his left arm held in a human vise, he was urged across the street to the police station. In the office a mounted constable, minus his tunic, was pounding on a typewriter.

"Keep your eye on this bird of passage, Gleeson," ordered the sergeant. The constable rose to stand beside the prisoner. His superior sat down at his own desk and wrote rapidly on an official form. Then he said, glaring at the prisoner:

"You are charged with (a) giving fictitious answers to lawful questions put to you by a police officer, (b) being insolent to a police officer in the execution of his duty, (c) having no visible means of support, and (d) loitering outside a licensed premises. Lock him up, Gleeson."

"There is an *e* within brackets, but I had better not mention it," Bony could not resist pointing out, and then another human vise became clamped about his upper arm and he was conducted to his Little Grey Home in the West—one of two whitewashed cells in a building at the rear of the station. The constable heard him laughing as he walked back to his typewriter.

Bony sat down on the broad bench which was to serve him as a bed. His clear blue eyes were bright and twinkling with mirth whilst his long slim fingers made a cigarette with the usual hump in the middle. Often had he been threatened with arrest by policemen who knew him only as a station hand, but this was the first time he had been jailed. His cell was clean but too warm for comfort beneath its iron roof, the air being admitted only through a barred opening in the roof and a small iron grill in the door. Philosophically he placed his swag of blankets and personal gear as a pillow for his head and laid himself along the bench and smoked whilst pondering on the advisability or otherwise of presenting his credentials to Sergeant Marshall. Eventually he would have to do so, but there were certain advantages to be gained by remaining incognito for a week or so.

He had been there for probably an hour when he heard movement outside the door as though a box or case was being placed against it. A moment later he saw a pair of large dark grey eyes gazing steadily at him through the grill. He swung his feet off the bench and sat up.

"Good afternoon," he said politely.

The steady appraisal continued, enquiring, assessing. Bony stood, whereupon a sweetly childish voice ordered:

"Stay where you are or I'll go away."

"Very well," he said, and sat down. "Now that you have looked me over carefully enough, what do you think of me?"

"What's your name?" came the faint echo of the sergeant's voice.

"Bony."

"Bony! Bony what?"

"Just Bony. Everyone calls me Bony. What's yours?"

"I am Rose Marie. I'm eight. My father's a policeman."

"Rose Marie," Bony repeated slowly. "What a beautiful name."

"It is not my real name, you know," said the person outside the door. "My real name's Florence. Young Mr. Jason gave me the Rose Marie name. I'm glad you like it. I do too. So does Miss Leylan. What are you in there for?"

"For having been rude to a sergeant of police."

"Oh! That'll be my father. He doesn't like people being rude to him. Why were you rude?"

Bony related the incident of his arrest. Then he chuckled, and unexpectedly, the person outside laughed with him.

"You didn't mean to be rude, did you?" she asked, swiftly serious.

"No, of course not. I was trying only to be funny. Can I come to the door now? It's rather difficult talking to you from here."

"You may."

The large grey eyes examined him with even greater interest when his face was brought to the level of the door grill, and, noticing the trickles of perspiration on his dark brown face, Rose Marie said with anxiety in her voice:

"Is it hot in there?"

"Somewhat," replied Bony ruefully. "How is it out there?"

"Goodo here in the shade. Would you like a drink of tea?"

He nodded, his eyes wide with anticipation and containing a little admiration, too, for Rose Marie's hair was light brown and

13

appeared to reflect the sunlight beyond the shadow of the jail. Her face was perfectly oval and fresh and winsome.

"I'll make you a drink of tea," she told him solemnly. "You must be thirsty in that hot old place. You wait! The kettle's boiling. I promised Mother I'd have it boiling time she got back from the parsonage. I won't be long."

He watched her cross to the rear of the station, noted her firm carriage and steady, deliberate walk, a mannerism of movement evidently copied from her father. There in the sunlight her hair gleamed, the twin plaits hanging down her back seemingly ropes of new gold. Ten minutes later he watched her return, carrying a tray covered with a cloth. She set it down upon the ground before the door, and then looked up at him and said firmly:

"You promise not to run away when I open the door?"

"I do, of course."

"Cross your fingers properly and promise out loud. Hold them up so's I can see."

Bony obeyed and loudly promised not to run away, with the mental reservation that he would not run away for a hundred pounds.

There was no further hesitation. Rose Marie moved the box from the door, slipped the heavy bolt, opened the door wide, and came in with her tray.

"My!" she exclaimed, putting the tray down on the bench. "It is hot in here."

"Better leave the door open," he suggested. "All the hot air will then go outside. Oh! I see that you have brought two cups and saucers. And cake! You know, Rose Marie, you are being very kind. Are you going to have tea with me?"

They sat one at each end of the bench with the tea tray between them. With the precision of an experienced hostess the little girl set out her service of cups and saucers and plates. They had two blue stripes round their edges, and the tea cosy of white wool also had its two blue stripes. It was evidently not the first occasion that Rose Marie had served afternoon tea.

"Do you take milk and sugar?" she asked, imitating her mother.

"Thank you . . . and one spoonful of sugar, please," replied

14

the delighted Bony, the romantic heart of him charmed. "You have a very nice tea set."

"Yes, it is pretty. I knitted the cosy all by myself to match the cups and things. Miss Leylan says I made four mistakes in knitting the cosy. Can you see them?"

"No, I can't. I don't see any mistakes. Miss Leylan must have been mistaken. Who is she?"

"She comes in from Wattle Creek Station three times a week to our school. She's the sewing mistress. I like her. Her brother owns Wattle Creek Station, you know. Will you say grace, please? Mr. and Mrs. James always do when they take tea with Mother."

"I expect you could say it better than I could," he said hastily, adding when the grace had been offered: "Who are Mr. and Mrs. James?"

"The minister and his wife. Mr. James is a lazy good-for-nothing dreamer, and Mrs. James is a slave to him. That's what Mother says. Someday I am going to ask Mr. James what he dreams about. Have you any brothers and sisters? I haven't. I heard Mrs. James tell Mrs. Lacey one day it was a shame that I didn't have a brother or a sister."

Bony shook his head. He was conscious that his table manners were being studied, and hoped they were being approved.

"No, I have no brothers and sisters," he told her, and related how he had been found, when a small baby, in the shade of a sandalwood tree in the far north of Queensland, and how he had found a mother in the matron of the mission station to which he had been taken. That produced many questions which had to be answered, for was she not his hostess and he her guest? His reward was the information that Constable Gleeson was her father's only assistant, that the elder Mr. Jason was considered "queer" by her mother, and by her father the essence of a broken-down actor, and that young Mr. Jason had given her the name of Rose Marie because he loved her and was going to marry her someday, and that Detective Sergeant Redman who had come from Sydney was "just a horrid man."

"Why was he horrid?" Bony asked, his own impression of Redman not having been good.

"'Cos he was." Grey eyes flashed and the twin hair plaits

were jerked into a half swing. "He was ever so rude to young Mr. Jason. I hate the big police bully. That's what Mr. Gleeson calls him. I told Sergeant Redman that I hated him too, and he only laughed at me. When I told young Mr. Jason about that he said he would punch Sergeant Redman on the nose if he came here again and laughed at me."

"But why was Sergeant Redman rude to your young Mr. Jason?" Bony pressed.

"'Cos young Mr. Jason wouldn't answer all his silly old questions."

"Oh! What were the questions about, do you know?"

"About poor Mr. Kendall who was killed out in his hut."

"But young Mr. Jason wouldn't know anything about that, would he?"

"Of course he didn't," Rose Marie replied indignantly. "No one liked that beastly Sergeant Redman. My father didn't like him. Father said, said—well, you promise not to tell?"

Bony nodded.

"Cross your fingers," he was ordered.

Obediently fingers were crossed to the satisfaction of half-angry grey eyes. Then gravely and slowly she said:

"My father said that Sergeant Redman might be good at pinching thieves down in Sydney, but he was no damn use here in the bush on a murder case. I heard him tell Mother so."

Bony fought to conceal the shock he received, and with feigned horror he asked:

"Did your father say 'damn'?"

"Oh yes. He often does when he's upset." Footsteps fell on the ground beyond the open door, and Rose Marie murmured: "Oh my!"

Into the doorframe loomed the figure of Sergeant Marshall. He stepped inside the cell. Rose Marie's little body stiffened into rigidity. Her hands were clasped and nursed in her lap, and over her face spread an expression of resignation, such as she had probably seen on her mother's face when she waited for a storm to break.

Bony stood up. From regarding his daughter, Sergeant Marshall surveyed the evidence of the afternoon tea. The silence was tense. Then the policeman exploded.

"Well I'm damned!" he said, giving a pause between each word.
Bony said stiffly, although his eyes were twinkling:

"I must remind you, Sergeant, that you are in the presence of a lady."

II. Bony Gets Down to Business

"FLORENCE, take those things back to the house and then wait for me at the office."

"Yes, Father."

Sergeant Marshall stood stiffly erect, his red neck swelling over the collar of his tunic, reminding Bony of an iguana when annoyed. The sergeant's eyes were like small brown pebbles in his brick-red face. With delightful dignity Rose Marie stood up and, with wilful unhaste, collected the afternoon tea service, picked up her tray, and sedately marched out, her back like a gun barrel, the plaits of her hair giving never a swing. Then, to Bony, the sergeant said:

"Good job you never made a break for it."

"You know, it never occurred to me," Bony told him gravely. "By the way, I have a letter for you."

The sergeant's eyes narrowed, and his big body appeared to rise slightly on springs in his feet. Other than that he made no move. Neither did he speak whilst watching Bony unstrap his swag, although he was prepared to jump should the prisoner produce a weapon. His eyes narrowed still more when he was presented with a plain foolscap envelope inscribed with his rank, name, and station.

It was an instruction to him from the chief of his division to render all assistance to Detective Inspector Napoleon Bonaparte, who was reopening the investigation into the death of one George Kendall.

Still stiffly erect, the sergeant returned the instruction to its envelope and the envelope to a tunic pocket. His eyes were no longer small, nor was his face brick-red—it had become distinctly purple. Redman had told him one evening in the office something about this Napoleon Bonaparte and had said he was the best detective Queensland, or any other state, had ever produced. And he, Richard Marshall, first class sergeant, and the senior officer of Merino Police District, had locked him up, because . . . He fought for composure.

"I regret having charged you, sir. I didn't know," he said.

"Of course you did not know me, Sergeant," Bony agreed soothingly. "Sit down here beside me and let us talk of cabbages and murders and things."

"But . . . but . . . oh, my aunt!"

"What is the matter with your aunt?" mildly enquired Bony, and then smiled.

That smile cracked the ice. Slowly, over the big man's face spread a grin. He snapped his fingers and began to laugh, low and full of sound. Bony's gaze fell to the task of rolling yet another cigarette, and the sergeant became less sure of his superior's amiability because he could not now see his face. He said soberly:

"Bit of a shock, sir, finding that I've locked up a D.I. Took you for an ordinary half . . . ordinary station hand. Saw you were a stranger in my district, and we want the station compound fence painted and the cells whitewashed."

"Labour scarce?"

"No, but money is."

"And so you arrest a stranger in this town, get him seven or fourteen days' detention from a tame justice, and then provide him with a paintpot and -brush, three meals and a bed, and two bob a day to take over to the hotel half an hour before closing time. I know. Good idea. The swagman gets a nice rest and the taxpayer has a drop of his money saved out of the ocean he provides. But you want always to be sure not to lock up police inspectors or union bosses. Supposing I had been a boss of the painters' union?"

"That would have been too bad—for the union boss."

"How so?"

"He would have had to do a spot of work or . . ."

"Or what?"

"Sweat it out in this cell."

"He would have worked," Bony predicted confidently. "Better

work than sweat. I've had some. And don't you go and scold Rose Marie. She saved my life with her tea and cake. Yes, I thought that your compound fence needed paint, and the work will provide me with a reason for being closely connected with the police. When do you intend to arraign me before the local magistrate?"

"Eh!" barked the sergeant.

"When will you prosecute me for (a) giving fictitious answers to lawful questions, et cetera, including (b), (c), and (d) in brackets?"

Two vertical lines became painted between the sergeant's brows. He said slowly:

"You are not being serious, sir?"

"I am. You will press all those charges. I will plead guilty. You will whisper a word or two beforehand into the ear of the beak, asking him to give me fourteen days without the option of paying a fine. I will lodge here, eat of your wife's excellent cooking—your own physical condition indicates that she is an excellent cook—and every evening at five-thirty you will pay me two shillings to spend over at the hotel. And then instead of everyone holding their horses in the presence of Detective Inspector Napoleon Bonaparte, they will talk quite freely with poor old Bony, the latest victim of the ber-lasted per-leece. It is all so simple."

"But what if the heads hear about it?"

"Who's running this show, you or me?"

"I'm supposed to be running the district," said the sergeant, a little doubtfully.

"You are. And I am running the investigation into the death of George Kendall. We are going to run in harness, and run well. The killing of Kendall wasn't just a plain, ordinary booze and bash murder. Had it been, I would not have been here talking to you. There are aspects of this Kendall case which not only interest me but which escaped Detective Sergeant Redman, and, I venture to say, you too. For instance, you and Detective Sergeant Redman, and others, all believe that Kendall was murdered in his hut at Sandy Flat on Wattle Creek Station. I have not been there, ever, and I know that he was not murdered in his stockman's hut."

19

"But the blood on the floor . . . all about the body!" objected the sergeant.

"Oh, of course, the blood!" Bony agreed calmly. "Was anything done to establish if it was human blood or animal blood? Of course not. The man lay in blood, and therefore it must be his own blood. So say Detective Sergeant Redman, and you, and others. Well, well, you may all be forgiven for believing that Kendall lay in his own blood. But first things first. Allow me to introduce myself.

"I never arrive on the scene of a crime, the investigation of which has baffled others, in my official uniform and accompanied by experts. Most often no one outside police circles knows what I am and cares less who I am. Publicity is not my forte. As my own chief commissioner says so very often that repetition of the obvious wearies me, I am not a policeman's bootlace. But, Marshall, I am an investigator of violent crime in Australia's outback, and so here I am about to investigate the murder of Stockman Kendall. Now tell me about yourself. How long have you been stationed at this district?"

"Eleven years, sir. A long time."

"You didn't get along too well with Redman, did you?"

"Well, no, sir, I didn't," Marshall admitted, his mind instantly imagining an adverse report on him by Detective Sergeant Redman. "You see——"

Bony cut in, nodding his head to emphasize his words:

"Yes, I know. Redman is a city man. He has no bush background like you and me, and Gleeson, your constable. Redman is used to bullying loose women and thieves for information. We have had to use our grey matter and obtain our information from such things as sand and birds and tracks. Wouldn't you like a change to a big town or city?"

The sergeant nodded. Bony's clear blue eyes and dark face seemed to blaze into a flashing smile and the other man's mind began simultaneously to work along two lines of thought: one that this famous detective could do him an extra good turn, and the other that only now was this half-caste revealing to him his personality. It was as though the smile was a lamp showing a man seen previously only in half-light. When Bony continued speaking, even his voice changed from the soft tones of his

20

mother's people to the fuller cadences of the white man used to authority. Already Sergeant Marshall was becoming aware of his own mental inferiority. Bony was saying:

"Men like you who have gained valuable administrative ability are often the forgotten men of our state's police force. You see, I have so often worked pleasurably with men of your type. You rule over an area of thousands of square miles, efficiently and without fuss, and the chiefs are unconcerned because you do not give them concern. I have given my chief a great deal of concern —and I am an inspector. I will show you how to earn promotion and a move to a large town or city where Rose Marie will receive a better chance in life. You and I will co-operate. We understand each other and the bushlands. Redman was a child—here in our element."

Marshall again nodded.

"That's so," he agreed.

"Well, then, if you can spare the time from your labours of collating statistics about sheep and fences and bores and income taxes and stinkweed and other stupid things not connected with the maintenance of law and order, I would like you to relate to me in chronological sequence the facts concerning this murder. Redman's report is full enough, but I want to hear the story from a bushman."

"All right, sir. The statistics can wait."

"Er . . . before you begin. Would you be good enough to call me Bony. It can be Robert Burns's nickname . . . save me from all Scotchmen! Everyone calls me Bony, from my children up to my chief commissioner."

Once more Marshall nodded. Bony was an entirely new experience, one that he was liking more and more. He cleared his throat.

"On the night of October eleventh last," he began, "there was held in the local hall a social and dance. In point of attendance it was most successful, nearly all the townsfolk being present as well as most of the people from the surrounding stations. Mrs. James, the wife of the parson, organized it in aid of the aborigines' missions, and what she organizes is always successful.

"There was also present George Kendall, a stockman employed on Wattle Creek Station, riding from a hut at a place

21

called Sandy Flat, which is three miles due east of Merino and close against the Walls of China.

"Nothing much of Kendall's history is known. He came east from the Darling River stations about a year ago, and got the job on Wattle Creek Station. He was unmarried and apparently had no relatives. His age was thought to be about thirty-eight. He was a good stockman. He never drank to excess, and he never gave us any trouble. He was a gambler but a poor sportsman, and his movements that night of October eleventh were as follows:

"He arrived in town about six o'clock and checked in at the hotel for the night. He stabled his horse at the rear of the hotel, had a few drinks at the bar, then had dinner, and later was seen by Gleeson, my constable, playing poker for matches with three travellers. He left the hotel with the licensee and his wife to go to the function at the hall, which was timed to begin at eight, the social part lasting till ten o'clock and the dancing continuing from then until midnight."

"There was a full moon that night?" Bony interposed.

"Yes, there was a moon . . . a full moon, I think."

"What were the weather conditions?"

"Clear sky and a wind."

"About what was the velocity of the wind?"

"I couldn't say. It was not a very strong wind that night."

"No matter. I can find that out later. Proceed."

"I didn't go to the chivoo," Marshall continued. "I had a lot of those damn-fool statistics to make up, but Gleeson was on duty outside the hall and he had my permission to have a dance or two. He's fairly popular, although you wouldn't think so to look at him. Stickler for duty and regulations is Mounted Constable Gleeson.

"My wife went with Florence, our daughter. According to Gleeson, the chivoo was in full swing by eight o'clock. There was a whist drive going on in one portion of the hall, and children's games were being conducted in another part. Now and then someone would be asked to go to the stage and give a song or a recitation.

"When Kendall entered the hall there was a children's game called musical chairs going on. Our girl was in this game. Mrs. James was playing the music on a piano and every time she stopped all the children rushed to the chairs, one of which was always short. Kendall went over to watch the game when Mrs. James was playing and the children were dancing round the chairs in a circle. It turns out that when Mrs. James stopped playing Florence hesitated in choosing a chair to run to, and Kendall pushed her with unnecessary violence so that she tripped and fell.

"The child wasn't hurt, but the push ruined her chance of getting a chair. The parson, Mr. Llewellyn James, admonished Kendall for interfering, and Kendall said: 'I was only showing the silly brat what chair to go to.' With that, young Jason, the son of the garage proprietor, walked up to Kendall, put a hammer lock on him, and marched him from the hall. There might have been a fight outside had not Gleeson been there, and to Gleeson Kendall explained that what had happened was an accident. Young Jason went back inside, and after Gleeson had a few words with him, Kendall went in.

"At half past nine they served supper, and after supper all the children left and the dancing began. It was when Gleeson was having a dance that Kendall said something to young Jason and they went quietly out and fought in an adjacent allotment. Result: Kendall won and Jason wasn't seen again that night.

"The following morning when the hotel yardman went to the stables he found that Kendall's horse had been taken away, and the maid found that Kendall's room had not been occupied by him. Late in the morning of October twelfth the owner of Wattle Creek Station and one of his hands called at the hut at Sandy Flat to leave rations for Kendall. They found his horse standing saddled and bridled outside the horse paddock gate, and they found Kendall lying dead on the floor of his hut. The table was upturned and a chair broken. The door was closed. Kendall lay in a pool of blood, and the doctor who examined the body said that he had been killed with a blunt instrument, his skull badly smashed."

"What time did you arrive on the scene?" Bony asked.

"Four minutes to two o'clock."

"What were the weather conditions?"

"Fine with a wind blowing from the west."

"How strong was the wind?"

23

"Medium strength, I suppose. Not strong, but strong enough to blow dust."

"Are there any aborigines in the district?"

"Yes, but they come and go. When here they usually camp at Wattle Creek."

"Where were they when Kendall was murdered?" asked Bony.

"They were camped on Wattle Creek . . . below the home-stead."

"None of them was outside the hall that night of the social?"

"No. Two were brought across to Sandy Flat the next day to see if they could pick up any tracks, but by that time the wind had erased any tracks made by Kendall. As I told you, you will have to see the place to know why they failed. By the way, would you mind telling me why you are so sure that Kendall wasn't killed inside the hut?"

When answering, Bony smiled.

"I will tell you something, but not everything," he said. "I discovered the fact from one of the photographs taken by the police photographer who accompanied Redman, the picture of the front of the hut."

"I saw that one. I saw no evidence."

"Neither did Redman. But I did. It is why I am here."

"But what . . . ?"

"One day I'll show you the evidence in that picture, without which I would not have consented to undertake this investigation." Noticing Marshall's raised brows, Bony expanded into grandiloquence. "You see, Sergeant, I have never permitted myself to stultify my brain with common murders. I pick and choose my cases, not for their simplicity but for unusual circumstances governing them. My superiors often argue about my attitude, and speak of discipline and matters which fail to interest me. Sometimes they threaten to sack me, and that interests me even less. Look at me. You see—what? Come, tell me."

Marshall hesitated, and Bony continued:

"You see a half-caste, a detective inspector in a state police department. I was given the chance of a good education by a saint, the matron of a mission station to which I was taken when abandoned as a baby. I passed from a state school to a high school, thence to the Brisbane University, where I won my Master of

Arts degree, and so proved once again, if proof is necessary, that the Australian half-caste is not a kind of kangaroo. But I had to conquer greater obstacles than social prejudice. I had to conquer, and still have to conquer, the almost irresistible power of the Australian bush over those who belong to it.

"You have been in the bush long enough to have felt that power yourself, and you are a white man. A similar power is exercised over seafaring men by the sea, but it is not so strong as this power of the bush. The only counterpower preventing me from surrendering to it is pride, with a capital P, and faith in myself. Without pride in my scholastic attainments and pride in my success as a crime investigator, the bush would have had its way with me. My record is unblemished by failure, and that is behind the faith in myself. Once I fail to solve a crime mystery, such as this Kendall case, I lose that faith in myself which holds me up with head high, and the great Detective Inspector Napoleon Bonaparte becomes Bony the half-caste nomad.

"I will not consent to investigate cheap and tawdry crimes of violence, or lesser crimes, because my pride would be shamed, and also I have to avoid the fear of failure which might grow in me did I accept any and every assignment given to me by my department. Once I forget that I am a police inspector and a Master of Arts, I become Bony the half-caste, and the banshee of the bush would lure me back and down into its secret cave, to stand naked before it and to recognize it as my lord and master."

There followed a period of silence which Marshall did not find to his liking. His long career as a policeman in the interior of Australia had made him *au fait* with the growing problem of the half-caste and the half-caste's problems. He knew that they were invariably intelligent, and that it was their white fathers who were degraded and not their black mothers, members of what was originally one of the most moral races that ever walked this earth. He was aware, too, that these people were mentally capable of competing successfully with the white man—were they but given the chance. Again came the voice of the man who had fought and suffered and triumphed over two enemies—the bush and the white man.

"Kendall was killed and the bush concealed the tracks of his murderer from you and Redman and any other white man and black man who might try to wrest the secret from the bush. But it will not baffle me, because I am neither wholly black nor white. I have the white man's reasoning powers and the black man's eyesight and knowledge of the bush. The bush will give up its secrets to me. I believe that someone is calling for you."

The sergeant stood up. Both men heard the rapid footsteps approaching the lockup. In those steps was urgency. Bony rose to his feet too. Then Constable Gleeson appeared at the door.

He spoke quietly, evenly.

"Mrs. Fanning is over at the office, Sergeant," he said. "She states that she went over to her father's hut to take him a roasted joint and that he is lying on the floor. She says that there is blood on the floor under his head, and that she thinks he is dead."

"We'll go along, Gleeson," Marshall said, astonishingly unruffled. He turned to Bony, to see him with his two hands together and the finger tips touching his chin. He looked quite happy.

"It sounds promising," Bony murmured.

"Might be anything. Will you come?" Marshall asked.

"You forget that I am a prisoner of the state, but you could conscript me as a tracker," suggested the detective. "Introduce me to Constable Gleeson, and then we will all take a little walk."

III. *The Book of the Bush*

WHEN Edward Bennett was found dead in his hut on the outskirts of Merino he was in his eighty-second year. In life he had looked but sixty, in death, according to the Merino undertaker, he looked—well, not peaceful.

He had retired from hard work at the age of seventy. His wife was dead. His only daughter, married to the Merino butcher, had said to her willing husband: "Father must come and live with us." Old Bennett had snorted: "Be hanged if I will. I'm living in me own house." Both father and daughter had said the same thing fifty times during the succeeding twelve years.

Old Bennett had built himself a two-roomed hut on the eastern edge of Merino, some few hundred yards north of the hall, which stood on the lower left-hand corner of the street. It faced over the vast area of country falling gently away toward the Walls of China, which appeared to be much higher than actually they were; and it was, therefore, less than a quarter of a mile from the post office, where the ancient battler had drawn his old-age pension.

Mrs. Fanning, the dead man's daughter, having been told to go home, the police party proceeded down the street and collected Dr. Scott. With the doctor between the two policemen, and Bony walking behind, they passed two stores, several houses, the school and the hall, thence to gain a quite distinct path hardened by the dead man's feet when walking to and from his hut.

"I expected it," the doctor was saying. "Told him he was liable to drop dead any minute, and advised him to listen to his daughter and go and live with her."

"Have you examined him recently?" Marshall asked.

"Only last week. He then said: 'I'm not going to ruddy well be petted and pampered like a prize bull. When I die, I'll drop like an old working bullock.' And that, Sergeant, is probably how he died."

Bony did not enter the hut with the policeman and the doctor. To him, of primary interest was this open page of the Book of the Bush awaiting his reading. What had happened within the hut could be established by the three men who had entered it. What may have happened outside the hut no one of them could establish better than he.

The hut was built of four-gallon petrol tins cut open and nailed as sheets to the wood framework. The roof was of stouter corrugated iron. The building was enclosed by a brushwood fence in which was only one low gate in the front. Inside the fence old Bennett had laid the rubble of termite nests, watered and tramped it level, and thereafter had kept it swept. It was almost cement-hard, and the tracks of no man would be registered upon it.

Outside the fence the ground was sandy and in places ribbled like the sand left by the receding tide. From the gate the sandy path wound away towards the hall, which it skirted to gain the street, and on it were the old man's tracks and those of his daughter, who was wearing rubber-soled canvas shoes.

No two persons walk alike. The gait of every human being

27

varies from normal when he is sick, and again when his mind is controlled by strong emotion. An aborigine, on seeing the imprint of a naked foot, will seldom fail to name the owner of the foot that made it.

Following a request put forward by Bony, the police party had proceeded to the hut away from the path, and Bony, who walked after the three men, had automatically observed their boot prints on the ground. Until this case was concluded he would not fail to recognize the tracks made by those three men, as well as those made by Mrs. Fanning, any more than he would fail to recognize their faces.

Marshall wore boots size nine. He walked with greater pressure on the back of his heels than elsewhere, and the toes were almost in alignment with the heels. The heel pressure denoted a man who had received rigorous training. The doctor's toes were placed outward a little more than that of the average white man, and the greatest pressure was at the extreme tip of the toes, denoting an eager, easily excited mind. His stride was much shorter than that of the sergeant, indicating that he was a short man or fat. In point of fact he was shortish and tubby. Gleeson placed his toes slightly inward, with greatest pressure on the inside of the soles. His boot print could have been made by any stockman accustomed to much horse riding, but the regularity of his stride and directness of his walk indicated a man trained in a military camp—in his case the police barracks. His boot size was seven: the doctor's size was eight.

The dead man's tracks were on the path beside which were the holes made by the point of his stick. His tracks were all about the outside of the fence, to and from the wood heap and the office. There were, too, the tracks made by a heavy dog from the right forepaw of which a toenail was missing, and those made by a lighter-weight dog. At present there was only one dog barking from beyond the wood heap. There were the tracks made by the feet of two white children whose visit had been made at the shortest two days previously.

Bony walked over to the wood heap to visit the dog, which was chained to an old iron cistern.

It was a kelpie. She greeted him vociferously, straining at her chain at his approach, and inviting him with impatience to loose her. She was the lightweight dog, obviously owned by old Bennett, and there was no need to examine her right forepaw to find all the nails there. The dog minus the toenail was probably a town dog who had come to visit her.

Bony returned to the path by skirting the rear of the hut. He made a second tour, the hut forming the hub, he the rim of the wheel fifty yards out from the hub. Now he was walking on his toes, his body bent slightly forward, his head hunched between his shoulders and his face tilted downward, his blue eyes never still as they surveyed that narrow section of the Book of the Bush over which he passed. And when almost opposite the gate, he read a sentence on this page of the book which immediately aroused his interest.

As has been stated, the hut faced toward the east across three miles of open country falling gently to the foot of the Walls of China. Here and there were giant red claypans, hard as cement and separated by narrow ridges of loose sand. Old man saltbush were scattered about the scene, and widely spaced water gutters, now dry, zigzagged slightly to the northeast to join a dry creek bordered by box trees.

What aroused Bony's interest was a peculiar mark made on a sand ridge separating two claypans. It was not distinct and the depression was very slight, but those keen blue eyes could see the crisscross lines forming a patch in symmetrical pattern. The mark had been made by hessian sacking, but the sack itself was not to be seen, and no human tracks were there to prove how the sack had been removed.

Now walking quickly, he followed the edge of the claypan round to its opposite side, where the sand ridge was only a foot wide, separating it from another and larger claypan. He traversed the edge of this one, and on its far side came to a wider stretch of sand. There in five places he saw the mark of the sack. Still there was no sign of the sack itself, but beside the sack marks were the imprints of the dog having a toenail missing. The dog had come from the creek to the northeast.

Bony proceeded to backtrack the dog, and quickly came to see that the animal had been tracking the thing that had made the sack marks. From the spacing of the sack marks, which never would have been noticed by other than an experienced tracker, it

29

became obvious that a man had wrapped sacking about his feet that he might pass over these pages of the Book of the Bush, leaving only the minimum impression of his passing, impressions lighter than those made by a small bird.

He returned to the place where he first saw the sack mark, and then, with apparent aimlessness, he wandered to and fro on a zigzag course toward the gate. He saw the mark again, twice, the second mark approximately eight feet from the gate.

Turning, Bony went back on his own tracks to the farthest point out, and from there he continued to backtrack the dog because that was easier and the dog had stuck to the man's tracks. The sack-footed man had approached the hut from the north, and when almost a quarter mile from the hut the tracks came from the southeast, from the road running out from the town. Near an old man saltbush the dog had sat to scratch, and on the ground close to the mark Bony found hairs which established the colour of the animal.

He continued to backtrack the dog and man, saw the tracks deviate to the southwest, and so found that the sack-footed man had left the end of the macadamized section of the road passing through the township.

The sun was westering. He saw the police party were leaving the hut, so he rolled a cigarette, lit it, and strolled up the street in which now were people shopping and gossiping. Some regarded him with faint curiosity, others said "Good dayee" to him. Children were driving two cows and a mob of goats down the street. A car overtook him, and the driver said something to one of the children, who thumbed his nose in reply. Outside the garage a tall man in engineer's overalls was serving a truck with petrol. A Major Mitchell cockatoo spread its multicoloured crest at him and called softly, "It's time for a drink."

Quite a friendly town was Merino. Beneath the pepper trees edging the sidewalks were seats on which people were lounging in the cool air of late afternoon.

In his prison cell Detective Inspector Napoleon Bonaparte waited for Sergeant Marshall. When he arrived Bony asked almost casually:

"Well, how was the man killed?"

"Excuse me for saying so, but you haven't displayed much interest," Marshall ventured, his eyebrows fractionally raised.

"Oh, but I have," Bony countered, faint mockery in his voice. "I was confident that two policemen, assisted by a doctor, could establish what had killed the victim. My contribution was, if possible, to establish who killed him."

The sergeant refrained from expressing a thought, and he said: "Edward Bennett wasn't killed. He just died. He fell and struck his head on the doorstep. Dr. Scott says that the fall itself did not occasion death, which was caused by heart failure."

"This Dr. Scott . . . good man or indifferent?"

"First-class. I don't hesitate to accept his opinion . . . and the death certificate which he says he will sign."

"And your own opinion, position of the body, and the rest?"

"Gleeson and I agree with the doctor," replied Marshall. "Old Bennett obviously took bad and tried to leave his hut for assistance. He got as far as the door and then dropped to hit his forehead on the step. He must have been dead before he fell."

"When?"

"He has been dead from twelve to twenty hours. Died last night."

Bony blew a smoke ring lasting but a second.

"How was the body dressed?" he asked.

"In pyjamas."

"The bed—where is it?"

"In the inner of the two rooms."

"The old man died just inside the only door of the hut, the door giving entry to the outer, the living, room?"

"That's so. There is no door between the living room and the bedroom."

For an appreciable period Bony did not press his questions, and Marshall took from his tunic a notebook and pencil and began the addition of notes. Bony smoked his cigarette to its last half inch and tossed the stub out through the doorway before he spoke again, which was to ask what arrangements had been made for the body.

"I have given the dead man's relatives charge of the body, and it will be buried tomorrow afternoon. The inquest can be held the following day."

"Ah me!" Bony sighed. "I have been anticipating a nice murder, having about it circumstances similar to those of the Kendall case. There is, I think, no greater tragedy than when a mischievous boy pricks the toy balloon belonging to a trusting child. I am feeling not unlike the child whose balloon has been pricked."

A slow grin spread over the sergeant's face, for the twinkle in the bright blue eyes belied the seriousness of the voice. Then abruptly Bony chuckled, and Marshall could not but chuckle in sympathy. Then Bony said:

"You must make sure tomorrow that I am sentenced to fourteen days' hard labour with paintpot and -brush. I am going to enjoy my visit to Merino. Will the beak at court be amenable to reason?"

"He'll give you a month if I put it to him."

"Better leave it at fourteen days. By the way, can you tell me who owns a fairly large dog having brown and white hair?"

"Yes," promptly replied the sergeant. "Young Jason owns such a dog."

IV.   A Funeral at Merino

At TEN o'CLOCK the next morning Mounted Constable Gleeson entered Bony's cell to conduct him to the courthouse, saying without a smile:

"Your trial is about to begin, sir."

When Bony laughed Gleeson smiled frostily, and in proper order they marched across the compound to enter the courthouse by a side door, from which steps led upward to the dock. On this occasion, however, the prisoner was told to halt just within the door. The court was sitting, and when the name Robert Burns was called by the clerk and repeated by Sergeant Marshall, prisoner and escort moved forward to take position beside the solicitors' table. The clerk read the charge, divided into four subsections, and then asked how the prisoner pleaded. On hearing the plea of guilty, he turned to Sergeant Marshall, who prosecuted, and Marshall then intimated that he wished to give evidence.

Having entered the witness box and taken the oath without

assistance, he related how he had found the prisoner sleeping off the effects of alcohol, and the resultant conversation following his being awakened on the bench outside the hotel. The prisoner's interest was centred entirely on the magistrate.

He sat alone on the bench, the court record book before him, his hands clasped and resting on the book. His face was long and narrow, the forehead high, and the top of the rounded head covered with sparse dark hair sprinkled with grey. His nose was thin and straight and appeared to part in dead centre the straggling black moustache. Hair and moustache, together with the dark eyes now directed towards Sergeant Marshall, emphasized the pallor of his face, an oddity in this part of Australia.

Marshall concluded his evidence and waited.

The magistrate transferred his gaze to Bony, the black eyes solemnly regarding the prisoner in a fixed stare. For a man whose hands bore the marks of manual labour, his voice was astonishingly full and rich when, speaking with deliberation, he asked:

"Have you anything to say to this witness?"

"Yes, your honour," replied Bony, who then turned to Marshall and said: "You said, on oath, that after you asked me my name I opened my eyes and yawned. I suggest to you that I opened only one eye, the left."

"I didn't say anything about opening your eyes, or one of 'em," Marshall stated with surprise plainly expressed on his weather-beaten face. "I said——"

"Read over the witness's evidence," ordered the magistrate.

The clerk read it.

"Well?" asked the magistrate, again regarding Bony with those searching dark eyes.

"Must have been mistaken," admitted Bony.

"Any further question to put to the witness?"

"Only that I wasn't doing any harm sleeping on the bench."

"What else have you to say for yourself?"

"Nothing, your honour."

"Humph! Ah well! We cannot have people sleeping on benches on our sidewalks in broad daylight. You are sentenced to ten days' detention."

"What! Only ten days? No option?" exclaimed Bony.

The clerk's mouth sagged a fraction. Gleeson's stiffly erect body

33

trembled from the chest upward. The magistrate said sternly and still deliberately:

"You are granted no option of paying a fine. Ten days."

"Come on," said Gleeson, and he and his prisoner marched from the court back to the cells.

"Disappointed, sir?" asked the constable.

"Why, no. It has been a new experience, Gleeson. What is the magistrate's name?"

"He's Jason, the garage proprietor."

"Oh! So that is Mr. Jason."

"Peculiar bird," Gleeson said. "In his way he's all there, is old Jason. He's chairman of the bench and deputy coroner for this district, and a good man for the work, too. Likes himself a lot on the bench, but then, I'd like myself if I were chief commissioner."

"What's the wife like?"

"Never knew her. She was dead when he and young Jason came to Merino eight years ago. He's been an actor in his early days, I understand. The son is a bit of a trial."

"How so? Tell me about him."

"He is, I think, twenty-three. Dark like his father but not so tall and much stronger. Has a harelip and one shoulder is higher than the other. Surly disposition and has no respect for the old man. What with his harelip and one shoulder higher than the other, I suppose he couldn't be expected to have a sunny disposition. To make him worse, one leg is shorter than the other and he has a crooked spine. Still, he's active enough and as strong as a young bull."

"They live next door, do they not?"

"That's so. A woman goes in every day to clean up and prepare the midday dinner. I have heard the old man cooks the breakfast and gets the tea. If you are going to the funeral this afternoon you'll see the old bird in his funeral regalia, which is in keeping with the hearse. You are not going to forget it for many a day."

Half an hour after Gleeson had departed for the station office Marshall entered Bony's cell.

"What was the idea of arguing about eyes?" he asked.

"I wanted again to hear the magistrate's voice," replied Bony. "Why the ten days? Was I not to get fourteen?"

"Old Jason sometimes isn't as tame as I'd like him to be."

34

Marshall scratched his nose. "Was in one of his cranky moods this morning. Still, ten days is better than a five-bob fine, I suppose." The sergeant grinned and then said sternly, with faint mockery in his voice: "Now you . . . you're here for ten days and nights. You'll find time drag a bit, and in here it's a bit hot during day-time. If you'll do some painting for me I'll let you take your meals with me, and I'll give you a couple of bob a day to spend over at the hotel before closing time."

"Sounds fair enough to me," Bony agreed with mock sullen-ness. "Lead me to the paintpots."

Again Marshall grinned and suggested:

"Why not come over to the house for a drink of tea before you start? I'd like you to meet the wife. I told her who you are. She's safe. Wouldn't have married her if she hadn't been."

"Wise man."

"Perhaps. You married?"

"Yes. Three sons. Eldest at Brisbane Uni. Going to be a medical missionary to his grandmother's people. Good lad, Sergeant, but he's always chronically broke and always, therefore, touching me for a quid. The expression is his, not mine, I hasten to assure you."

A minute later he found himself being introduced to a woman as tall as her husband and larger. Her grey eyes beamed at him through steel-rimmed spectacles.

"I know all about you," she said after welcoming him and urg-ing him to be seated with her husband at the kitchen table, where she served tea and little cakes. "I am to call you Bony. Rose Marie told me all about the tea party in the cell yesterday."

"You are fortunate in being the mother of Rose Marie," Bony said, bowing slightly from his chair. Mrs. Marshall glanced at her husband, also seated at the table, and said:

"She is a sweet child, but she's terribly precocious. The things she gets to hear other people say is extraordinary. There's no need for me to visit to hear all the news. I only hope to goodness she doesn't relate to other people what she hears us say."

"We'd better be careful what we talk about when she's handy," supplemented her husband.

"I gathered from what she told me yesterday that your daughter didn't like Sergeant Redman," Bony observed. "I do not think that odd."

35

"Nor did we," Mrs. Marshall said. "But Rose Marie hated him. Did she tell you why?"

Bony nodded, saying:

"It appears that Rose Marie likes young Jason, and that Redman bullied young Jason."

"Redman as good as accused young Jason of having murdered Kendall, but then he as good as accused a dozen people of having done that," Marshall put in.

"What is your opinion of young Jason?" Bony asked.

"He's a surly pup, and he's a long way from being handsome," replied the sergeant. "There is one great thing in his favour, and that is that children like him and trust him. Our Florence has long conferences with him; quite often she will sit with him on a box or against a petrol pump and talk and talk. And sometimes there will be half a dozen children in the conference."

"He tells them fairy tales," Mrs. Marshall said. "But are you actually going to do the painting about the place?"

"Of course," replied Bony. "Didn't you know that I have been sentenced to ten days' hard labour with paint and brushes?"

He rose to his feet. "A fortnight hence you won't know your police station. Thank you for your morning tea . . . and the breakfast you so kindly sent over."

"And I am really to call you Bony?"

Her large open face pleased him.

"Pro tem my name is Robert Burns . . . with apologies to every Scotchman," he said, smiling. "However, all my friends call me Bony, and I hope that I may include both of you among my friends."

After he had left her kitchen with her husband Mrs. Marshall sat down at the table, poured herself another cup of tea, and stared unseeingly at the hot stove, her mind seeing him bowing to her prior to his leaving.

At the expiration of the lunch hour, which began at one o'clock, Bony returned to the front fence from which he had begun to scrape the old paint. The previously clear morning sky was now filling with blue-black clouds having ponderous snowcaps, each cloud mass sailing like a galleon upon an azure sea. There was no wind, and the air was slightly oppressive.

Now and then he glanced down the street at the vast stretch

of snow-white sand hills. Although the twin lines of pepper trees and the roofs of the church and hall at the lower end of the street cut sections of the white sand hills from his view, they had come to dominate his mind. He had gazed at them the day before, and several times again this day, and on each occasion they had appeared in different guise: once like the misty crest of a breaking wave; once like pure marble and as inert; at present they appeared to be advancing upon the township like the face of a glacier.

When, a little before three o'clock, he left his work and walked to old Bennett's hut, a vast cloud shadow lay upon the land between the township and the Walls of China, which were sunlit and rested along the distant horizon like misty blue velvet upon which were the blue-black undersides of distant thunderclouds.

The dead man's hut and the large group of people gathered outside the gate were all bathed in the hot sunlight. The tin-sheathed dwelling gleamed like gold, smeared here and there with the fire of opals. Shimmering heat rose from the bonnets of several cars parked beyond the hut as though incense was being burned in honour of yet another representative of a great and vanishing generation.

"Looks like there'll be a storm before Ted Bennett's put away into his final bed," predicted one of the group of men to which Bony attached himself.

"Bit of a gamble," ventured another of the group. "Bet an even quid no rain holds up the planting."

"That'll do me," agreed the other. "And the winner spends the quid on a glass wreath for old Ted. He'd appreciate a wreath bought with a bet. Ah! Here comes Jason and his turnout."

"I've never seen it before, but I've heard about it," someone said, and another added:

"Having seen it, you're going to make special mention in your will to be planted by it."

At the lower end of the town appeared a long black object having about it much glass which sent forward little searchlight reflections of the sun. It was being driven over the tracks made by the cars already arrived, and eventually it rolled past the hut, was turned about, and halted opposite the gate and facing the direction from which it had come.

Originally the massive body of this hearse had rested upon a horse-drawn chassis, but it had been transferred to the chassis of a motor truck and now was grossly out of proportion. On the roof of black wood was the figure of a woman lying in an attitude of grief prostrate, whilst the once-silvered guide rails now were masked with white ribbon. In front of the hearse body, and dwarfed by its size and magnificence, was the low engine bonnet and the driving seat without back or roof.

Down from this roofless and backless driving seat stepped Mr. Jason. He was wearing a top hat of nineteenth-century vintage, the crepe about its middle failing to obliterate its emphatic waist. His frock coat was faintly green down the back and over the shoulders and its hem came two inches below the baggy knees of trousers that had been built for evening wear. The trousers were slightly short for the wearer, and the rear hem of each leg rested with persistent confidence on the top of the rear tag of each elastic-sided boot.

With solemn aspect Mr. Jason surveyed the gathered people before striding to the gate and entering the hut.

The driver stayed in his seat. He was a young man having a harelip and deformed body. He wore engineer's overalls and stared directly away over the engine bonnet, the butt of a rolled cigarette between his lips. A cloth cap, worn peak foremost in deference to the occasion, was none too free of grease.

"Gonna rain, Tom?" asked one of the wagerers.

Young Jason surveyed the sky, rolled his cigarette end to the opposite side of his mouth, spat without removing it, and replied:

"If she does we're all gonna get bogged."

Further discussion on the chances of rain was prevented by the appearance at the door of the hut of a clergyman wearing a black cloth gown. After him came bearers bringing out the mortal remains of Edward Bennett, which they placed on trestles in the front yard. The people drew nearer to the fence, the personal mourners, the bearers, and Mr. Jason and the clergyman grouping themselves about the casket. From a book the clergyman began to read the first part of the burial service in a high nasal whine, the end of his every sentence higher still in tone.

Not much more than thirty years old, he would have benefited by physical exercise. He looked flabby when his build and years should have suggested hardness of flesh and resilience of muscle. His pale eyes appeared dark in an unwholesome, square face at present devoid of all expression.

Distant thunder preceded the closing of his book with a sound equally significant. Mr. Jason signed with his hands to the bearers, stood back, and then stalked ahead of them out through the gate and to the rear of the hearse. There, with dramatic deliberation, he swung open the glass-panelled doors, stepped to one side, and in his full and rich voice directed the bearers when sliding the casket into the glass interior. He closed the doors with the slow deliberation with which he had opened them.

People began to walk over to the cars. Bony counted five. The minister got into one and was followed by two men. Mrs. Fanning and husband boarded another, and a tall, angular woman wearing a Merry Widow hat and a tightly fitting grey costume was escorted by two young boys to yet another car. Mr. Jason, standing beside the hearse, waited. He waited until the parson's car was drawn up behind the hearse and the other cars behind it, and not before he was satisfied that all were in order of procedure did he get up beside the driver of the hearse.

Even then he did not at once sit down. By standing he could look back over the top of the hearse for a final inspection of the mourners' cars. Then, without haste, he surveyed the silent crowd. Being apparently satisfied, he touched the driver's leg with a foot, and the driver started the engine. Thereupon Mr. Jason turned to the front, raised his right hand on high, maintained it there as though he were an orchestra leader, and finally brought it smartly to his side. That was the signal for all drivers to let in the clutch and so begin the last journey for old Bennett. Mr. Jason sat down, obviously having enjoyed the drama of the ceremony.

On low gear the procession moved away toward the road to the accompaniment of a long and loud roll of celestial drums.

The small crowd began silently to drift from the tin shack to the only street, silently, for old Bennett had been a sterling character and his generation had been great in Australia.

Unnoticed, Bony walked with the others, now and then glancing ahead to observe the hearse reach the road and turn eastward onto the earth track and so begin the downward run to the cemetery one mile from the township. Once on that road, the pace quickened, so that when Bony reached the end of the street the trails of dust raised by the vehicles hid all within a rising red cloud.

Haste certainly was indicated by the weather portents.

On reaching the police station fence, he stood with blowlamp and paint scraper in either hand, and gazed down the main street to see the Walls of China lying clay-white beneath a vast ink-black cloud from which rain already seemed to be eating up the northern extremity of the gigantic sand wall. The dust cloud raised by the funeral cortege hung steadily in the air above the track, and then abruptly from its left flank dust billowed as the vehicles turned left off the track into the cemetery. Gleeson, who came to stand beside the detective, said:

"They'll have to make it snappy or they'll get caught in the rain, and it would be no time, in rain like it is over there, before that track becomes a bog soft enough to stick up a rabbit."

"Like that, is it?"

"Worst bit of road in the district. What did you think of old Jason?"

"I like him better as a mortician than a magistrate. Look, the edge of the storm is drawing near to the cemetery. Observe how the colour of the Walls of China is changing just in front of the rain."

"Makes 'em look like a purple carpet all tuckered up, doesn't it!" Gleeson said. "I never get tired of looking at that range of sand. It always seems different. Ah . . ."

Out to the road came the first of the returning vehicles, others coming on fast after it in the misty edge of the rainstorm. Lightning flickered and darted to earth apparently immediately behind the last vehicle to leave the cemetery. Thunder began in a single splitting crack and continued in a prolonged roll, shaking the earth on which stood the township. Above Merino the face of the cloud mass threatened to topple forward and smother the township with snow and ice. From the breadth of a man's hand southward of it the sky seemed to be without height.

Men were called from the hotel, and they moved to the middle of the street to obtain a less obstructed view of the oncoming motor vehicles.

"Bet a level pound that the doctor gets back to town first," called one of the group.

The ghost of a smile came to Gleeson's mouth.

"If it wasn't against the law to bet in a public place," he said, "I'd back the hearse if I could be sure it was first to clear the cemetery and reach the road."

Bony chuckled.

"We are inside the station fence, and therefore we stand on government property, not a public place," he pointed out. "I am having ten shillings on the Jasons against the rest of the field, under any circumstances."

"Well, sir, if you set such an example, who the heck am I to quibble about the side of a fence . . . or ten bob?" replied the constable. "Sure, I'll take you."

"Well then, we may as well have our money's worth and see the race properly. Let us go to the centre of the street. Why did you favour the Jasons if they first reached the road?"

"Because young Jason wouldn't let any driver overhaul and pass him. He'd block any such attempt. Looks as though they left the cemetery just in time, doesn't it!"

The first of the oncoming vehicles was still half a mile from the lower end of the township where the macadamized street gave place to the earth road. Behind it nothing could be seen in the dust raised by its wheels save now and then when a black dot appeared to draw level for an instant before falling away again into the dust cloud.

"Must be doing fifty, sir," estimated Gleeson.

"And the rain is doing sixty, Gleeson," the delighted Bony pointed out. "It will soon catch up with them. And please remember not to call me sir. I am supposed to be a prisoner of the state. My friends all call me Bony. If you don't like to be a friend, call me Burns. Ha! Ha! That second vehicle almost got ahead." He was rubbing his hands with glee, and he shouted: "It's the Jasons leading. Come on, the Jasons!"

A voice roared from the group behind them:

"No, it ain't. The doctor's leading. I'm 'aving a bit on 'im. Five bob on the quack, Jack. Make a note."

Thunder crashed, rolled away over the mysterious Walls of China, only the southern portion of which could now be seen. The sound of it dampened men's voices into unintelligible murmurs. When it ended, a man shouted triumphantly:

"It isn't the quack. It's the parson. Come on, Jamesey. Come on, you beaut."

"I told you so! I told you so!" yelled a man farther down the street, a man who turned and waved his hat and then slapped it against a thigh. "The Jasons are leading. Good old Tom! Drive her, Tom. Step on it, lad. Let her have it."

The leading unit of the returning funeral cortege was now nearing the eastern end of the macadamized road. One drop of rain "tanged" on the garage roof. Then another pinged on the roof of the police station. Sergeant Marshall came out with his wife and stood at the gate. The group in the middle of the street took not the slightest notice of the presence of the police, and called betting odds and shouted and cheered.

"You win your ten shillings," Gleeson told Bony. "Now watch 'em clear the final hurdle."

The hearse appeared like a horse rising to take a fence as it was driven off the earth road upon the macadamized street. The car almost touching its rear doors also took the jump, as did the remainder.

A bad flash of lightning made the excited onlookers blink, and the ensuing thunder shook the air about them. Up along the street came the hearse. The car behind it swerved to its left and entered the driveway of the house next to the church. Bony now could see Mr. Jason's white face, and beside it the rounder face of his son. They both were crouched forward so that the faces appeared as ornaments above the engine bonnet. Mr. Jason was gripping the top of the low windscreen with both hands. The top hat was not visible.

Like a machine gun being steadily fired, huge raindrops fell upon the iron roofs and actually raised little balls of dust when they dropped on the sandy places on the sidewalks. The onlookers now could see Mr. Jason's moustache apparently glued to the windscreen, and they could see the cigarette end in the wide mouth of his son. It looked like the same butt which had been there when the cortege had left old Bennett's hut.

The hearse roared past Bony and the constable, who had gained the shelter of a pepper tree, and there, lying in state inside the vehicle, was Mr. Jason's top hat. Tires screamed when the turn was made into the garage, almost drowning out the roar of applause given by the onlookers from the hotel who now were gathered under its veranda.

The rain began in very earnest, its roar on iron roofs deepening in cadence and increasing in volume. The doctor's car turned off the street. The Fannings did likewise. The last car home roared to a halt outside the hotel, and the woman wearing the Merry Widow hat and the grey costume appeared from it like a Jill out of her box, to run round the front of it and dart into the main entrance of the hotel, followed by two small boys.

Then from out the garage raced Mr. Jason and young Jason. The father was carrying his top hat under an arm. The son was wearing his cloth cap back to front. They sped across the street in the cloud of rain and vanished into the hotel.

And as though all this violent activity was become a universal fashion, Bony left the shelter of the pepper tree and Constable Gleeson to run across the street and also enter the hotel.

V. A Wake without the Relatives

ON ENTERING THE BAR, Bony's swift appraisal numbered fourteen men in addition to the licensee, who in that instant announced that the drinks were on him.

The gloom within the bar was now and then banished by lightning which flickered against the windows, and men's voices were drowned by the resultant thunder which blotted out the roar of the rain on the veranda roof without. Men named their drinks, and one who took it upon himself to transmit the orders turned to Bony to ask his choice.

This man was not a bushman. He was wearing tweed slacks and black shoes. He had no coat and the striped cotton shirt he sported beneath a waistcoat was similar to those worn by city men.

"You're the feller who got ten days this morning, aren't you?" he asked with a friendly smile. "Never mind. Bit of bad luck.

43

The sergeant was telling me only yesterday that he'd have to get someone to paint his fence."

Bony's teeth flashed.

"I always try to meet adversity like a sportsman," he said.

"Good on you. That's the spirit. I'm Watson, the local press correspondent. Own the news agency and fancy goods shop in this town. Your name's Burns, isn't it?"

"That's so. Hope there are no Scotchmen present."

"Not Robert Burns? Lovely! You know, I get more fun out of this township than ever I did out of Sydney. Now don't be in a hurry to drink. Just wait, and you'll see something that you've never seen before."

Grey eyes peered good-naturedly through the gloom which, however, failed to mask the telltale caress of John Barleycorn on Mr. Watson's face. His bristling grey moustache had a hole in the centre of it, burned by smoking cigarettes down to the last half inch.

When the drinks were all set up, no one appeared to be abnormally thirsty. It appeared to Bony that everyone waited for a signal to drink to be given, for certainly no one was too bashful to drink first. Even the licensee waited, his elbows on the counter, his hands cupping his round and red face. All present seemed to be covertly watching Mr. Jason, who stood in the centre of the gathering.

He stood with his back to the counter. The tall hat was perched at an absurd angle at the back of his head. Leaning hard against the counter, he was cutting chips from a jet-black tobacco plug with a knife having a four-inch blade. His long-fingered hands were obviously strong, for the knife did its work with methodical ease.

Men discussed the homeward race of the funeral cortege with slackening interest as their interest in Mr. Jason increased.

He snapped shut the knife and placed it, with the tobacco plug, in his trousers pocket. Then with the palms of his hands he shredded the tobacco and crammed it with some care into the bowl of a cherrywood pipe. At his right elbow stood two glass mugs of beer.

The pipe loaded, Mr. Jason audibly sighed, long and deeply.

44

His face bore the evidence of grief and he appeared oblivious of those on either side of him.

"Watch," breathed Mr. Watson into Bony's ear.

From a pocket in the skirt of his remarkable frock coat Mr. Jason produced a box of matches, struck one, and laid it against the pipe bowl. Followed then a period of expectant hush as the assembly watched with extraordinary intentness Mr. Jason draw and puff until the pipe seemed on fire. Then he began to inhale smoke. He inhaled to the capacity of his breath three times without exhaling, upon which he turned slowly to the counter, laid down his pipe, and took up and drank the two mugs of beer. That was the awaited signal for all to drink.

"Fill them again, Landlord," requested Mr. Jason as he resumed his position with his back resting against the counter. Following the slurred drawl of men who lived in the open, the full tones of Mr. Jason's voice came strangely to Bony's ears.

Mr. Jason puffed out his cheeks and again sighed, this time with evidence of satisfaction. He pulled down the front of his black waistcoat and shot his cuffs. Then he glared at his son, who rolled a cigarette with one hand, lit it, and glared back at his father. His greasy cap was still back to front. His dark eyes never rested, and he recalled to Bony's mind the Hunchback of Notre Dame. Mr. Jason spoke, following a long, ear-shattering roll of thunder.

"That was the most indecent planting I have ever conducted."

From behind him rose the faint ghostly spiral of smoke from his pipe.

"The service was an insult to the departed," he continued sternly. "The speed of the cortege on the way to the cemetery was disrespectful to the late lamented, and the speed of the cortege returning from the place of burial, as well as its reception on arrival in the township, was thoroughly disgraceful."

Once again he turned round to take up a mug of beer and drink without apparently swallowing. With the fourth mug of beer in his left hand, he turned again to rest his back against the counter. The company drank, it seemed hastily, for all present excepting young Jason continued to regard Mr. Jason with unwonted interest. Young Jason said, a snarl in his thin voice:

45

"Well, we didn't want to get bogged, did we? I didn't fancy getting halfway there and having to carry the coffin for the remainder of the distance."

Now Mr. Jason began to exhale smoke. It issued from his lips in a faint stream, and it continued when he said:

"The service, I repeat, was an insult to the departed."

"Well, we can't argue the point about that, seeing that the parson ain't here to take it up," young Jason objected.

"There would have been time to have half filled in the grave, at least," persisted his father, tobacco smoke continuing to issue from him. He emptied the fourth mug of beer and set it down on the counter with a sweep of his arm. "It is my opinion that the whole affair was indecently hurried. I do not agree with Dr. Scott giving the certificate he did. If ever a man was frightened to death, it was poor old Edward Bennett. The look on his face was terrible. A man does not die of heart disease with a look like he had."

No one spoke at that. The daylight was growing brighter, and the rain was ceasing. Smoke continued to issue from Mr. Jason's mouth, astounding Bony by the amount he must have inhaled and by the period of time which had elapsed since he had inhaled. There appeared to be no limit, and the entire company were far more interested in Mr. Jason's remarkable feat than in what he was saying.

"You've got murder on the brain," young Jason sneered. "Just because that Kendall bloke was bumped off you're gonna believe that everyone who dies in Merino during the coming three years was murdered too. What's worrying you? We can complete filling in the hole tomorrow. Come on, gents. It's my call, Joe. Fill 'em up."

"Wait," Mr. Watson urged Bony. "The old boy hasn't finished yet. One minute fifty seconds that smoke's been coming out of him. Another twenty seconds and he's broken his own record."

"The record is?" Bony enquired.

"Two minutes and five seconds . . . made the day that George Kendall was murdered."

Bony now observed that Mr. Watson held a stop watch in his left hand. He was seen to shake his head when a dozen pairs of eyes stared at that watch. Mr. Jason opened his mouth, wide, and someone said hastily and loudly, as though to stop Mr. Jason yawning:

"Mr. Jason!"

Mr. Jason closed his mouth and the strain among the company relaxed.

"Well?" asked the funeral director.

"What do you think frightened old Bennett to death?"

"How do I know? It might have been brought out had there been an inquest."

Mr. Watson was smiling. His bristling moustache appeared to stand straight out from his face. Once more Mr. Jason opened wide his mouth, and from the door leading to the hall of the building a woman cried:

"The man died naturally of heart failure. Let the dead lie in peace."

But this time Mr. Jason did not instantly close his mouth. From it belched a huge volume of smoke which rose to the stained whitewashed ceiling, where it seemed to spread outward like smoke from a railway engine entering a tunnel. That was the grand finale, and Mr. Watson shouted triumphantly:

"Done it. He's broken the record, gents. Two minutes and thirty-seven seconds. Congratulations, Mr. Jason."

"Enough!" Mr. Jason cried. "Too many unseemly records have been broken today." He took two steps forward and lifted his hat to the woman standing in the doorframe. She wore a Merry Widow hat and a grey costume. Her face was so sunburned and weather-tanned that she might easily have been mistaken for a half-caste. Her age Bony found difficult to assess, but she stood upright, her figure slim and hard.

"Mrs. Sutherland," began Mr. Jason, "I accept your rebuke. The dead shall lie in peace. This, I fear, is a sorry wake and one which would not have had the approval of the departed. Will you not join us in drinking to the memory of a man who was a great Australian?"

"I certainly will, Mr. Jason, and with pleasure, but I'm not agreeing that old Ted Bennett was a great Australian," responded Mrs. Sutherland, and came two paces inside the bar-room. "Old Bennett was a hard doer. He was tough. He knew his onions. But I'm not agreeing that he was great."

47

Mr. Jason actually bowed, saying:

"Madam, we will all agree to disagree."

"Just as well," she announced grimly. "Yes, a little glass of wine, please, Mr. Morton."

Bony's interest in young Jason was heightened when that young man took up from the counter the glass of wine and stepped across with it to Mrs. Sutherland. She raised it on high, and her action was followed by the company. And in silence the toast was drunk.

"Who is she?" asked Bony of the local press representative.

"Oh, I forgot," Mr. Watson whispered loudly. "That's Mrs. Sutherland, who owns a selection a few miles to the southeast of the town. Husband died some four years back, since when she has run her own place; does everything from lamb marking to shearing. Tough girl, but very sound. Knows everyone."

"Thank you, Mr. Watson," said the woman in the Merry Widow hat. "But I don't know your boy friend. Please . . ."

Bony felt a hand grip his arm and he was urged across the barroom to be presented.

"This gent is Robert Burns," announced Mr. Watson. "Burns, this is Mrs. Sutherland, the first lady in our district."

"How d'you do!" she said, offering him her hand. Bony took it and felt a grip like that of a strong man. He assessed her age at forty, and noted the clear and steady eyes that regarded him not coldly. It was one of his great moments. His bow outdid that of Mr. Jason.

"I am happy to make your acquaintance, madam," he told her. "At the moment I am a jailbird, Mr. Jason having but yesterday sentenced me to ten days. I would not like to withhold my present status from the knowledge of one so charming as yourself."

Mrs. Sutherland almost giggled.

"That won't upset me," she said. "I know all the boys about these parts, and there's not one of them but oughtn't to have done a turn in jail. When you are free, ride out one day and see me. I'll kill something. Now I must be going. Good-bye, all. Be good and keep the grass down."

This time she did giggle, and then turned and walked from the bar with the unmistakable gait of a woman who has lived most of her life on a horse.

48

VI. The Prisoner's Visitors

To SERGEANT MARSHALL, administrator as well as policeman, Detective Inspector Bonaparte was an entirely new proposition, the antithesis of Detective Sergeant Redman.

Marshall knew no class of men better than policemen and plain-clothes investigation men who once were uniformed policemen. He was aware, and took pride in the fact, that the modern policeman is the product of a machinelike organization built up by generations of men engaged in the perpetual war against lawbreakers. There was no doubt in Marshall's mind that Detective Sergeant Redman was a good investigator. His record was proof of that. But Redman's training began as a constable on a city beat, where he had learned the rudiments of the warfare against criminals operating in cities, and he had continued in the same warfare, and against the same enemies, when promoted to the Criminal Investigation Branch. As an investigator here in the bush, however, Redman was a lesser quantity than Gleeson, who could recognize the tracks of any particular horse sufficiently well to follow them for miles, and who did know the difference between the tracks made by a dog and those made by a fox.

Here, in the vast untrammelled and uncultivated interior of Australia, the science of crime detection was as different from its city counterpart as the tracks made by a fox are different from those made by a dog. Here in the bush the sciences of fingerprinting, blood grouping, hair sectioning, and general photography were of relatively small importance compared with the sciences of tracking and of the effects of varying wind pressures upon the face of the earth.

Again, in comparison with crime in any given populated area, crime in the bush was negligible, and certainly not sufficiently prevalent to demand the institution of a special school of detection to deal with it. Which was why Sergeant Marshall recognized the extraordinary value to the police force of any Australian state of a man having Napoleon Bonaparte's mental gifts and inherited instincts.

49

Marshall had yet to experience personally Bonaparte's methods of crime detection, but he had heard sufficient about this Queenslander to appreciate their extraordinary success. That Bonaparte chose to enter Merino as a stockman, that he had artfully got himself charged in a court of law, and now was painting government property for two shillings per diem and his meals, did not appear to Marshall as unorthodox as it would have done to a police officer having no experience of the bush.

Certainly no one in Merino would ever imagine that the half-caste stockman painting the police station fence was a famous detective inspector investigating the murder of George Kendall. Bony had said after breakfast on the morning following the funeral of Edward Bennett:

"You administer a district comprising roughly nine thousand square miles, a district occupied by about a hundred and fifty people, of whom nearly two thirds live here in Merino. Without being disrespectful, I may call myself a fisher of men. I cast my net and in due time I bring in for examination all these people. All of them are fish. All are harmless fish except one that is a sting ray. It is not very exciting work. It is not comparable, for instance, to angling for swordfish. I don't go about armed with loaded guns and things, save on very rare occasions. The uniformed policemen do all the necessary shooting. The only shooting I do is with my mind. The mental bullets I fire cause a man to die at the bottom end of a rope."

Well, well! Was Bony even then getting ready to fire one of those mental bullets?

Seated at his desk, through the open window of his office the senior police officer of the Merino District could observe Detective Inspector Bonaparte industriously painting the police station fence fronting the street, and he could hear him cheerfully whistling "Clementine, My Clementine." When a few moments later the whistling ceased, Marshall saw that his daughter Florence had joined the painter. Unable to hear the conversation, he began work upon a report.

Rose Marie said to the catcher of sting rays:

"Good morning, Bony!"

"Good morning, Rose Marie! Are you off to school?"

"Yes. But I'm early. I can talk to you if you like."

Bony slapped the last drop of paint from his brush to the wood.

"How do you like the colour?" he enquired mildly.

"I hate it." The little girl's dark eyes gazed steadily at the light yellow of the new paint work. "It makes me feel sick."

"It makes me feel tired, Rose Marie. Now why should the government permit only the most artistic shades of colouring to be applied to the inside of Parliament House down in Sydney and send this fearful stuff to Merino? But never mind."

Laying the brush across the top of the paintpot, he sat down on the bare ground with his back to that part of the fence still to be painted, and began to manufacture a cigarette. Gravely the girl unslung her school satchel, placed it beside him as a seat, and joined him at his ease.

"Mother said that you're the most lovely man she's ever met," she told him.

"Indeed!"

"Yes. I heard her tell Father so after you left the kitchen last night."

"Oh! Where were you?"

"I was supposed to be asleep in my bedroom. It's next to the kitchen. Would you like to know what Father said about you?"

"Do you think I ought to know?"

"Yes, because it was nice. I wouldn't tell you if it had been nasty."

"Perhaps it would be better if you didn't tell me. You see, it might make me vain. What's your teacher's name?"

The question was asked through the faint haze of cigarette smoke. He observed the dark eyes regarding him with open trust. The small oval face was healthy and not yet burned by the summer suns.

"Mr. Gatehead," she told him. "He's a nice man, but his wife isn't. Mrs. Moody says that Mrs. Gatehead is a real useless trollop, and however he came to marry her is beyond reason. I like Miss Leylan. She's our sewing mistress, you know. She's in love with a minister who goes round Australia in a big truck. Miss Leylan thinks that I'm too young to be in love. Do you?"

"No. We are never too young, Rose Marie, and never too old to be in love."

"Thank you, Bony," she said solemnly. "You see, one day I am

51

going to marry young Mr. Jason. He's saving up his money to buy a Buick, and then we will be married by Mr. James, and young Mr. Jason will drive me straight off to the kingdom of Rose Marie."

"Oh! And where is that?"

The school bell began to clang and the child rose to her feet. Whilst she was adjusting her satchel she looked down at him with bright eyes.

"You promise not to tell?"

He nodded.

"Cross your fingers and promise . . . loud."

He obeyed. She said:

"The kingdom of Rose Marie is where I'm going to be queen and young Mr. Jason the king." She then proceeded to recite what she had learnt by heart. "You follow the new moon to where it sinks into the sunset glow. There is a lake of liquid gold, and in the middle of the lake is an island all green with tall grasses and flowering trees. The island is the kingdom of Rose Marie, and when we get there all the stars will fall and hold tight to the tops of the trees and be like those electric globes in Mr. Jason's garage."

"True?" asked the entranced Bony.

"Yes. Young Mr. Jason told me. My, I must run! The bell's stopped."

"You promise me something before you go?"

She crossed her fingers and promised.

"Promise that you will never again speak the word 'trollop.' It isn't a nice word."

"All right! I promise, Bony. Good-bye."

She left him, running, the bars of her golden hair floating behind her.

He was wishing that he had been blessed with a daughter in addition to his three sons when a dog came to stare at him.

"Good day!" he said to the dog.

The dog wagged its tail. It was a large rangy animal of nondescript breed, brown head, brown back, and white chest.

"What is your name?" Bony asked. "Come on, tell me your name."

The dog wrinkled his nose and suspicion left his eyes. He came nearer, willing to be friends.

"Come on, shake hands," invited Bony, and the animal dutifully lifted his right forepaw, his tail now a flail, the entire body of him expressing friendship.

One nail was absent from the paw clasped by Bony's hand.

Someone whistled shrilly, and at once the dog raced away to vanish into the garage doorway. Bony rose to his feet and fell to work on his painting. Five minutes later he observed Mr. Jason coming from the garage. And Mr. Jason stopped and said:

"Good morning, Burns. How's the work going?"

"Goodo, Mr. Jason. Rotten colour, though."

"I agree. It will be an eyesore in Merino," predicted Mr. Jason. "As the Bard of Avon said, so perhaps shall I: 'O, I have pass'd a miserable night, So full of ugly sights, of ghastly dreams.' I intend to write a strong protest about that paint to the police department."

Mr. Jason was wearing blue engineer's overalls, which seemed out of place when quoting Shakespeare. The expression in his dark eyes now was mild, almost paternal, when he went on:

"One does one's best to bring beauty into the outback, but so few appreciate one's efforts to beautify a place or beautify the mind with passages from the works of the world's literary giants. Take to reading, Burns. Read the works of Shakespeare and Milton and Wordsworth. Elevate your mind, Burns. Did you notice any peculiar circumstances relative to old Bennett's demise?"

"Er . . . no," replied Bony, a little set back by such a question following closely upon the subject of literature and the elevation of the mind.

"I saw you walking about the old man's hut the other afternoon," admitted Mr. Jason. "You are probably aware, having heard what I said yesterday, that I am not easy in my mind about that death. You did not, by any chance, observe any unusual tracks? I think, you know, that someone frightened old Bennett to death."

"But why frighten the old man?" argued Bony. "He had no enemies, did he?"

"I don't know. I am only going on what I observed on the man's face. You were, of course, asked to accompany the party by the sergeant?"

"Yes, he did ask me to go with him. I looked about all round the hut but I could see nothing strange, or of any value. I am not very good at tracking. Not so good as the full blacks."

"Ah, no, I suppose not. Well, I have to go along to buy some tobacco. Good day."

Mr. Jason departed down the street and returned on the far side. Twice he stopped and chatted with people. Several times he was spoken to beyond the normal greeting. What had Rose Marie said that her father had said of him? A broken-down actor. Well, he might have been an actor, but hardly a broken-down one, whatever that term might mean. There was a drover in western Australia who, during two months' association with Bony, had recited word-perfectly every Shakespearean play. And Bony knew of another who could repeat long passages of the opening chapters of Balzac's *Wild Ass's Skin*.

Yesterday's storm had left an aroma of springing life. It was as strong as the perfume of lilies in a quiet, night-shrouded garden, an elixir which rose from the rain-sweetened earth. A few fleecy clouds sailed the turquoise sky. There was even a mellowness in the heat of the sun. And away to the eastward, like the marble monuments of a vanished civilization, lay those Walls of China, arousing the wanderlust in Bony's blood, calling to him, inviting him to look upon the imagined wonders on their far side.

People were shopping in the few stores and gossiping in the shade of the pepper trees. Cars and trucks were arriving from west and east, to stop at the hotel as though their engines would fall out should they be driven past it. The mail car from Mildura arrived at eleven, from the west. It was the only vehicle to pass the hotel. It continued on to the post office, then it was turned and driven back to the hotel to unload its passengers. At the garage young Jason was kept busy pumping petrol and serving oil and examining engine defects.

At noon the humming of the blowflies was subdued by the burst of children's voices released from school. Rose Marie came flying up the street, to give Bony a wave and a smile before darting through the police station gate and into the house.

Everyone who passed along Bony's side of the street said "Good dayee" to him. The words of the greeting never varied, nor was it ever omitted. Several passers-by paused to speak to the painter and to sympathize with him in his bad luck at having been chosen by the sergeant to paint that fence.

In the afternoon there came the Rev. Llewellyn James. His greeting was minus the final long *e*.

"Good dayee," responded Bony, straightening his back and turning about to see a youngish man who gazed at him intently with pale blue eyes. He wore no hat, and his fine brown hair was unruly. His hands were large and white and soft, and from the crook of an arm dangled a walking stick. Grey flannel trousers and black lustre coat failed to hide his flabbiness. He spoke with the unmistakable accent of the Welshman.

"I regret being informed of your fall and subsequent arraignment before the court," he said. "However, I am glad to find you at honest labour in the pure sunshine, for which you must thank Sergeant Marshall. What is your name?"

"First I'd like to know who you are," Bony said with pretended sullenness.

"I am Mr. James, the clergyman."

There was now superciliousness in the voice, and an expression of hardness had flashed into the pale blue eyes. Bony thought that he knew his man and assumed humility.

"Sorry, Padre," he began. "My name's Robert Burns. I'm a stranger to this part of the state."

Mr. James smiled, and Bony could actually see the shaft of wit being fashioned in the man's mouth.

"No descendant of the great Scotch poet, I presume. I cannot trace the Highland burr in your voice."

It was a different Bony from the one who had spoken that morning to Rose Marie.

"I am Australian-born," he said. "My father may have been a poet. I don't know. I was reared in a North Queensland mission station, and I roam about Australia whenever I want."

Mr. James was made glad that he knew his parents. It was a feeling he found comforting and pleasant. He began to press questions as though fully entitled. What was Bony's age; what had been his education; what were his domestic responsibilities; and what was the reason of his being here in the southwestern quarter

55

of New South Wales? He did not enquire concerning Bony's religion. Presently he said unctuously:

"Well, Burns, remember that you would not have found yourself in your present predicament had you not succumbed to the temptation of taking alcoholic refreshment. It is the greatest pitfall to entrap the unwary. At the expiration of the term of your imprisonment, have you any employment to go to?"

Sadly Bony shook his head.

"Then I will speak to Mr. Leylan about you. He is the owner of Wattle Creek Station and is a great friend of mine. Can you ride a horse?"

"So long as it's a quiet one, Padre."

"Good! Well, we'll see about it. Meanwhile, ponder on your delinquency so that profit may emerge to you. Did I see you accompanying Sergeant Marshall and Gleeson and Dr. Scott to the late Mr. Bennett's hut the day before yesterday?"

"Yes, Padre, that's so."

"What were you doing walking round and round the hut when the others were inside?"

"Just having a look around, Padre."

"Oh!"

Mr. James appeared to be happier about Robert Burns. The word "padre" sounded well. He had been resolute in his attitude against serving with the armed forces, but he understood that the title was used by both the officers and the men.

"Looking around!" he echoed. "For what?"

"Nothing in particular, Padre," Bony replied, gazing over the minister's shoulder. "You see, the sergeant thought that, being half aboriginal, I might find tracks that were peculiar, sort of, the sergeant thinking at that time that the old man might have been killed."

"Ah . . . yes . . . certainly. And you are a tracker?"

"Just ordinary, I suppose. I'm not much good at anything."

"Perhaps not, Burns, but we must all try to make something of our lives." Into the minister's voice had crept a whine. "Keep to the straight and narrow path. I will not forget you. It may be possible to reclaim you, for I observe only a trace of degradation in your face. Now I must be away. Good day to you."

Bony essayed his first smile.

"Good dayee, Padre," he responded. "I'll think over what you have told me. As I read somewhere: no man ever becomes a saint in his sleep."

Mr. James had proceeded towards the garage, and now he turned sharply to look back with swift suspicion at the half-caste, who was dipping a paintbrush into the pot. He came to the verge of saying something, checked himself, and went on his way.

Bony began his work mechanically. His eyes were engaged with the footmarks left on the soft earthen sidewalk by the Rev. Llewellyn James.

VII.   A Scar on Nature's Handiwork

ON THE SEVENTH DAY of his "imprisonment," Bony suggested to Sergeant Marshall that they visit the hut at Sandy Flat in which the body of George Kendall had been found. The suggestion was readily accepted by the sergeant, who had been tied more than he liked to his desk.

That Bony should wait seven days before indicating a desire to visit the scene of the crime he was in Merino to unravel was to Marshall peculiar, to say the least, but those seven days had not been spent merely in painting government property. There had been the prolonged study of large-scale maps of the district to imprint on Bony's mind the situation and layout of every surrounding station property, every road and track, every water hole and well. There had been hours spent on Detective Sergeant Redman's reports and on the statements he had gathered. And Bony had got to know nearly every man and many women who lived at Merino.

It was a little before eleven o'clock on the morning of December fifth that they left Merino in the sergeant's car, in the boot of which Mrs. Marshall had herself placed a hamper and a tea billy. The day was warm with a clear heat; it would have been hot were it not for a fitful wind coming from the west. Once clear of the town, Bony said to the sergeant, who was wearing flannels and an open-necked shirt:

"I am a great believer in intuition. For instance, intuition never fails to warn me when my eldest son is about to ask for financial accommodation."

"Doing well?" enquired Marshall, now hopeful that following a period of "closeness" Bony would be confidential during this trip.

"Very well. I am, secretly, proud of him. For that reason, when intuition warns me that a loan is about to be requested, to avoid paining him by a refusal, I make excuses to rush away. What is your opinion of the Rev. Llewellyn James?"

"Not much."

"Do you mean that the opinion is not much in length or of value, or that the opinion is not favourable?"

Marshall removed his attention for a second from the twisting track to regard Bony's not unhandsome profile. Then he chuckled, saying:

"Even now I can't tell whether you are serious or pulling my leg. I don't like the Rev. Llewellyn James."

"Officially or privately?"

"Privately, of course. Why be legal this morning?"

"I am in the mood for exactitude," Bony told him, although his voice indicated the opposite. "What is the general opinion of James held by the people?"

The sergeant did not at once answer this question.

"The best way to deal with the subject," he began, "is to make a comparison with the previous parson. James has been here four years and a bit. He arrived eight months after the other man left. The previous man was very well liked. He was elderly and a really great man who inspired love as well as respect. You know what is wanted in a parson by bush folk. To get on well with bush people, a parson has to be a man's man as well as a churchman. James may be a good churchman, but he's not a man's man."

"You do not seem confident that he is or is not a good churchman?" pressed Bony.

"That's so. I don't go to church. My wife does, however, and she says that James is better than no minister at all, and also that what he lacks is compensated by his wife."

"Oh!" Bony made no other comment for a period. Then he said lazily: "You would not have had time to spare, as the

58

statistician of every government department, to study criminology. That is a study thought unsuitable for real policemen, and so no time is allowed for it. I used once to compile data on the physical features of murderers and near-such, when it was proved how remarkably high is the percentage of killers having light blue eyes. James, you will recall, has light blue eyes."

"Eh!" exclaimed the startled sergeant.

"Don't let it worry you. Millions of people having light blue eyes go through life without committing a murder. We must not allow our natural reactions to Mr. James to cloud our common sense. I mentioned the matter only for interest value. So that is the cemetery! Well! Well! It tells us its own history."

"What does it tell?"

"It is all elementary, my dear Watson. In bygone years people hereabouts died and were taken to their rest over there. Then came the motorcar, to transport sick people swiftly to the hospital at the much larger town of Mildura. And so only very poor persons, and those who died suddenly or from accident, have been buried at Merino. Right?"

"Yes. Before Kendall was buried there the last was several years ago."

"It is likely that another will be buried there shortly."

"What!"

"Imagination, Marshall, just imagination. It runs away with me sometimes. Hullo! Here is the left-hand turning."

Instead of taking the road turn to the north, Marshall stopped his car at a gate through which a lesser track continued eastward towards the Walls of China. They were now two miles out from Merino and three miles from the homestead of Wattle Creek Station along that north road. The great barrier of white sand dominated the scene far more powerfully than it dominated the township, rising several hundred feet in a series of whaleback ridges. The sparse scrub trees and bluebush and saltbush growing on red soil verged on the limits of vegetation.

Bony alighted and opened the gate in the five-wire fence, stayed to regard the track beyond whilst the sergeant drove through. Not since the rain had a vehicle been driven down this track, the wheel ruts semifilled with drift sand making progress slower for Marshall's car.

59

"Those Jason men are singular in their individual ways, don't you think?" remarked Bony.

"You're telling me," agreed the sergeant succinctly.

"Which of them is the boss? I went into the garage the other morning and was just in time to hear young Jason tell his father to 'get to hell away from that.' Old Jason was standing by the engine of a truck. The engine was running and he was peering in at it under the raised bonnet. When the son shouted at him from a wall bench the father straightened up and moved away after switching off the engine. He said nothing; made no attempt even to remonstrate with his son for speaking as he did."

"They're a peculiar pair," Marshall further agreed. "The son is the motor mechanic, and a good one too, and the old man doing all wheelwrighting and coffin making. He's a bit of a brick, in his way, for he takes a lot from the lad and seldom asserts himself. Pities him, I suppose, for his deformities, and the son resents it."

"Where do they come from?"

"Bathurst, I think."

"Redman doesn't record their origin, although in his reports he is hostile to young Jason. There is a lot in origins, you know. The history of murders and lesser crimes doesn't begin five minutes before they are committed. The origin of some murders began generations before the—er—blunt instrument was used."

Now the country was swiftly changing. The trees were thinning out and the barley and spear grass were giving place to tussock grass, that wiry, seemingly indestructible grass growing in clumps in the drier, more inhospitable parts of the inland. The red sand was becoming heavier, and on the east side of every clump of tussock grass the sand was raised into a small mound. Quite abruptly the trees and bush shrubs ended in an irregular line, and the car passed out onto a half-mile-wide ribbon of plain land bordering the Walls of China. The red sand gave place to white sand, and now the tussock grass gave out. Nothing grew here on the white sand foundations of the Walls of China. The white plain was gouged and tossed by the fingers of the wind into ugly chaos which made astonishing contrast with the beautiful curves and mouldings of the sand ridges rising tier upon tier to the lofty summit lines sweeping away in great undulations to north and south.

Ahead stood a corrugated iron hut, with, a hundred yards south of it, the windmill over the well and the iron reservoir tank perched on its high stand. The lines of troughing radiating from it appeared like the fire-hardened hafts of aboriginal throwing spears, black on the white sand.

The door of the hut was in its east wall. Beyond it by a dozen yards was a construction of cane grass in which was kept the cool safe for the storage of meat. And beyond that, some three hundred yards away, was the base of the sand range.

Marshall halted his car between the hut and the meat house. The hut was the usual monstrosity of iron nailed to a wood frame. There was not even a window to it, an opening in its west wall being closed at this time by a trap on hinges.

"What a salubrious resort at which to spend the summer vacation," observed Bony. "How one would enjoy the summer breezes, the rarefied air, the perfume of flowers, the song of birds. Don't get out yet."

"Quiet enough, anyway," Marshall said, reaching for pipe and tobacco.

"Were it not for the blowflies and the crows somewhere up there on the Walls of China, there would be no sounds our human ear could register," Bony noted, and became busy with tobacco and paper. "You wouldn't think, would you, that in this place of spotless white—if we can disregard that hut—a man could meet with a violent end? Ah me, how truthfully it was written: 'The evil men do lives after them.' For years and years to come men will say: 'A murder was committed here.' They may even say: 'Two murders were committed here.'"

Marshall had struck a match, had brought its flame against the tobacco in his pipe, but he did not draw upon it.

"What's that?" he demanded.

"What is what?" countered Bony mildly.

"What was that about two murders being done in this place?"

"Oh, I was just letting my imagination have a little freedom. But let us be serious. Take note, and profit by it, of the difference of my approach to the scene of a crime from that of your own and Redman's. I sit back in the comfortable seat of this car and leisurely smoke a cigarette whilst observing the scene of a crime now several weeks old, and give my imagination a slack rein.

What did you and Gleeson and Redman do? What was your approach?"

Marshall grunted.

"Go on, I'll buy it," he urged.

"Firstly, then, you and Gleeson arrived here in a car with such speed that the car probably skidded to a halt. You threw open the doors, leapt out, and rushed pell-mell into the hut to take a look-see at the body. Secondly, Redman and his colleagues arrived in manner similar but probably much faster. It is unlikely that they gave themselves time to open the car doors. It is likely that they fell out before the car was stopped, bounced on the white sand and, with the maintained velocity, shot into the hut to stare at the alleged bloodstains and make notes in small books. Ah . . . me! Why will men persist in thinking that accomplishment is regulated by muscular activity?"

"Search me," responded Marshall, who knew that Bony's picture was actually an exaggeration. He had got his pipe alight, and he half turned to look at his companion, to see the well-moulded nostrils of the slender nose appreciating the aroma of tobacco smoke.

"Listen, Marshall, for sometimes I talk downright common sense," Bony went on. "That hut is not a house, or a flat, or an office. This Sandy Flat is not a city. Therefore an investigation of a crime committed here must be conducted on vastly different lines. Let us assume that at this very moment there is in that hut the body of a murdered man, and that we are about to investigate the circumstances under which he died, and, further, to establish who killed him.

"Now you and Redman—Gleeson might not because he is accustomed to bush work—would rush into that hut to note the position of the body and the interior generally, because the interior of that iron monstrosity is a room, or the scene of the crime. You would search for the weapon with which the deed had been done, and for clues which might identify the killer. Now wouldn't you?"

Marshall nodded his agreement. Bony looked at him thoughtfully.

"But what do I do?" he asked blandly. "I leave the body to a uniformed constable, and the cause of death to the doctor and

62

the coroner, and to the experts at headquarters I leave the finger-prints if any, the weapon if any, and objects more closely associated with the crime. In a city the scene of the crime is of paramount importance, for there the scene of a crime is confined to a room, an office, a flat, and, if on a street, to a space within a few feet of the body.

"Here in the bush the scene of a crime is extended far beyond its immediate locale. Someone has had to go to the scene of the crime in order to commit it, and, afterwards, to leave the scene of the crime. As the criminal does not grow wings, he needs must walk, and he does not walk about without leaving tracks of his passage for me to see. To the city detective his fingerprints: to Bony his footprints. So you will now understand how it is that I am much more interested in the ground outside a house or hut or camp than I am with the interior.

"Again assuming that there is a dead body in that hut, what do we note about its exterior?" Bony continued after flicking a spent match towards the hut. "We see that Redman's photographer made quite a good negative of the hut with the door closed, precisely as we see it today. I am almost sure that photographing the hut with the door shut was a fluke, and a very lucky one, too. Anyway, the picture shows that now blurred mark on the door which you and I see from this distance. By the way, what do you make of that chalk mark?"

"Don't know," responded Marshall, to add: "Looks something like a game played by Florence and her mother called noughts and crosses, doesn't it?"

"I agree, Marshall. I suppose that the perspicacious Redman calculated that the dead man occupied his spare hours playing the game of noughts and crosses with himself. It was a probable assumption which he adopted on the grounds that the dead man was mentally deficient to live in a place like this. So that once more is stressed the absurdity of sending a city-bred man to investigate a bush crime, for Redman would not know that there are men who find contentment in living here. Redman makes no mention of that game of noughts and crosses in his reports. To him the game meant nothing, but to me it shrieks to high heaven the intelligence that George Kendall was brought to that hut a dead man."

Marshall sighed audibly. He was beginning to find this passive attitude a little boring.

"Patience! Patience!" Bony cried. "What else do we see?"

"Sand. Ruddy sand. And the hamper and tea billy are in the back of the car."

"Cannot you see certain marks on the ground?" urged Bony. "You will remember that it rained heavily that afternoon when Edward Bennett was buried. That was six days ago. It rained so heavily that the natural water holes were filled with water, and, consequently, no animals have since come to drink at these troughs. Neither was there cause for anyone to come here from the station homestead to make sure that the troughs were being supplied with water. Since the rain fell the wind has blown at a velocity exceeding ten miles an hour on only two days, the last being yesterday. The rain and wind wiped clean this page of the Book of the Bush for such as me to read.

"Observe . . . again. On this clean page of the Book of the Bush are printed the boot prints of a man. He did not arrive here by the road we came by. He came from the north, skirting the sand range. We may assume (a) that he came from Wattle Creek homestead and (b) that he was bushman enough to travel across country and (c) that he knew the position of this hut and well. Is that clear to you?"

When the frowning sergeant did not reply Bony slowly continued:

"The man reached the hut along its north wall, and he came to the door and went inside. He went inside, I repeat, and he closed the door and he has not come out."

"Then he must be still in there?" asserted Marshall.

"Naturally. The tracks proved that he arrived and went in. There are no tracks to prove that he has come out."

"Well, what's it all mean? You seem to know."

"Let us get out of the car."

On alighting from the car, Bony stood beside its rear mudguard and invited Marshall to join him. The sergeant's interest was kindled.

"You see," Bony continued, melodramatically waving his hands, "you see a work of wondrous artistic beauty, a work revealing the ultimate in balance and mathematical exactitude.

There the perfect beauty of line etching the Walls of China against the sky, and all about us the same beauty of line in the miniature waves of the sand ribbles. To the undiscerning eye, in all this vast picture presented to our eyes today, there are no straight lines save those made by man when he erected that hut, the tank stand and the mill and the lines of troughing. Even that natural gutter over there which carried water the other day down from the higher land is not straight for even an inch. It would seem that the Master Potter is incapable of moulding a straight line. Satan's hell is probably built on straight lines—the flames even having no curves in them. Do you see the spent match which I flicked away a moment ago?"

"Yes."

"Look at the ground immediately to the left of the match. What do you see?"

"Nothing. The ground is smooth."

"I can see straight lines immediately to the left of the match, and also beyond the match and this side of the match. I am confident that when we approach the door of the hut we shall see straight lines also imprinted on the nice, clean, and apparently smooth sand. Come with me to the match, and with it I will trace the straight lines for you to see more clearly."

Bony squatted beside the match and the sergeant bent down beside him. With the point of the match Bony indicated lines so finely drawn that even then Marshall found difficulty in visually following them. When they stood up Marshall waited for his superior in bushcraft as well as in rank to speak.

"There are no straight lines in nature," Bony repeated. "Therefore those straight lines were made by a man. Let me read this new writing on this page of the Book of the Bush. A man walks direct from Wattle Creek Station to that hut, goes inside and then comes out again, shuts the door, and walks backwards away from it, at the same time carefully wiping out his boot prints with the aid of lengths of sacking strips tied to the end of a stick. Why he left like that, why he was so anxious to prevent others seeing that he had left, is a problem which can wait awhile. We can, meanwhile, read it in another way. The man from Wattle Creek went into the hut and has not come out. A second man came and went, and flailed out his tracks from the sand in order to prevent others

65

from knowing that he had visited the place. Being human, he could not do other than make straight lines with his flail. I am almost sure that there were two men, and that one of them is still inside the hut."

"Well, let's go and find out," pressed the sergeant, interest now at fever point.

"Slowly! Slowly!" murmured Bony, and Marshall noted that when he walked towards the closed door of the hut he walked on the toes of his feet and his hands were clenched tightly. They halted two yards from the door.

"Again I offer thanks to that police photographer for unwittingly introducing me to a nice meaty case," Bony said softly. "The man who so carefully flailed out his boot prints was most careful not to tread on the tracks made by the man who is still inside. Look! He reached the hut at its southeast corner, or left by it, and he did not put foot on the low doorstep, as the man did who is still inside. When you open the door, Sergeant, you are going to receive a surprise."

Sergeant Marshall now was standing stiffly erect. His face was a mask in which his eyes were unwinking orbs. He said, ice in his voice:

"I think I can smell the surprise."

"I have done so for the last half hour. Will you open the door, or shall I?"

"Me . . . I'm no chicken," growled Marshall as he advanced to open it.

"One moment. The door handle. It may possibly have retained the fingerprints of the man with the flail."

"Of course," snapped Marshall. "I'm a fool."

He whipped a handkerchief from a pocket, wrapped it about the brass handle, and with a firm grip turned it and flung inward the door.

Their gaze became riveted for an instant on a pair of old boots suspended about twelve inches from the floor. Then, slowly, their gaze rose upward, up the trousered legs, up the old blue shirt, up to the awful face of the man hanging from a crossbeam.

A great swarm of blowflies came out through the open doorway to break the silence with the hateful buzzing of their wings.

"Do you know him?" Bony asked with apparent calmness.

"No. Never seen him before. What do you think—suicide or murder?"

"I give murder first preference because of the man with the flail. He was probably here when that poor wretch arrived. I would that the interior was much larger, but we must go inside."

The interior measurements of the hut were ten feet by ten feet. More swiftly than he had moved for some time, Bony stepped by the suspended corpse and reached the far side, where he quickly raised the trap-door opening which served as a window. Then he turned about to survey "the scene of the crime."

"Ah, the obvious story is as follows," he said. "The man entered the hut. Then he tossed his swag onto the bunk and removed from it the two leather straps. Having done that, he dragged the table almost beneath the crossbeams, climbed up on it, joined the two straps together after making a noose with the end of one passed through its own buckle, fastened the end of the other to the beam and slipped the noose over his head and about his neck, and then stepped off the table. But why, if he arrived with the intention of committing suicide, did he close the door? And if he had no intention of suiciding when he arrived, why did he not visit the well for water? For he did not possess a water bag."

"You think he was hanged, then?" Marshall asked.

"I think he was hanged. You had better go back for Dr. Scott and Gleeson. Phew! Let's get out."

Having hastily closed the trap window, they went outside and closed the door.

"What about making arrangements for having the body removed to the morgue?" Marshall suggested. "The Jasons can do that."

"Wait! Er—no. Not a word about this affair to anyone in Merino, not even to Gleeson and the doctor until you have left with them. And also, not a word to a living soul, now or in the future, about that game of noughts and crosses on the door, and about the blemish of straight lines on Nature's handiwork. They shall remain two little secrets to be shared only by you and me."

VIII. Tracks on the Walls of China

DURING THOSE SECONDS of horror following the opening of the hut door, Sergeant Marshall changed from the very human being he had permitted himself to become back to the coldly calm, efficient police administrator. He refrained from saluting only by a fraction of time before striding to his car and driving away across the waste of white sand to the fringe of bush and scrub timber.

There had also occurred a subtle change in Bony. The easy and apparently careless movement familiar to Sergeant Marshall was replaced by taut, spring-controlled action—the difference marked in a cat when, following its master about a garden, it sights its prey within stalking distance.

Despite his long association with crime in its worst degree, he had never become indifferent to the proximity of death, for beneath the veneer of the cultured white man the black man's fear of the dead lurked deep within his subconsciousness. It was, therefore, with unusual haste that he set to work to remove the door handles, thankful that the screw gave easily to the point of his penknife.

He had seen a pair of old trousers in a far corner of the hut, and for the second time he edged past the swinging corpse, the soul of him in revolt. When he regained the open air he wrapped the door handles within the trousers and the parcel he pushed under the raised floor of the hut near the doorstep. The door he wedged shut with a wood chip from the wood heap. And then, with a feeling of thankfulness, he crossed to the cane-grass meat house, peeped inside at the safe on its tall legs set in jam tins filled with water, and finally squatted on its south side with its wall as a back rest.

It was noonday and the shadow cast by the meat house would not have covered a plate. He was oblivious to shadow and sunlight; the making of a cigarette was entirely automatic. He was unconscious of the nearer, the inner, languorous silence which lay heavily over the dazzling white scene of white sand, but the buzzing of the blowflies was a constant and sinister reminder of what was within the hut, whilst the noise created by a party of distant crows at first made no impression on his mind.

A state of ecstasy lifted him up, urging him into activity which had to be resisted. What he had predicted to Sergeant Marshall but an hour since, that another would be buried shortly in the cemetery, would take place. For a lie will beget lies, and murder will beget murder. And now he knew for certain what he had expected, that the man who had killed Kendall had not fled but remained in or close to Merino.

The whys and wherefores of this latest death could be divided into two sections: those concerning the dead man and the circumstances of the discovery of the body; and those concerning the living man who had so carefully obliterated his tracks. The dead could wait, could be left to Dr. Scott and Marshall, and to Coroner Jason. The living was his concern, for that living man who flailed out his tracks was the quarry he, Napoleon Bonaparte, was here to hunt. It was the ecstasy of the hunter that was now lifting him up, that was coursing through his veins like a fire, liquid fire refined by generations of the most cunning, the most patient, and the most relentless hunters this world has ever known.

Rising to his feet, he walked to the place where he had outlined with a match the marks made by a flail of strips of hessian sacking. Slowly he followed the regular series of marks over the steps made by a man, visualizing the action of the flail on the fine sand. First the hard pressure on the ground to fill in the deep indentations, then the lighter touches with the ends of the strips. The flail could smooth the sand, leaving the faintest marks for only the most expert of trackers to see, but the flail wielder could not re-create the delicate sand ribbles made by the fingers of the West Wind.

Time must have been necessary, and also daylight. The operation was carried out most probably immediately following the dawn of the day, for the wind of yesterday would certainly have covered those hair-fine marks had they been made the morning before. Presently he stopped to find himself close to the well.

The marks led him to the windmill over the well, and from there to the stand on which was the iron reservoir tank. There

was an iron ladder giving access to the wooden platform on which
the tank rested some fifteen feet above the ground. The mark
were closer here at the foot of the ladder, as though for some
reason or other the man had gone up that ladder to the tank. The
marks continued on past the ladder and Bony continued to follow
them east towards the Walls of China. And at the foot of the
Walls, where the foot of the lowest sand dune rested on the plain
the flail marks ceased and there began larger, light indentation
which at this shadowless time of day were barely more easily fol
lowed.

From this point back to the hut the flail had been used. From
here on and up the Walls the man had considered the flail un
necessary to wipe away the tracks made by his feet encased in
loose hessian.

Whether the man had come down this way or had gone back
this way Bony could not determine; therefore he could not know
if he was following the man's tracks or backtracking him, and the
only way to find out was to continue.

On the soft and fine sand of the slopes the imprints were hardly
deeper than the cover of a book and as large as the impression
made by an elephant. They led him up a minor gully between the
lower dunes, twisting about to take still other gullies, until finally
they reached the comparative flat top of the Walls of China. On
ward they went directly eastwards over the field of dazzling white
sand. Bony halted to take stock of his position.

The sunlight was reflected by the iron roofs of Merino situated
midway up the vast rise of land reaching to the western horizon.
The bush lay like an old and moth-eaten brown carpet, the holes
in it red with the sandy soil; and the green of the pepper trees
lining the street of the township made striking contrast. To the
north, close to the huge sand range, were the roofs of Wattle
Creek homestead, and the sun glinted on the fans of a windmill
in action. At Bony's feet was the little iron hut and mill at Sandy
Flat; whilst to the south, also close to the Walls of China, roofs
and a windmill marked the home of Mrs. Sutherland.

It appeared mathematically impossible for the entire bulk of
this mighty sand range to have been raised from the strip of white
sand country upon which it was founded. As yet he could see no
eastern limits, for the bushlands to the east were lower than the

"roof" on which he stood. Here and there pillars of sandstone rose like monoliths from the "roof," some twenty feet, others thirty feet high. And those pillars possibly indicated that the Walls of China had not been raised by the wind but by an earth upheaval, that out of the bowels of the earth this section of white sand had been heaved to become the sport of the west wind, to wear it out and away from the hard cores.

Bony turned to the east and continued to follow the almost invisible tracks of the man who wore sacking about his feet. Ahead, about midway to the farthest limits seen of the sand range, a party of crows were vociferously engaged with something lying on the sand. The object he could not see, but their antics proved that something did lie there. Some of the birds were flying in erratic circles; others were on the white sand like blots of ink on paper.

The man tracks did not extend directly to the object of interest to the crows, but when they reached a point close to it, he left the tracks and walked the short distance to ascertain what it was. At his approach the birds whirled upward in flight, cawing angrily, some to alight on the sand and continue their loud protest at his intrusion.

In a small and shallow declivity lay the body of an animal which Bony instantly recognized as young Jason's brown and white dog with the nail missing in its right forepaw. The crows had ripped out its entrails, but the manner in which the dead animal lay revealed clearly that it had died from taking a poison bait.

Bony considered, thoughtfully gazing over the roof of sand and thereby maintaining the anger of the crows. He could see nothing other than the roof of the Walls of China, limited to the east and west by the blue of the sky, to the south and north by endless slopes and summits of whalebacks lying in shimmering, faintly purple opalescence. And here and there those strange cores of sandstone behind which could shelter a corps of spies . . . or one man armed with a rifle.

Within yards of the carcass the crows had obliterated the last tracks made by the living animal. Bony found them at the edge of the crow-disturbed area, and backtracked. He came to the place where the unfortunate animal had lain in a spasm of agony and, still farther along, to another where it had endured probably its first. Continuing to backtrack, he reached the slight indentations made by the man who had visited Sandy Flat, and then it was established that the man had been on his way to Sandy Flat from the east country, and that the dog had been following his trail when it picked up the poison bait.

Question: Was the bait dropped by one of the station men to destroy a dingo, or had it been dropped by the man to prevent the dog with one toenail missing from following him and thus probably drawing attention to his own tracks so carefully smoothed out by a flail made with strips of sacking? The answer could be established by enquiries made at Wattle Creek homestead.

The answer was in favour of the poisoning having been done by the man who wore sacking on his feet. Was that man the owner of the dog? That was possible but not probable, for Bony had himself seen that same dog following Mr. Jason, Constable Gleeson, two stockmen, and Fanning, the butcher.

When Bony continued with his work it was to backtrack not only the man's faint impressions but also to backtrack the perfectly plain tracks of the dog. He was led to the eastern side of the Walls, their leeward side, and here the flank of the sand range abruptly fell more sheerly than the slope of a house roof down to hard white claypans.

Beyond the claypans, many covering unbrokenly an acre or more, lay a strip of wire-grass country varying in width from half to a full mile away to the edge of thick mulga scrub.

Bony pursed his lips. Had he been a profane man, he would have sworn, for it was useless to attempt to track across that dense growth of wire grass growing to a height of eighteen inches, grass so springy that beneath the tread of a rhinoceros it would rise again within the hour.

The man and dog had obviously come up from those claypans and, most probably, from across that wire grass, which would bend but never break and then stand up again within the hour. They could have traversed either the claypans footing the Walls or the wire-grass country for miles from the south or from the north, and now to continue backtracking them would be time ill spent. Where man and animal had climbed up the steep face of the sand cliff, huge dislodgments had scarred the perfectly symmetrical face.

Having established from which point the man had travelled to the hut at Sandy Flat, it remained for him to ascertain in which direction the man had left. Even that was less important than other work to be done. And after all, with all his minute care to avoid discovery, the man had failed to frustrate Napoleon Bonaparte, failed in his attempt to lead justice to believe that the unfortunate man within the hut had committed suicide, if, indeed, he had been hanged.

Bony walked southward slowly, rolling the inevitable cigarette now that the tenseness of the chase was relaxed. The great cores of sandstone were not found on this side of the Walls. He stood looking downward upon a huge claypan containing water two inches deep, and down he went in a flurry of sand to reach its edge and follow it round to see if the dog had taken a drink there. The tracks of sheep were left on the softer edge of the pan against the water, and there, too, were the tracks made by two dingoes and many birds and several horses. There were no tracks of the dog having a toenail missing from its forepaw.

Once again up on the Walls, he continued walking southward, and then, approximately a mile south of the tracks made by man and dog across the roof, he found the tracks of the man returning from the westward side, alone.

Looking upward at a crow winging softly towards those now far-distant blots on paper, he said:

"Some people hate you and your kind. I don't hate you. How often have you black devils led me to a clue of great importance. Well, you to your carcass, and me to my little brain teaser. A man takes extraordinary pains to leave no trace of his walkabout over these beautiful Walls of China at a time when a man is hanging from a crossbeam of a lonely stockman's hut. Interesting . . . most. As Charles would have said, it's a monty that that poor devil was hanged and did not hang himself. But if I had not discerned those faint straight lines where there are only curved lines, it is probable that the death would have been recorded as suicide."

He began the walk to the northwest which would take him directly above Sandy Flat well.

It was as deserted as when he had left it. There was no sign of the returning police sergeant's car on the track he could see running from the left-angle turn up to the township. He sat down on a ledge at the base of a sandstone pillar and rolled another cigarette. And two minutes later he vented a long-drawn "Ah!"

Riding towards him at an easy canter was a woman on a grey horse. She was coming from the south, and so clear was the air he could see the tracks made by her horse on the slope of a whale-back more than a mile away. She and her horse disappeared in a declivity, to reappear three minutes later much nearer to him. She was, apparently, riding towards the homestead of Wattle Creek.

When she saw him she reined in her mount to a walk and drew near. Bony was on his feet and the hazel eyes of the rider were quick to notice how his hat had been removed . . . not a prevalent male courtesy in Australia.

"Good morning!" he said, adding hastily: "Or is it good afternoon?" He sighted his own shadow, and then noted the position of the sun. "Why, it is twenty minutes past two."

Involuntarily the girl looked at her wrist watch.

"Why, it is twenty minutes past two o'clock!" she exclaimed. "Oh! Good afternoon! You made a remarkably good guess."

Bony smiled broadly. The smile lay deep in his blue eyes and lingered about his mouth, revealing his perfect teeth. Then, before the smile had quite departed, he said boastingly:

"I never guess . . . when I am serious. Have you ridden far today?"

The impertinence of his question went unnoticed. She sat still, looking down at him, whilst telling him that she had ridden out from the homestead that morning to make sure that a mob of horses were getting water. Although he had boasted that he never essayed a guess, he guessed that this girl's age was in the vicinity of twenty-eight or -nine. She was slight of figure, and she sat her horse as though long accustomed. Khaki jodhpurs and silk blouse, the absence of a hat revealing light brown hair drawn to a bun at the back of her head, showed modern Australian womanhood at its best. She was not actually good-looking, but Bony had long reached an age when beauty of personality was more appreciated than skin beauty. And personality this girl certainly had.

She appeared oblivious to his degree as stockman, as well as to the fact of his birth. That she should overlook these matters, he prided himself, was due to his own charm. He knew that he could be charming when he wished. . . . She said, puzzlement leaping into her eyes:

"But what are you doing here? On foot and no swag! Have you lost your horse?"

"No. I got the day off, and so decided that I would tour these extraordinary sand walls."

"They are certainly well worth a visit. Who are you working for?"

"His Majesty's representative, the governor."

"The governor!"

Gravely he bowed his head in assent. When he looked upward he was again smiling, this time impishly, and through her mind sped the thought that only now did she realize that he was not wholly white. He was saying:

"You see, I insulted the police force over there in Merino, and the police force hailed me before Justice Jason, who ordered me to be held in durance vile for ten long days . . . and nights, by the way. Thereupon the police force suggested—suggested, mind you, not ordered—that were I to paint the police station fences a sickly yellow colour I would be given three meals a day by Mrs. Marshall and two shillings a day for beer at knock-off time. To-day, however, to celebrate the halfway period of my penal sentence, I asked for the day off, threatening that if I were not granted the holiday I would immediately go on strike. If the coal miners can go on strike over stupid and trivial things, why can't I?"

The girl tossed back her head and laughed, and he noted how her nose wrinkled at its bridge and how her eyes seemed to dance in the light.

"The threat of leaving the police station only half painted was sufficient even for Sergeant Marshall," he went on. "You would appreciate that could you see the new yellow paint over the old blue tints."

"I have heard something about you," she told him, abruptly serious. "Mr. James, the minister, spoke to my brother about you. Asked my brother if he could find you a job after your release."

"You are, then, Miss Leylan?"

"Yes. What is your name?"

"I am known as Robert Burns." Bony raised a hand and

75

mimicked the parson at Merino. Then he adopted a Scotch accent and denied his descent from the poet. "For some reason unexplained," he went on, "all my friends call me Bony. I prefer it that way. It saves a lot of arguments with Scotchmen."

"You speak very well—Bony. Good school?"

"My father gave me a sound education," Bony replied gravely. "Do you think your brother will give me a sound job?"

"Probably. I didn't actually hear what he said to Mr. James. I left them together. Mr. James didn't mention the matter when I saw him this morning."

"You saw him this morning?"

"Oh yes. We met by chance away out east from the Walls of China a little before I found our horses. The silly man had blown his horse. It was in a lather of sweat and he was rubbing it down with a piece of hessian sacking. If I'm any judge, he would have to walk his horse back to town."

"Your brother is a great friend of his, I understand," Bony suggested.

She laughed again, and not until some time later did she realize how easily this stranger had made her forget her native caution.

"Not exactly. My brother says that the minister makes his toes itch to be up and doing. We like his wife. You will find her a splendid woman. Well, I must be going. Good-bye."

"Good-bye, Miss Leylan. By the way, do your men lay poison baits on these Walls of China?"

"No. Why?"

"There is a dog dead over there, and I thought it might have picked up a bait."

"Indeed!" She turned and gazed in the direction indicated by him. "I'll ride over and have a look at it."

"I have seen it before. It's a town dog."

She heeled her mount round, waved a hand to him, and rode away.

He turned from watching her to see the dust of a car coming down the slope from Merino, and to murmur:

"Well! Well! So this very morning Mr. James was wiping down his blown horse with a piece of hessian sacking. And Mr. Leylan is not a great friend of Mr. James, after all. Well! Well! Our official interest in Mr. James goes on and on and on."

IX. Dr. Scott Examines the Body

DR. MALCOLM SCOTT was short, tubby, and sixty, white of hair, and had a fresh complexion which defied the sun. Why he came to practise in Merino no one knew and he never bothered to explain. He arrived, had a comfortable house built between the bank and one of the stores, and quietly settled down to enjoy life in his own manner and alleviate the superficial sufferings of a people notoriously healthy.

It could be assumed that Merino would have assimilated Dr. Scott. To use the vernacular: "What a hope!" Dr. Scott assimilated Merino, for he became its first citizen in all activities excepting those connected with the law. He got to know everyone and everything about everyone, or nearly so. And he had the knack of keeping everyone in his place so that he could be familiar to all while none dared be familiar to him.

He was out of town when Marshall reached Merino, necessitating a wait for an hour, by the end of which Mounted Constable Gleeson's iron control was beginning to crack. On arrival at Sandy Flat, they discovered Bony sitting on the doorstep of the hut.

"I hope you brought back the hamper and tea billy," he said pleasantly, when they had left the car and stood before him. "I am beginning to be hungry."

"Stomach! Stomach! Stomach! It's always stomach," snorted the doctor. "Can't you forget your stomach and enjoy good health? And what a place to have a stomach, too! Now where's this body?"

Bony rose to his feet, and before pushing inward the door he said gravely:

"It awaits you."

The three men grouped themselves behind Dr. Scott, who surveyed the body through his steel-rimmed spectacles.

"Coo!" he exclaimed softly. "What's your opinion, Marshall?"

"Haven't decided," replied the cautious sergeant. "We'd better

77

go in. Have a look, Gleeson, at the way the straps were joined and then tied to the crossbeam. Note the general layout. I'll open that trap window."

Bony did not again enter the hut. He heard Marshall tell his constable to photograph the corpse and the use made of the dead man's swag straps, and then he walked to the car and took out the hamper and billy can.

"Ever seen him before, Gleeson?" Marshall asked.

"No, Sergeant."

"How old would he be, Doctor?"

"About fifty."

"Colour of eyes?"

"Hazel. Grey hair . . . was dark brown."

"Any distinguishing marks—without stripping him?"

"Yes. First joint of little finger of right hand missing."

"Thanks. We'll leave the contents of the swag till later, Gleeson. There seems to be nothing else. No fire lit for weeks. He didn't even have a meal here. Couldn't have been here long before he died. Shall we take him down, Doctor?"

"Yes. Get my bag from the car, please, Gleeson. Afterwards we'll want some hot water—and soap—plenty of it. I see half a bar over on that shelf."

Ten minutes later they heard a distant voice shout:

"Lunchoh!"

Marshall, who was standing just inside the door, turned about to see Detective Inspector Napoleon Bonaparte, the noted crime investigator, standing beside a fire he had made over by the tank stand. In the shadow was the unpacked hamper and a steaming billy. Beside the fire were two petrol buckets of heated water.

"Ready for a drink of tea, Doctor?" he asked over his shoulder.

"Drink anything . . . now," snapped Scott. "Ugh! Filthy business! Let's get outside."

They were thankful for the hot but fresh air without, and the sergeant wedged shut the door. They walked across to the tank stand, and it seemed to them that they had left a noisome dungeon.

"Gentlemen! Lunch is served," Bony said in welcome, and, strangely enough, they were glad to hear the tone of gaiety in his voice. "There is the dish I brought from the hut. Hot water aplenty. I forgot that soap, Marshall. Sorry. Towels are minus."

Dr. Scott glared.

"Seen you somewhere," he said impolitely. "Why, hang it, I remember. You're the fellow who was painting the police station fence. The colour makes me sick every time I look at it."

"It causes Rose Marie to feel sick too," supplemented Bony. In fifteen minutes he was saying to his guests, who were seated on the ground beside the contents of the hamper:

"Tea in this china cup for you, Doctor. And this other china cup for you, Sergeant. Gleeson and I will drink from these tin pannikins I brought from the hut. It's all right, Gleeson. They are station property, and I have scoured them well with hot water and sand. What a beautiful day!"

In after years, whenever the doctor recalled this scene, invariably he remembered the manner in which Bony appeared to evolve from a nebulous figure painting a fence, through the clearer stage of seeing him seated on the doorstep of a hut in which was suspended the body of a man, to this moment when smilingly he proffered to him a cup of tea. Subsequently he always felt like a man who mistook his host for the butler.

He said to Sergeant Marshall: "You could arrange for the inquest to be held tomorrow. Seems all straightforward."

"It will depend upon my superior," Marshall countered.

"Your superior?"

"Permit me to intrude—again," murmured Bony. "I am going to take you into my confidence, Doctor, because I need your co-operation. I am a detective inspector of the Queensland C.I.B. on loan to this state to look into the circumstances of the death of George Kendall. My name is Napoleon Bonaparte."

"What's that?" exclaimed Scott.

"That is actually my name. Sandwich?

"I have made myself *au fait* with your history, Doctor, and I am entitled by it to be confident that you will maintain what is at present a police secret," Bony said. "For twenty-eight years you practised in Sydney, where you were widely and favourably known. You came to Merino ten years ago for domestic reasons. Your chief interest in life is the study of biochemistry. Finally: you are known most favourably to the police force at Merino."

Dr. Scott seemed bereft of motion, for he held the teacup in a

79

fixed position about the level of his round chin whilst gazing at Bony with wide eyes. Then he barked:

"It's like your impertinence, inquiring into my career as though I were a criminal." His face was flushed. "My reasons for coming to Merino are my own. My hobbies are my own. My financial affairs are my own. I'll have you know——"

"I had to be assured that I could ask you for assistance on the side of justice," Bony cut in. "You will shortly appreciate the reason for caution, and the irritation caused in you by my cautiousness will probably be balanced by matters of great interest to you as a scientific man."

"That's all right, then. I'm all for law and order, myself."

"Good! Another sandwich. What about you, Sergeant? Gleeson?"

For a little while they ate in silence, the three men appearing to wait upon the half-caste who so assiduously attended to their needs. Dr. Scott still was a little ruffled, and still affected by the surprise sprung upon him. Marshall seemed happy to take a minor position, and Gleeson continued to be like one whom nothing could visibly affect. Then again came Bony's softly modulated voice uttering the slightly pedantic sentences.

"It would seem that in this district there is a quite ruthless killer, a man far removed from the exasperated husband who slays his nagging wife, and far removed, too, from the unthinking thug who waylays and bashes on dark nights. I would not have consented to undertake this investigation were I not assured that the killer of Kendall was a man having intelligence, and, further, that in spite of appearance Kendall was not killed over in that hut."

"But I came here that day and saw the body lying on the floor in its own blood," expostulated Dr. Scott, and Gleeson appeared to freeze.

"Yes, yes! I know you did, as well as others. I know for a fact that Kendall was not killed inside that hut. His body was taken to it and put on the floor and blood, probably sheep's blood, was poured on the floor to indicate that the man had been killed there. Where he was killed I don't yet know, and I have yet to establish why. The point of greatest interest is why the killing was staged in the hut, why such efforts were made to divert police attention from the place where the murder was done. Would it be possible, Doctor, for you to identify the blood on the floor from the dried residue?"

"I am uncertain," replied Dr. Scott. "I will certainly try."

"Thank you. If you succeeded it would set all your doubts at rest. Now let us pass to the case of Edward Bennett. He was one of your patients. Tell us what you know about him, professionally."

Dr. Scott handed round his case, filled with expensive cigarettes. Then:

"Old Bennett was my very first patient after my arrival in Merino. The condition of his heart was not robust and I warned him to go easy. But his type never goes easy, and I knew that my job was to keep him going as long as possible. Only a week before he did die I told him to cut his hotel bill by half."

"He was found in his pyjamas on the floor just inside his front door," Bony continued. "He died sometime during the night, according to your estimate, as I know quite well that only an estimate can be given of the length of time a human body has been dead. Would it be possible, do you think, that old Bennett could have died through shock, let us say, when he opened his front door?"

"Quite possible. Bennett had been staggering on the edge of his grave for several years."

"There are, of course, many others in Merino who knew the state of the old man's heart?"

"Yes. He himself made sure that everyone knew it."

"Thank you. Now, gentlemen, go back to that afternoon when you three entered Bennett's hut and found him dead, and consider my suspicion that someone knocked on his door in the dead of night, and that, on opening it, he received such a fright that his poor weak heart failed. How does it appear to you?"

"Are you inferring that someone frightened him to death?" asked Gleeson, his eyes narrowed.

"Let us leave that for the time, Gleeson, and concentrate on the possibility that Bennett died from shock and not from the normal failure of his heart action," Bony countered.

"Knowing nothing to change it, my opinion remains that Bennett died from angina pectoris, which was not a secondary cause," the doctor argued. "I think I can put myself in his place that night. Sometime during the night he became ill, and he lit his bedside lamp and swallowed two of my tablets. A little later he became worse and decided to leave the place and seek assistance, of me or of his daughter. He got as far as the door when death came to him."

"If that were so," Bony began demurringly, "would he not have slipped an overcoat over his pyjamas? The night was not warm. He did not even put his feet into the slippers which were placed neatly beside his bed when he retired."

"Yes, there is all that about it," Scott admitted.

"His dead face looked as though he had received a bad fright," said Gleeson.

"I accepted the look on his face as having been due to the last sharp agony," argued the doctor. "People suffering from his complaint sometimes die very hard. Still, I am not now hostile to the idea that old Bennett received a fright which caused his diseased heart to stop. That he died from heart failure is certain."

Gleeson flashed a look at his sergeant, his eyes still narrow and, as usual, his face maintaining its mask.

"Assuming that the main cause of Bennett's death was fright," he said, "was the fright given him accidentally or deliberately? I remember that the old man was at the dance social. He left early, and he was seen, later, holding Kendall's coat during the fight with young Jason."

"It would appear, Gleeson, that the thought is in your mind that the man who killed Kendall subsequently frightened old Bennett to his death," remarked Bony. "You may be right. It would not surprise me if you were. If we assume that you are right, then we should not accept too readily that that swagman hanged himself."

"It was suicide," snapped the doctor. "Men are not murdered by being hanged."

"Why not?" asked Gleeson pointedly.

"Why not?" echoed Scott. "How the devil do I know? Why should anyone hang the man? Why not hit him with an iron bar, or knife or shoot him?"

Gleeson was stubborn.

"Supposing he was stunned by a head blow, and then hanged

to present his death as suicide," he pressed. "If you will excuse me, you jumped to the conclusion that he hanged himself. You did not examine his head."

"Neither has an examination been made of the stomach," Bony added. "He may have been poisoned before being hanged."

"Imagination," snorted the doctor.

"Perhaps," conceded the constable. "You would be justified in calling it imagination if it hadn't been for the killing of Kendall. If Inspector Bonaparte is correct when he says that Kendall's body was brought here from some place the murderer didn't want to have investigated, and how the inspector makes that out beats me, then this hanging business may not be what it appears to be. By the way," to Bony, "have you looked around for tracks?"

"Yes, Gleeson. There are none other than those made by the dead man." Marshall blinked his eyes. "Those tracks indicate that the dead man came from Wattle Creek homestead direct along the foot of these Walls of China. Those you see laid over the Walls were left by me. I went up there to find out what the crows were so excited about. They had found young Jason's dog. It had picked up a poison bait."

For the first time expression was registered on Gleeson's face. He looked like a man whose thoughts were being proved.

"Young Jason's brown and white dog?" echoed Marshall.

"What on earth would that dog be doing up there?" demanded the doctor.

"Possibly following his owner," replied Gleeson.

"Or young Jason's father, or the butcher, or the parson, or Rose Marie," said the smiling Bonaparte. "I have seen that dog following many people."

"So have I," said Marshall in support.

"It must have been following someone and that's important," asserted Gleeson.

"In which case I would have seen the tracks made by the person followed," Bony pointed out frankly. "However, I am going to suggest that you remain here while Marshall and I run up to the homestead to enquire about the dead man, and during our absence you could hunt for tracks. I may possibly have missed them. I think, Doctor, that you might examine the body in the light of what we have discussed. Do you think you could have

83

your report ready for the inquest tomorrow morning? There would be nothing else to delay it beyond tomorrow, eh, Marshall?"

Both the doctor and the policeman agreeing that the inquest could be held in the morning, Bony beamed upon them in turn. He was almost gay when he said:

"If old Bennett did die of fright produced by the threat of murder, and if that man in the hut was first killed and then hanged, and if Kendall's body was taken to that hut from some other place where he was murdered, we are entitled to assume that in this district there is a tiptop, first-class, dyed-in-the-wool murderer. You know, gentlemen, I am beginning to enjoy myself. The answer to the question: 'Who dunn-it?' is going to be most interesting. Now, Doctor, who do you think it will turn out to be?"

"Rev. Llewellyn James," was the doctor's prompt reply.

"Dear me!" exclaimed Bony mildly.

"Yes. The fellow would murder anything. He's a hypocrite, a malingerer, and a fraud. Says he suffers from a weak heart, but he's too cunning to let me examine him. Sits most of the day on his veranda reading books, and lets his wife chop the wood in the back yard. He's as strong as a young bull, and he could hang that man with the greatest of ease."

Bony chuckled. He turned to Sergeant Marshall.

"What about you?" he pressed.

"Good job these guesses are off the record," growled Marshall. "I think I'll vote for Massey Leylan. He's young and strong, and he has a violent temper."

"My guess," said Gleeson, accepting Bony's invitation, "is young Jason. There is a certain amount of evidence pointing to him. Sergeant Redman picked on him too. Bad-tempered, sullen fellow. Strong despite his deformities."

"Now we have three likely-looking coves all ready for the neck-tie ceremony, as the late William Sykes would have said," pointed out the delighted Bony. "Henceforth I will take an especial interest in them."

Gleeson asked Bony who was his guess, and Bony was evasive.

"I am a personage of such terrific importance that I dare not hazard even a guess off the record," he said smilingly. "Were I to name the elder Jason, the hotel licensee, or the butcher, or even you, Gleeson, you would condemn the named person out of hand.

I can accept your choice with an open mind; you would accept mine as a certainty. However, if I favour anyone at all it is Mrs. Sutherland. When she invited me to call on her one day she said she would kill something."

At that they all laughed, and Marshall said:

"She always says that when she invites anyone to her place," he said. "Of course she means that she'll kill a fatted calf or a chook or something."

"That is what I thought," Bony agreed lightly. "Now we had better be off to Wattle Creek homestead, where you, Marshall, can telephone to the Jasons about the body, and I can visit the cook. Will you be coming, Doctor?"

"No. I think I will remain here and take another peep at the corpse."

X. The Guest of Sam the Black-mailer

As a man Sam the Blackmailer would never be cast for a screen lover, but as a cook he was superlative . . . when he liked to exert himself. He was known from one end of the Darling River to the other, and no squatter alive was game enough to offend him, for at the least offence, real or imaginary, a superlative cook would demand his cheque and make posthaste for the nearest pub.

Be it known that cooks are not as plentiful as peas in a pod; they are more rare than rich squatters who breed Melbourne Cup winners. Sam's bread and yeast buns were a delight to eat, whilst his pastry simply floated down the throats of men long used to soddy damper and mutton stews thickened with pure sand.

The story of how Sam the Blackmailer came by his sobriquet has come down through the mists of time in various forms, the most authentic being that when he asked for his cheque of an employer whose rich wife lived in the city he was told that there was no money with which to pay him. Thereupon Sam hinted in his gentlemanly manner that if the cash was not forthcoming in thirty minutes he would write to the wife concerning her husband's carrying on with a lubra. The husband was innocent, but the money was paid . . . quick.

Sam was tall and thin. His face was as white as his bread, and his unruly, straggly moustache was the colour of beer. When he sat down it seemed that he coiled himself, and when he got up he took an appreciable time to uncoil himself. He had never been known to wear other than white flannel trousers and cotton singlet, and when his great flat feet were thrust into cloth slippers he was the monarch of all he surveyed.

The men's eating room at Wattle Creek Station was akin to that on the majority of stations. It was a dining room cum kitchen combined, and at half past three o'clock it was Sam's duty to have tea and cake (brownie) ready for the hands working about the homestead.

This afternoon he heard a car arrive and stop outside the station office three minutes before the time to call the men. He was about to coil himself upon a petrol case preparatory to peeling the dinner potatoes when he changed his mind and sauntered to the door, there to lean against the frame to observe the well-known figure of Sergeant Marshall being welcomed by Massey Leylan. Bony he did not recognize, but he did see that Bony was not dressed as a policeman, and when his employer and the sergeant went into the office he whistled with his fingers and then beckoned the stranger to him.

His next act was to lurch from the doorpost and amble to the short length of railway iron suspended from a tree branch. This he struck with an iron bar, giving it one terrific clout as though it were his greatest enemy, who needed only the one blow. He was seated at the end of one of the long forms flanking the dining table when Bony entered, followed by several hands.

"Good dayee, mate. Come and have a drink er tea," he said to Bony. "Pannikins on the wall there. Tea here in the ruddy pot."

Bony nodded his thanks, took down a shining tin pannikin, and poured himself tea.

"Sit down, mate," invited Sam the Blackmailer. "Ain't never seen you before. Bushman?"

"Yes. Looking for a job . . . or was," replied Bony, helping himself to brownie.

"Cripes!" exclaimed one of the hands. "Ain't you the bloke what was run in and made to paint the police station fence?"

"My fame as a painter of police station fences has, apparently, gone out far and wide," modestly admitted Bony, beaming upon them all.

"Ruddy shame," snarled Sam the Blackmailer.

"Oh, the work is easy enough, the hours not long," Bony said lightly. "And I get my meals at the sergeant's table, and his wife's a good cook. Plus two bob a day to spend over at the hotel half an hour before closing time. I needed a spell. I'm getting it."

"I still say it's a ruddy shame," persisted the cook. "The ruddy gov'ment ought to be made to pay union wages, that's what I says. What did they shoot you in for?"

"For several things all at the same time," Bony replied laughingly, and recounted how he had been awakened by the sergeant, and the answers he had given to his questions.

"That's what old Marshall would do," asserted a thickset man, and the cook demanded to know what Marshall was doing here at Wattle Creek.

"To ring up old Jason and ask him to take a truck out to that hut at Sandy Flat for a body that was found hanging from a beam," Bony answered carelessly. He was lounging over the table and methodically stirring the tea in his pannikin, but he registered the effect of the announcement on each of his hearers. "A swagman hanged himself in that hut last night."

"So!" Sam the Blackmailer said softly, and his brown eyes seemed unnaturally large. There was complete silence following Sam's exclamation, broken only by the cawing of crows and the methodical action of an engine pumping water. "Now what d'you know about that? Is he a medium-sized bloke, grey hair, getting along for half a century, and dying of consumption?"

Bony nodded. They thought it not strange that what was to them of tremendous interest appeared to him to contain little if any interest. His table manners would have brought a swift reprimand from his wife. The men saw merely a half-caste stockman, dressed perhaps not so flashily as some, but one with those they knew in easy movement, mental imperturbability, and a seeming dislike of parting with information. They plied him with questions.

"That'll be him," he told them.

"How did he do it?" demanded a youth who wore spurs that tinkled like cracked bells every time he moved his kangaroo-hide riding boots.

"Buckled his swag straps together . . . after making a noose through the buckle of one. Got up on the table, put the noose round his neck, tied the other end to the beam, and stepped off the table. You fellers know him?"

"Can't say as we know him," replied Sam the Blackmailer. "He was here last night having his dinner."

"He was over at the hut afterwards," supplemented the youth.

"That's right," agreed the thickset man. "Me and Johnny was pitching to him for a coupler hours."

"Where did he come from, did he say?" Bony asked casually.

"Said something about having come out of the 'ospital at the Hill," answered the youth. "Come to think of it, he didn't give much away about himself, did he, Harry?"

The thickset man agreed. Bony spoke, softly, indifferently. "He must have left this homestead pretty late last night. What time did you see him last?"

"He left our hut about ten. He was camped up at the wool-shed," volunteered Johnny. "Never said anythink about going on that night. Come to think of it, he passed through here some time back. Don't you remember, Sam?"

"Can't say as I do," replied the cook, whose mind seemed to be away from the subject.

"Anyway, he's dead now," Bony put in. "He made a very good job of himself."

"Ruddy shame—bloke like that being on the tramp," snarled the cook.

"Might sooner be on tramp in freedom than penned up in a hospital," remarked an elderly man. "Hospitals are good places to be out of."

"I remember——" began Johnny, and then cut off.

Sam the Blackmailer glared at him.

"Well, what d'you ruddy well remember?"

"About that swagman. He never come through here like I thought. I seen 'im over at Ned's Swamp that time me and Jack

88

Lock went over there to fetch them horses. Yes, that's where I seen 'im before."

"Ned's Swamp is a run on the other side of the Walls, isn't it?" enquired Bony, who knew quite well that it was so.

"Yes. Me and Lock went over to the homestead—sixteen miles across. That's where I seen that swagman. I remember, too, when that was. It was three days before George Kendall was murdered. Funny!"

"What's ruddy funny?" growled the cook.

"George Kendall was murdered six or seven weeks ago and that swaggy told us he'd been in 'ospital for the last three months. Didn't he, Harry?"

"He did so."

"Must have been wanderin' in 'is ruddy mind," asserted Sam. "Must 'ave 'ad a lot on 'is mind last night when he was here, to go and 'ang 'imself like that."

"He didn't seem to have anythink on his mind when he was talking to us, did he, Harry?"

"No," replied the thickset man. "He did not. He was cheerful enough. Talked about going down to Melbun for Christmas. Got a sister down there. Didn't——"

"Cripes, now!" almost shouted the youthful Johnny.

"Don't let it ruddy well 'urt cher," urged the unsmiling cook. "And look at the time. The ruddy boss will be sacking the lot of you if you don't do a get-back to work."

Johnny's eyes were big, expanded by the idea in his brain, and he had either to get it out or explode. He said, when on his way to the door and back to his work:

"I wonder if that swagman killed old Kendall, and then had to go back to the scene of 'is crime? Then he got overcome by remorse and did 'imself in."

The thickset man chuckled.

"You might be right, Johnny me lad, but don't go gabbing about it to the police," he advised, winking at Sam. "Besides, blokes these days don't hang themselves through remorse. You been reading too many of them Charlie Garvices. You stick to the sporting news in future."

"Kendall!" exclaimed Bony with raised brows. "Was Kendall killed in that hut?"

"Too ruddy right he was," asserted the cook. "He was bashed about somethink awful. His blood was all over the place, wasn't it, George?"

The elderly man nodded and stroked his grey moustache with the stem of his pipe.

"All over the floor, anyway," he corrected. "It was the boss and me who found him. We was going farther out, away across the Walls that day, and we called in at Sandy Flat with rations for Kendall."

"The police never got anyone for the crime, did they?" asked Bony.

"No, they didn't, and they ain't likely to now. A d. came out from Sydney, but he didn't do no good—leastways it never came out," cut in Sam the Blackmailer. "There was a bit of a blue at the social and dance the night before, and Kendall was mixed up in it. It seems that Kendall pushed Rose Marie, the sergeant's daughter, and young Jason took aholt of 'im and marched him outside. They had a fight afterwards. You seen 'im?"

"Young Jason? Yes. He doesn't say much." The remaining men left for their work, and Bony asked: "What kind of a man was Kendall to work with?"

Sam gazed straight into Bony's blue eyes, paused before saying:

"There are some blokes what was borned to be husband of a nagging wife. There is other blokes what was borned to have sixteen kids. And there are some other blokes which are borned to be murdered. Kendall was borned to be murdered. The surprising thing is that he was murdered so late in life."

"You don't say," Bony observed.

"I do say. By rights Kendall ought to have been murdered when 'e was much younger . . . say about two days old," proclaimed the cook. "Kendall was just natcherly a nasty bit of work. He never could say a good word for anyone. Australia 'as the best Labour gov'ment what ever lived, and Kendall didn't even have a good word for it, let alone local man, woman, or child. We 'ere was all very glad when the boss sent 'im out to Sandy Flat."

"How often did they take Kendall out his rations?" Bony asked without apparent interest.

"Every month. Why?"

"Just thinking I might ask the boss here for a job. A man out at Sandy Flat would kill his own meat?"

"Of course. There was ration sheep in the yards when Kendall was murdered. Everyone was so excited at Kendall being flattened that them sheep was forgotten for nigh a week. Three of 'em there was. They reckoned that Kendall musta got 'em yarded just before he went to town that evening, 'cos there was a full carcass in the safe. Having killed one, he ought to have let the others go. Musta forgot."

"Well . . . well . . . and now he's dead. And now that swagman is dead in the same hut. Don't you think it funny that swagman left here in the middle of the night to tramp to Sandy Flat?"

"Come to think of it, I do," agreed Sam the Blackmailer.

"How long was he here? Any idea?" persisted Bony.

"Yes, I know that one. He arrived the afternoon before and camped up in the woolshed. He called in here when we was having dinner, asking for some bread and meat. I give 'im a handout."

"If it was roaring hot weather, he could be expected to travel at night. But why go to Sandy Flat? There's no public road past that well and hut, is there?"

"There's no public road, but there is a track what begins again t'other side of the Walls, a track that goes on over to Ned's Swamp homestead."

"So actually that swagman spent a full day here?"

"Yes. That's so, mate."

"What road's this place on?"

"On the road to Pooncaira. Dry track too. There's another road what branches off just north of the woolshed what goes to Ivanhoe. You worrying about getting a job?"

"Not exactly," Bony said carelessly. "Went down to Melbourne and went broke. You know, pawned a watch for me fare up to Mildura, and I'd like a couple of months' work somewhere."

"Ask the boss. He'll put you on."

"I will. Want to write a letter, too, when I get back. When does the mail go out?"

"Went through here yesterday. Left Merino yesterday. Won't be another till Sat'day." Sam uncoiled himself and clawed at the table to get himself to his feet. He stood then, looking down at Bony, and he said paternally:

"Don't you go taking a job out at Sandy Flat. That's no ruddy place for no 'uman being, what with a murder and a suicide being done there."

"I wouldn't lose no sleep over it if I did go there," Bony stated, getting to his feet. "Suppose I'd better get back to the car. Thanks for the lunch. See you sometime."

"Yep. In the ruddy pub, prob'ly. Hooroo!"

On leaving Sam the Blackmailer, Bony walked back to the car, and then strolled along the creek bank to the woolshed and shearing shed, a quarter of a mile distant. He came first to the woolshed, now empty of wool, its great doors wide open, and before them a makeshift fireplace.

There was no one within. He stood for a moment in the doorway, surveying the dim interior. It was cool within and smelled of wool in the raw. On one side were two hydraulic presses; along the other was a stack of wool tables.

Before going in he walked over to the fireplace, knelt, and felt the white wood ashes with the back of his hand and found them cold. He saw Sergeant Marshall and the squatter crossing from the house gate to the men's quarters, and he guessed the sergeant would be making his enquiries concerning the dead swagman. Sam the Blackmailer was a certainty for the inquest the next day.

Knowing that he still had time at his disposal, Bony entered the woolshed, glanced at the inside of the heavy door posts, and eventually reached a far corner where three sheepskins lay side by side, obviously placed there to form a mattress. He lifted up each one. Nothing lay beneath them. Nothing had been left by the dead man . . . if there was to be excluded a half-completed game of noughts and crosses drawn in chalk on the nearer of the two woolpresses.

XI. A Great Day for Mr. Jason

AT TEN O'CLOCK the following morning Main Street, Merino, was unusually animated, for in addition to the business people and those engaged in shopping there were men from Wattle Creek Station to give evidence at the inquest. These now were seated on the hotel bench and at the edge of the sidewalk, all of them a bodyguard over Sam the Blackmailer, who had to be kept sober against his will.

At ten-thirty the courthouse was packed.

On a form against the rear wall of the building were seated the Crown witnesses: Johnny, Sam the Blackmailer, the thickset man, whose name was Harry Hudson, and Bony. These were kept in order under the stern and officially cold eye of Mounted Constable Gleeson, who guarded the public entrance, or appeared to be so doing. When he shouted something like "Hip!" everyone stood up, and up to the bench mounted Mr. Jason.

He was dressed in a navy-blue double-breasted lounge suit, a white handkerchief flowing from the pocket, his trousers neatly pressed, and black shoes upon his feet. His hair was parted down the centre, and his black moustache gleamed with a smear of oil. He looked an efficient public servant; the opening preliminaries proved him to be what he looked. When he sat down he wiped his glasses with the clean handkerchief, neatly restored it to its pocket, arranged the pile of foolscap upon his left, placed a sheet of it on the blotter before him, tested a pen, set it down, and leaned back in his chair to survey all the people as though it were the first time he had seen any one of them.

Sergeant Marshall conducted the case for the Crown. The first witness to be called was Sam the Blackmailer, and Sam the Blackmailer was given a hearty send-off by his fellow witnesses, and the promise of one little drink by Johnny if he gave his evidence without stuttering. The suggestion of such a promise that young man would not have dared to make in Sam's own kitchen.

As Mr. Jason was compelled to take down in longhand all evidence and questioning, the proceedings were slow and tiresome. The cook at Wattle Creek Station deposed having given the dead man bread and cooked meat on the evening of December third, and having given him rations on the evening of December fourth. This was not strictly accurate in accordance with what Bony had been told: viz., that on the evening of December fourth the swagman had been invited in to dinner by Sam the

Blackmailer. It was probable that the cook did not want his employer to know of that invitation.

"Did the deceased appear to you to be depressed?" asked Mr. Jason, regarding the cook severely over his spectacles.

"No, he was cheerful enough."

Marshall waved Sam the Blackmailer off the witness stand and then called for John Ball. Johnny related the conversation in general which took place at the men's hut between the deceased and himself and Harry Hudson.

"What time did he leave the men's hut that night?" asked Marshall.

" 'Bout ten as near as anythink," replied the witness.

"Did the deceased appear to you to be depressed at that time?" asked Mr. Jason.

Johnny replied in the negative.

"Did you observe which way the deceased went after he left your hut?" asked Marshall.

"Yes. He walked towards the woolshed."

Harry Hudson, the next witness, corroborated Johnny's evidence and he was asked the same question by Mr. Jason about the dead man's state of mind. There was elicited from this witness nearly everything that Bony had heard at the men's dining table the previous day. It all amounted to very little.

Bony was called, an unusual experience for him, to detail the discovery of the body, and it was noticed by many, especially by Watson, the press representative, that he was the first witness who was not frequently requested by the coroner to pause that the evidence be recorded in writing. When he had finished, Mr. Jason asked:

"What was the reason that you went to the hut at Sandy Flat?"

"I was ordered by Sergeant Marshall to accompany him."

"Indeed! That does not answer my question." Mr. Jason set down his pen and leaned back in his chair of justice with obvious physical relief. In his full and rich voice he said: "I will repeat the question."

"I had no particular reason, sir," Bony stated. "I am at present in custody, and I was ordered by Sergeant Marshall to accompany him."

94

"Very well."

"Stand down, please," ordered Marshall.

When Bony reached the witnesses' form he found there only Harry Hudson, who announced in a loud whisper that Johnny could no longer "hold" Sam from the hotel.

Having been sworn, Constable Gleeson recited the list of the articles comprising the dead man's swag, and in detail described how the hanging had been accomplished. He submitted the photographs he had taken. Mr. Jason accepted the prints and gazed at them with great interest, much to the curious envy of the public.

At the solicitors' table sat Mr. Watson, the local press correspondent. He continued to write furiously, and it was evident that he could easily outpace Mr. Jason. He stopped, for about the second time since the proceedings had begun, when Dr. Scott was called to the witness stand.

The first part of the doctor's evidence corroborated that of previous witnesses. Then:

"The body having been taken down," he continued, "I examined it externally and estimated that life had been extinct for from twelve to twenty hours; in other words, that death had occurred sometime the previous night. There were no marks of violence, other than that made by the ligature round the neck, and a recent injury on the back of the right hand.

"The ligature was fashioned with the deceased's swag straps, comparatively new and one inch in width. The depression round the neck made by the ligature was hard and brown in colour, the upper and lower borders having a faint line of redness or lividity. Where the buckle came hard against the neck beneath the left ear the skin was rasped and ecchymosed, and where each buckle hole in that part of the strap had rested against the skin there was a distinct circular mark indicating absence of pressure."

The little doctor ceased speaking, and the silence in the court was broken only by the busy pen in Mr. Jason's hand and the rustling of paper when Mr. Watson flung a filled sheet away from himself to the floor in dramatic manner.

"The body having been brought to the morgue here in Merino," Dr. Scott proceeded, "I made a second external and

95

an internal post-mortem examination. I found that the lungs were much engorged with blood, and that there were no injuries to the spinal column and cord. That would indicate that the body did not drop far when deceased stepped off the table. Actually the drop was not more than five inches. However, I found serious fracture of the larynx, the *os hyoides,* which is of especial importance because these injuries are very rare in hanging and quite common in strangling cases."

Mr. Jason put down his pen before he could have caught up with the doctor's evidence and stared blankly at witness. Bony cast a swift glance at Mr. Watson, and Mr. Watson was standing up on his island of paper sheets, his mouth open, his pencil held on high. The silence was so profound that the cackling of a kookaburra in a near-by tree seemed to thunder on the eardrums. Down went Mr. Watson like a poleaxed bullock, to sprawl over the table and continue to write with even greater rapidity. It seemed that Mr. Jason waited for the kookaburra to cease its cackling laughter before he sent his rich and full voice over the head of the public.

"What, Doctor, does that infer . . . exactly?" he asked.

"It infers that the deceased died of asphyxiation produced by strangling, and not asphyxiation produced by hanging. The mark made by the strap was in accordance with death from hanging, and in front of the neck the mark was higher than the larynx. It was, therefore, not the strap which injured the larynx so much that it was fractured.

"With the aid of a glass I found a second mark with very little ecchymosis, save at the back of the neck. It was this second mark which indicated clearly how the larynx was fractured, and here and there along this mark round the neck there were small areas of ecchymosis in a kind of crisscross pattern, indicating that this ligature was not a strap or a rope but a strip of some material.

"I examined deceased's mouth and his hands. Under his fingernails and also in the congealed blood on his injured hand I found fibres which microscopic examination prove to be jute fibres. It would appear that deceased was strangled to death with a strip of hessian."

"Hessian!" repeated Mr. Jason loudly.

"Yes sir, hessian. It would seem that deceased was first

strangled with a ligature of hessian sacking, and then his body was hanged from the crossbeam of the hut."

"You infer that the deceased was killed and did not kill himself?"

"That is what I infer, sir."

Mr. Jason's voice had lost all its richness. It was become almost a screech.

"That deceased was murdered by being strangled and that then his body was hanged to simulate murder? Is that your opinion?"

"Those are the facts, sir," Dr. Scott said slowly and distinctly.

The cackling of the kookaburra without would have made a welcome entry into the dead silence within the court. Even Mr. Jason's angry pen seemed to make no more sound than a hissing snake at the bottom of a well. Presently he laid down his pen and looked up.

"Have you anything more to add?"

"No sir."

"Any more witnesses, Sergeant?"

Marshall replied in the negative.

"You cannot establish the identity of the deceased person?"

"Not yet, your honour. Enquiries are being made in Broken Hill, where, it is thought, the man was recently in hospital."

Mr. Jason pondered. Mr. Watson hurried outside, Bony guessed to go to the post office. His telegrams to his papers were going to cause irritating commotion. Mr. Jason's voice broke in upon his thoughts:

"I adjourn this enquiry for one week . . . to ten o'clock on December thirteenth."

No one in the courtroom moved, other than Mr. Jason, who, with grave deliberation, gathered his papers together and placed them in an attaché case. Then he glared at the gathering over his spectacles for an appreciable period of time before rising abruptly to his feet.

Only when he disappeared through a door at the end of the Bench did the people present get noisily to their feet and stream outside, everyone talking as though to relieve overtaut nerves.

"What d'you know about that?" Hudson asked Bony. "Getting interesting, ain't it? Coming over for a drink?"

"Not just now. Mrs. Marshall will have the lunch ready, and I'm not missing that part of my wages," Bony told him. "See you later, perhaps."

Hudson grinned.

"All right. But I mightn't be able to see you . . . clearly. So long."

He began his afternoon work on the police station fence promptly at two o'clock, and five minutes later he observed Dr. Scott and Marshall accompany the coroner to the morgue behind the station residence. They were there a bare ten minutes, and then returned to the office, where, Bony guessed, the doctor would sign his certificate and Mr. Jason would give his authority for the burial of the body.

At three o'clock he learned from Marshall that his guess had been correct and that the unnamed swagman was to be buried at four that afternoon.

"I'll have to go," Marshall said. "Care about coming too? I could conscript you as a bearer."

"Yes, I think I'll go. Any reply to our telegrams?"

"No. Bit early."

At one minute to four o'clock the ancient hearse was driven out of the garage and stopped at the police station gate. Young Jason was at the driving wheel. He wore his cloth cap right side foremost. He was arrayed in his working overalls. In the corner of his mouth was the unlighted cigarette end. Mr. Jason was in his funeral regalia, the metamorphism of his outward garments being almost as remarkable as that from his character of deputy district coroner.

Having alighted, Mr. Jason shot his cuffs, set his top hat more firmly on his dark head, which advancing years seemed slow to whiten, and stared at Bony. Young Jason rolled the cigarette end to the opposite side of his mouth, got to the ground, and stood glaring at his father.

Two men crossed the street from the hotel. Harry Hudson and the hotel yardman, engaged for the afternoon by the Merino mortician. Bony became a third, with young Jason the fourth. They carried the coffin to the morgue, where Mr. Jason with his usual solemn decorum supervised the encoffining of the remains. The main street of the township was thronged by waiting spectators. Those in the street opposite the police station saw Mr. Jason coming ahead of the four bearers carrying the coffin to the hearse. He looked something like a major-domo leading a distinguished guest into the presence of his master or a drum major at the head of his band.

"The coffin must weigh more than the body," remarked Harry Hudson, his voice a little thick. "How much will the old man get for this planting, Tom?"

"About as much as when we plant you," came the surly reply from young Jason. He was ahead of Bony, who saw that despite his ungainliness and the shortness of one leg, he did his work with ease.

"You ain't looking forward to planting me, are you?" Harry mildly enquired, liquor mellowing him and not rousing his temper.

"Can't say that I look forward to planting anyone, especially on a hot day," stated young Jason sourly. "I leaves the anticipation act to the old man."

"He seems to enjoy a good and hearty plantin'," observed the yardman. "I 'ad a nuncle once who went to every funeral about the place, grew flowers specially to take to 'em, and it was a fair-sized town, too. 'E just loved funerals, but your old man, 'e just loves 'imself at one. Properly enjoys 'em."

Mr. Jason, having arrived at the rear of the hearse, threw wide the doors and stepped back. The bearers slid the coffin into the interior. Thereupon Mr. Jason reverently closed the doors, his white face and dark moustache, his top hat and frock coat perfectly in tune with the vehicle in which he took such evident pride.

Young Jason crawled into his driving seat. His father stood up beside him . . . as if to enjoy his great moment. He surveyed the people gathered under the pepper trees, the bearers, and Gleeson, who was standing at the police station gate. Mr. Jason waited, a frown settling about his eyes.

"Do we stay put all day?" asked his son loudly. "I promised old Sinclair his truck at five."

"The cortege has not yet assembled," Mr. Jason said as loudly and with emphatic disapproval.

"But we can go on," argued his son.

"Wait."

"Oh, all right, blast it," growled his son, and lit his cigarette end.

Sergeant Marshall came driving out to the street in his car, and he waved to Mr. Jason to proceed, but Mr. Jason was adamant. He remained standing, posed as though gazing upon the figure of grief recumbent on the roof of his hearse, but actually glaring at the sergeant, who drove his car in a circle to bring it to the rear of the hearse where the bearers got in with him.

Again Mr. Jason surveyed the throng. Then he turned to the front, raised his hand with the tall hat clenched in it, nudged young Jason with his foot, and before he could sit down nearly fell over the seat when the driver viciously let in the clutch and accelerated down the street at unseemly speed.

Just beyond the township the minister's car shot out to the street from the parsonage, thence to keep a respectable distance to avoid much of the dust.

"Young Tom's making no bones about this planting," observed the yardman. "The old bloke will be rampant mad time we hit the cemetery. He likes to enjoy his funerals."

"He enjoyed giving me ten days," Bony said lightly.

"Takes 'imself seriously, does old Jason," asserted Hudson. "Not a bad fault either. Used to be a nactor, once, in his young days. Tom once told me that his old man still has albums full of press notices about his acting, and every Sunday evening he reads 'em all through. Funny old bird, all right."

"Got a lot of good points," remarked the sergeant. "Remember how he helped Ma Lockyer and her kids when her husband was rolled on by his horse?"

"Yeh. And that never come out till long afterwards, did it? An' I understand that he acted as nurse for old Doc Scott when Boozer Harris nearly died that time with whiskeyitis. I was working on Tintira then. I ain't saying anything against old Jason."

Presently the hearse reduced speed and entered the cemetery and drew up beside the grave dug that morning. Mr. Jason dismounted, carrying his hat in the crook of an arm. They removed the coffin from the hearse whilst he uttered little cries in a soft voice:

"Steady now! Slowly does it! Honour the dead! The dead know all things and we nothing. This way! Now here . . . down here. That's right! Gently now!"

The hot north wind teased his black hair and played on his moustache like invisible fingers on a harp's strings. His white face emphasized the dark eyes which gleamed with the anger his voice did not betray. When he stepped back Mr. James stepped forward.

The wind also played with the unruly brown hair of the Rev. Llewellyn James, and with the skirt of his crepe gown. The light blue eyes had not failed to notice Mr. Jason's anger, the sergeant's stiff military bearing, the unassuming figure of Napoleon Bonaparte, and the loose stance of the bushmen bearers.

He produced a book, coughed, began to read the burial service in his singsong nasal voice, and Bony wondered why a man should adopt such a voice when conducting a religious service. Mr. James read rapidly. He made no pauses between sentences. It might have been he who had promised old Sinclair his truck by five o'clock. And then the book was closed with a little snapping sound, and Mr. James stepped back.

Mr. Jason placed his top hat on the ground, and upon it placed a stone to keep it there. He removed his frock coat, took up one of the shovels, and assisted his son to fill in the grave. The minister joined the policeman and began to ask questions concerning the dead man, to which Marshall returned evasive answers.

"Give us the shovel, Mr. Jason," suggested Harry Hudson. "I'm used to hard yakka." And the filling in proceeded apace, young Jason working with evident haste to get the job done. Mr. Jason came to stand with the sergeant and the minister, anger still smouldering in his eyes.

"Will you relieve my son, Ted?" he asked the yardman. "We have a pressing job to get out."

"Righto, Mr. Jason. Give us your shovel, Tom."

Young Tom ungraciously flung down his tool. The yardman grinned without mirth. The young man ambled to the hearse, started its engine, and roared away out to the road and up the gradient towards the town.

"Your son needs a little tighter rein, Mr. Jason," remarked the minister undiplomatically.

"There are more than my son in this district, Mr. James, who need to have faults corrected."

"Meaning, Mr. Jason?"

"That people who live in glass houses should not throw stones, Mr. James," replied Mr. Jason. "Pray, do not let us wrangle here among the dead."

"But, Mr. Jason——"

"Please!" cried Mr. Jason commandingly, and the minister turned and walked to his car.

On the homeward journey Mr. Jason sat beside the sergeant and Bony occupied the rear seat with the yardman and Harry Hudson. They left the cemetery without speaking, but when on the track the sergeant said conversationally:

"We all seem to have been kept pretty busy lately."

"To be sure," responded Mr. Jason. "Three deaths and three burials all within five weeks, and that after several years with no deaths. The vagaries of life are often mystifying. As Longfellow wrote:

> *"There is a Reaper whose name is Death,*
> *And, with his sickle keen,*
> *He reaps the bearded grain at a breath,*
> *And the flowers that grow between."*

"Death is certainly a reaper," murmured Marshall, and Mr Jason stretched forth his right hand and quoted with rich articulation: " 'O mighty Caesar! Dost thou lie so low? Are all thy conquests, glories, triumphs, spoils, shrunk to this little measure?' "

"I think we could do with a drink," announced the yardman sotto voce. "The day's gettin' warm. Give me a coupler deepnosers, an' I'll recite 'The Passing of Dan McTavish' in eighteen verses and a bit."

They all went into the hotel—even Sergeant Marshall and Bony, the jailbird. And everyone at the bar delayed drinking until Mr. Jason had loaded his pipe, lit it, and had inhaled with tremendous satisfaction. No longer was he angry, but to Mr Watson's great disappointment he did not beat his previous record.

XII. The Battle of Pros and Cons

"WE SUFFER from a number of disadvantages not experienced by crime investigators in a city," Bony said in that quiet, unassuming voice of his. He had completed the making of half a dozen cigarettes, and now he glanced up at Sergeant Marshall, who was seated on the far side of the office desk. The door was closed and the windows were closed, too, although the evening was warm.

"One of those disadvantages," he went on, "is seldom recognized by the unthinking. The unthinking immediately rush to the conclusion that a killer is more easily discoverable in a small community than in a large one, whereas in fact the smaller the community in which a killer has operated the greater the difficulty in locating him—that is, if he has a brain. Fortunately you and I have opposed ourselves to a killer having a brain, and, also fortunately, we have to locate him in a small community. Those two facts give us cause for self-congratulation, eh?"

"Well, if you know where we are or what's it all about, I don't," grumbled Marshall. "And I can foresee trouble in that letter of yours to D.H.Q. telling 'em in most uncivil-servicelike manner to keep out."

Bony leaned back in his chair and chuckled.

"My dear man, we don't bother about D.H.Q. when we've got such a splendid job like this on our hands. Don't worry so. We can't help little Mr. Watson telegraphing the account of the hanging to his papers, to be followed by the certainty of city reporters barging in and messing around when we want everything to go on quietly. And if Pro Bono Publico writes to the local press and demands to know why the killing is not being investigated by a Redman or two from Sydney, well, we must shut our ears to the clamour. It might force me out into the open through an announcement that the great Detective Inspector Napoleon Bonaparte is on the job, but that is a fence we will take when it is reached. This is my case and yours, and no one is going to be allowed to interfere with it or with us."

"But my district inspector——"

Bony waved his hands.

"Copy my example," he urged. "Never permit yourself to be concerned with inspectors and chief commissioners and people of that class. They are all right in their places."

"So am I . . . so far. Anyway, it's your funeral."

"Not quite so morbid . . . after this afternoon," Bony implored. "Now let's get down to a battle of pros and cons, and when we have finished you will see that matters have not been allowed to slide as much as you think. To begin.

"You are not aware that I sent those door handles to Sydney from Mildura Post Office, are you? How do we know that the killer is not a member of the post office staff? Already I can see that you appreciate the significance of hunting for a killer in a small community like Merino. There are only a hundred and fifty people in all your district, and only eighty persons, including children, living here in Merino."

"How did you get those handles away?"

"I addressed them, together with a long covering report, to a friend of mine in Sydney who will himself deliver the package and report to headquarters. I stuck up a commercial traveller and gave him five shillings to cover registered postage. I should get back the receipt tomorrow."

Bony inhaled deeply. Then he placed the cigarette on the edge of the desk—the ash tray was a jam tin—and, interlocking the fingers of both hands, rubbed the palms together and beamed at Marshall.

"We've got a holt on a first-class murder investigation," he said softly and with tremendous satisfaction in his voice. "The killing of Kendall and that swagman, together with the possible intended killing of old Bennett is not the work of a man who kills his nagging wife, or another who slays his sweetheart because she has been untrue to him. This feller you and I are after is in the same class as Jack the Ripper. He's an aristocrat, not a sniffling lounge lizard. Come now, look up cheerful. We have every cause to be cheerful."

"Damned if I can see anything to be cheerful about," snorted Marshall. "Still, tell me some more, and then I might."

It was as though Bony's countenance was a sunlit landscape

over which a swift cloud cast a shadow. Good humour vanished and he became almost grimly serious. He said:

"I read somewhere a truism that without the night we cannot see the stars. To see the stars we have to wait for the night, and, peculiarly enough, in all big investigations the investigators have to wait for complete darkness to fall upon them before they begin to see light. This case is not yet dark enough for us to see any light, but it is growing darker and we shall see the light eventually. Let us gain an appreciation of just the degree of darkness that we have reached.

"Now I have been through Redman's collection of statements and his long general report. What he knew when he left Merino is only a fraction of what I know, and you know but a fraction of what I know. From Redman's material, I cannot see how Redman came to suspect young Jason above others. Because a man fights with another who is subsequently murdered, we cannot even assume that he killed him, even although he was licked in the fight. In actual fact a man who fights is less likely to kill than one who declines to fight. What is your opinion?"

"I never considered young Jason," replied the sergeant. "I've always thought it might have been one of the two men, or both, who played cards with Kendall that night of the social dance. And I stress the word 'might.' "

"Did you ever employ your mind with the motive for Kendall's murder?"

"Yes. Loss at cards. Kendall was a bad man. He might have cheated that night, but not so's an accusation could be made against him. Remember the statements made to Redman by the men who played against him?"

"I do. They both stated that Kendall won over fifteen pounds in less than two hours, and that they thought he cheated but weren't sure. I have given those two statements some consideration, but we have to offset them by police reports on the characters of those who signed them. Both are well known in this district; both are stated to be good citizens.

"I haven't concentrated on the killing of Kendall as much as I would have done had it not been for subsequent developments. I began with the most remarkable feature of Kendall's death; then got myself ten days in your lockup because that remarkable feature goes to prove that Kendall's murder was out of the ordinary and was done by a resourceful man. I saw, before I left Sydney, that I would require absolute freedom to make enquiries among people who did not know me."

"What is the remarkable feature?" asked Marshall, impatiently waiting for Bony to get to the meat. Bony grinned mirthlessly:

"The game of noughts and crosses on the door of the hut at Sandy Flat," he said.

"Ah! I remember you mentioning that more than once."

Bony abruptly leaned forward and began to shuffle the pile of documents on the desk between himself and the sergeant. "Here it is—this photograph of the front of the hut," he cried. "See the drawing of the game with chalk on the hut door. It is done with white chalk, and not the red or blue raddle with which sheep are marked, indicating that the chalk was carried about for just that purpose by the man who drew the game. Take a glance at it."

Marshall studied the now familiar picture.

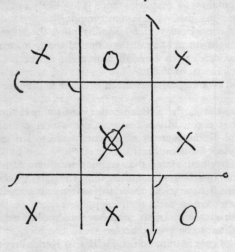

"Observe closely that game of noughts and crosses," urged Bony. "The assumed players did not complete it, for there is neither a nought nor a cross in the centre of the left-hand section.

See the position of the ticks and the little curved lines and the dot at the right extremity of the lower horizontal line. Those additions to the game itself are done but roughly as though carelessly by a player when pondering on his move to be. Consider the number of variations which could be made with the crosses and the noughts and the small additions. Why, one could concoct a cipher with such material. And that, my dear Marshall, is just what it is."

Marshall looked up from the picture and stared at Bony.

"You can read this cipher?" he asked, less as a question than as a statement.

"I can read it," claimed Bony. "I have seen that cipher on homestead gates, on telephone posts, and burned on chips of wood or bark and left in the vicinity of homesteads and near small townships. There is one on the gatepost just the other side of the town dams which states that you are not a hard policeman but are given to charging swagmen in order to get work done by them whilst in custody.

"The cipher is used by only the genuine swagmen. As you are aware, a goodly proportion of the men travelling these outback tracks are honest station hands looking for a job, or going back to a job from a bender at a wayside or town hotel. There is, however, a minority of swagmen, better known as sundowners, who never work and who must walk hundreds of miles in the year tramping from station homestead to homestead, where they obtain rations or a handout. It is this minority who have evolved the noughts-and-crosses cipher to leave information for others of their class.

"You see how it goes. A sundowner arrives at a gate in the fence enclosing the homestead area or the township area. He looks for the cipher on that part of the gate or telephone post which the road user would never see, telling him that the police are bastards, or that the station cook is generous, or that the station owner should be avoided.

"Mind you, that cipher is not now universally used, and with the passage of time it has become more complex, so that it is almost as difficult to read by one familiar with the original cipher as it is to read fortunes from the cards. However, to revert. That particular example scrawled on the door at Sandy Flat hut comprises a statement both clear-cut and definite."

"Go on," urged Marshall, when Bony paused to light a cigarette. "How do you make it all out?"

"It would take a long time to explain, and the necessity doesn't arise now. I will, however, point out a few simple things. The semicircle at the left extremity of the top horizontal line means meat. The quarter circle connected to the top horizontal line and the left-hand perpendicular line means dead or death. The short line drawn at an angle at the top of the right perpendicular line represents brought—brought to this place. And the V at the bottom of the same line represents police, or a policeman's helmet. And so on and so forth, including the positions of the noughts and crosses.

"A most important meaning, or message, is conveyed in the central square, where the cross is overlaid by the nought, or the other way round. That is the clear danger sign: get out, clear out, don't be seen hereabouts. In effect the cipher reads: 'A dead body has been brought to this hut for the police to find. Danger. Clear out. Touch nothing.'"

When Marshall again looked up from studying the photograph, he said admiringly:

"Where did you learn it all?"

"Oh, from a swagman who thought I was another of his clan. To proceed. We may presume that the man who scrawled that game of noughts and crosses on that door had seen someone take the body of Kendall into the hut, and then had watched that somebody kill one of Kendall's ration sheep, catch the blood and pour it on the floor about the head of the man, and hang the carcass in the meat house. The first part of the presumption I adopted when first I saw that photograph, the second was yesterday when I learnt that a fresh and uncut carcass of a sheep was hanging in the meat house the following morning. Scott supports the second part. He says that, in his opinion, the sample of blood he scraped from the floor of the hut where the body lay is animal blood, not human.

"Recall. The drawer of the game of noughts and crosses states clearly that a dead body was brought to that place. He doesn't state that a dead body is in it. It was brought there. Therefore he must have seen it brought there, and most likely he saw the face or recognized the figure of the man who carried it into the hut.

However, I am breaking away from fact to supposition when I say it is likely that the watcher recognized the man who brought the dead body and placed it in the hut.

"Given two facts, an investigator is entitled, pro tem, to assume a third with which to connect them," Bony went on. "My assumed fact is based on this deduction. The man who saw him who brought the body to the hut knew him and subsequently began blackmail. He arranged that that same hut should be the place of meeting of himself and his victim, or that it be the place where the money was to be deposited by the victim.

"That swagman, remember, did not leave the station homestead until after ten o'clock at night. That was the night of December fourth, three nights before the full moon. When he walked into the hut to meet his blackmail victim, or to obtain the blackmail money, he walked into death. For he was strangled with a strip of hessian and his body was hanged with his own swag straps. But, Marshall, remember that the motive for the killing of that swagman, our assumed motive, is merely supposition, and we may yet be grievously wrong. Interested?"

Sergeant Marshall's despondency had long since vanished. Now his eyes were wide. He said:

"As I mentioned to you when arresting you, quoting a favourite saying of an American friend, 'You've said a mouthful, bo.' But please tell me what makes you think that the killer lives here in Merino?"

"I wasn't sure about that until after I arrived here," Bony replied. "I might be rash in saying that I am sure about it even now. You remember the marks made by hessian-covered feet about the hut at Sandy Flat. Those same hessian-covered feet made similar marks about the hut occupied by old Bennett that night he died. The same man walked off the eastern end of the macadamized road running through Merino, and he walked back to that end of that macadamized road after he had paid a visit to old Bennett."

"Ah! Ah!" breathed Marshall.

"I believe that we are also entitled to assume that the killer of Kendall knew that old Bennett knew of the murder, and that the murderer went to old Bennett's hut to silence him. When the old man opened his door, the poor weak heart did the foul work for him. But why the killer waited a little more than a month before acting as he did would be absurd even to assume. You light the lamp. I'll draw the blind."

When they had resumed their chairs and Bony had made yet another of his cigarettes with the hump in the middle of it, he went on:

"Perhaps you can now appreciate this case of ours as being not one suitable for the attention of a city detective. And I hope that now you can appreciate the fact that the murderer of Kendall and that swagman can be any man living within the boundaries of your district, if not within the boundaries of Merino. He may turn out to be Dr. Scott, either of the Jasons, the schoolmaster, the minister, even Gleeson, even you, Marshall. Gleeson, by the way, was exceptionally intelligent in his questioning of Dr. Scott yesterday, was he not? The murderer is hardly likely to be an obvious choice of our guessing. We can, however, think that he is fairly strong, one able easily to lift and carry a man of medium or light weight. He was able to carry Kendall, whose body weighed nine stone six, and he easily lifted the swagman's body, weighing seven stone four pounds. He is not old or a weakling, but he is not necessarily big and very strong.

"We could reduce the number of possibilities by making a list of every able-bodied man in the district, but I hardly think it would be of immediate assistance. However, you might do that sometime."

"I'll do it. It won't be difficult," asserted the sergeant.

"Good! Now I want you to make an enquiry. The day before yesterday the swagman camped in the woolshed at Wattle Creek homestead, and that afternoon the mail car passed through that homestead on its way to Merino from Pooncaira. It stopped there to pick up the Wattle Creek mail, and doubtless there were letters in that station mailbag addressed to persons in Merino. The book-keeper, who would collect the letters from the station box to put into the mailbag with the office mail, would be familiar with the handwriting of the station hands. He might well remember seeing a strange handwriting, say that of the swagman, and he might remember to whom in Merino the letter was addressed. The addressee of a letter posted by the swagman to a person in Merino might be the victim of his blackmail. There is just a chance we may get a lead there."

"Shall I ring up or go out to see that bookkeeper?"

"Better go out. Should you see Mr. Leylan, you might mention to him that your jailbird is a good worker and civil, and that he would like a job at stock work. Mr. James has already spoken to him about me. I would much like to get a job riding from the Sandy Flat hut."

Marshall's eyes narrowed.

"Don't know that I'd like to live in that place," he said.

"Perhaps you would not. I know that I will not. But since when is a detective thought to have nerves like other men? I will live there if it can be arranged, because I want to examine the country east of the Walls of China.

"There is something else, too. If we could prove where Leylan spent the night that the swagman was killed, we could remove him from our imagined list of probabilities, take him into our confidence, and so arrange for me to go to Sandy Flat without any botheration.

"By the way, when you were having an interview with Sam the Blackmailer, I was inspecting the Wattle Creek woolshed. On one of the woolpresses I discovered another noughts and crosses sign. It contained the information that the men's cook was generous to swagmen, and that the boss could be touched for a plug of tobacco. That was all."

Sergeant Marshall leaned back in his chair and stretched his arms. On his red face was a smile of satisfaction.

"Well, I'm glad we are getting somewhere, or rather that you are getting somewhere, for I have got nowhere. This job's becoming mighty interesting."

"They all become interesting if they don't break too easily," Bony asserted. "I don't like investigations which run easily, meaning that I have pitted my intelligence against a dolt and, therefore, have wasted my gifts and the exercise of my intellect. Now I am going along to implore your wife to give me a cup of tea, and then I'm off to bed. Tomorrow I am to interview the Rev. Llewellyn James. As I have previously intimated, I don't like the Rev. Llewellyn James, but it doesn't follow that because I don't like him he is the murderer of Kendall and the swagman and the frightener-to-death of old Bennett. Never let your personal dislikes interfere with your profession, Marshall. That is apt to cloud your judgment."

XIII.   Windmills and a Woodcutter

BONY HAD COMPLETED the painting of the paling fence fronting the police station compound and had begun work on the division fence separating the compound from the residential property owned by Mr. Jason. This division fence was constructed of corrugated iron sheets nailed to a wooden framework which was now receiving Bony's attention.

At half past nine on the morning of December seventh it was already hot. From the street came the noise of cars and a truck, and from within the garage came the sound of iron being hammered. Merino was engaged with its morning business; it was as though everyone wanted to get it done before the promised hot afternoon began.

It was Saturday morning, and from the kitchen door there issued Rose Marie, dressed in a blue and white cotton frock, with a large floppy-brimmed sun hat shading her face. She pushed a small pram in which were installed two large dolls. Sedately, and conversing in motherly fashion with her charges, she pushed the pram across the compound to where Bony was working.

"Good morning, Bony!" she greeted him gravely, her grey eyes seeming very big within the shadow cast by her hat. "Mother said that you might like to see my babies, Thomas and Edith."

"That was very thoughtful of her and very nice of you, Rose Marie. How are you this morning? I wondered where you were, when at breakfast. Did you sleep in?"

"No. I had to take a hot breakfast over to Mrs. Wallace," replied the child in her precise phraseology. "Mrs. Wallace has been very sick, and it's Mother's turn to send her meals over."

"Indeed!" Bony murmured encouragingly.

"Yes. Mrs. Wallace lives alone. Everyone likes Mrs. Wallace, and when she fell sick heaps of people looked after her. She told me that she never knew there were so many angels in Merino."

Bony slapped the last of the paint on his brush against the wood and turned to look at her before again dipping the brush into the pot.

"I am glad to hear about your errand," he said. "You know, I thought that your absence at breakfast was due to that box of chocolates."

"Oh no! I only ate four. Won't you say good morning to my babies?"

"Of course. But which is whom?"

The presentation having been made, and Bony having duly admired Thomas' hair and Edith's blue eyes, he proffered to Rose Marie a bright two-shilling piece, saying:

"By this time your money box should be getting quite heavy."

"It is so," agreed Rose Marie. "There's seven silver coins now in my box, and what with all the pennies it will soon be full. Thank you, Bony. I'll have a lot of money when I take it all out, won't I?"

"Yes, you will. But there are still two more two-shilling pieces to go in yet. I hope there will be room."

"Mother says you are spoiling me," she told him, sitting Thomas more uprightly in the pram. "She caught me putting in the silver coin you gave me on Thursday. I had to tell her who give it me."

"Gave it me."

"Gave it me. She said that I ought never to spend them because they are all the wages you are getting. But I'll never spend them just because . . ."

"Because what, Rose Marie?"

She smiled at him, a beautiful, shy smile, and said:

"Because you gave them to me, Bony. They're keepsakes."

"Oh!"

He went on with his work and did not observe her rearranging the coverlet over Edith. Presently she said:

"What will you do when Father lets you out?"

"Do! Why, I hope to get a job somewhere near Merino. In fact, I am going to see Mr. James this afternoon about one."

He glanced swiftly at her, in time to see the child make a face and then become busy with Thomas, informing that baby that he was a naughty boy and would be deprived of a chocolate if he persisted in trying to get out of the pram. Then she said a little hesitatingly:

"After Father lets you out and you get a job, will you come to Merino one Sunday and take me to church?"

Without consideration Bony assented.

"Remember you promised to—a long time ago—with your fingers crossed."

"I did?" Bony exclaimed, turning round to look at her with well-feigned astonishment.

"You know you did. Don't you remember?"

"Hum! I do seem to remember something about it."

Bony turned again back to his work, and neither spoke for nearly a minute, when the little girl asked:

"If I ask Father to let you go tomorrow evening, will you take me?"

The thought flashed through Bony's mind that this child was going to become an intelligent woman. She was actually conducting an attack. He raised his defences . . . like a man, thinking that he would successfully resist the attack. Evasively he said:

"I don't know. You see, I am supposed to be in prison. Anyway, it would be a matter of you taking me . . . if your father did let me out."

"I would like you to, if you would." The attack was being pressed with resoluteness, and, already becoming faint, he asked:

"Do you want me to go especially, tomorrow?"

"Yes," came the answer distinctly. "Tomorrow night. Mother won't let me go at night. But she might . . . if you wanted to take me."

"Why do you want especially to go tomorrow night?"

"Because Miss Leylan's sweetheart is taking her. You see, he's a bush evangelist."

"Oh!" murmured Bony, now suffering from a sense of deflation.

"Yes. His name's Frank. He goes everywhere in a big covered truck teaching from the Bible. Miss Leylan says he's coming to Wattle Creek today. I've never seen him, but Miss Leylan says he's very nice and brave and kind. He's got an organ on the truck, and big 'lectric lights he puts on at night to preach by. He's bringing his truck to Merino next week."

On the flying carpet of memory, Bony was away on the roof of the Walls of China, looking up at the winsome face of a young woman on a horse. Then he was back again, here with Rose Marie, a silly little disappointment in his heart that this child did not after all want him to take her to church for his own sake.

Idly he asked:

"What is the bush evangelist's other name?"

"Oh! All his names go Frank Lawton-Stanley."

"Eh!" Bony jerked round to face Rose Marie, to repeat: "Frank Lawton-Stanley! Is that so? Well . . . well! Yes, I'll take you to church tomorrow evening. I'll take you even if I have to break jail. Happy?"

Rose Marie was smiling, and within the shadow cast by her hat her grey eyes were very bright.

"Thank you, Bony. I knew you would," she said, to add shrewdly: "Do you know Miss Leylan's Frank?"

"Promise not to tell."

She promised . . . with her fingers crossed.

"Yes, I know the Rev. Lawton-Stanley," he told her. "You'll like him, Rose Marie. If you would like me to, I'll present him to you after service."

"Oh, Bony, will you? Is he old?"

"Not as old as I am. He's got brown wavy hair and hazel eyes that look at you very kindly most times. . . . You are going to like him."

"Most times," she echoed. "Not all times?"

He laughed outright. Then:

"Rose Marie, I'll tell you a secret. I had a job once away out in Queensland, and the Rev. Lawton-Stanley came along and in the morning he asked me to put on the boxing gloves with him so he could get exercise. I put them on. You won't know what they are like. He was a better boxer than me. Oh yes, you are going to like him. He's a proper man."

"Is his father a minister too?"

"No. His father lives in Brisbane and makes hundreds and hundreds of windmills every year."

"Does he?"

There was plain dismay in her voice, which caused him to look sharply at her, to see her staring hard at Edith.

115

"What's the matter?" he asked.

"Nothing. Will Miss Leylan's sweetheart want to sell his father's windmills when he comes to Merino?"

The subject of windmills was quite obviously a disturbing one to Rose Marie, and Bony was further astonished by this precocious child putting her question while pretending to be happy again with Thomas. He told her that it was unlikely that the bush evangelist would want to sell his father's windmills, adding:

"But what if he should?"

"Oh, nothing," she replied hastily.

"Don't you want me for a friend any longer, Rose Marie?"

From beyond the pram she looked at him to dismay him with the tears in her eyes. He knew then that he had lost the battle to her, that she had won all along the line, and with concern in his voice he said:

"Now, now, Rose Marie! This won't do. Come and sit beside me whilst I make a cigarette."

He almost threw the paintbrush into the pot and then sat down on the clean reddish sand with his back resting against an upright, and she sat down at his side, little caring if Thomas and Edith did fall from their pram.

"Tell me the trouble about windmills," he urged her softly. "You know, there can be no secrets between good friends like we are."

"Are you sure Miss Leylan's sweetheart won't want to sell windmills when he comes to Merino?" she pressed him.

"Yes, of course. A minister doesn't sell windmills or anything else. Why?"

"I can't tell you, Bony."

"Oh! Why not?"

" 'Cos I promised young Mr. Jason with my fingers crossed I wouldn't."

"Did you? Then, in that case, you mustn't tell."

Sunshine broke through the misty rain.

"And you won't make me?"

"Make you? Certainly not. If you promise anything you must keep to it. We must never break a promise."

"And you'll still take me to church tomorrow night?"

"I promise . . . with my fingers crossed . . . see. And if Miss

Leylan's sweetheart is there, I will certainly present him to you as the—er—second lady in Merino."

"The second. Is my mother the first?"

"I heard Mr. Watson say that Mrs. Sutherland was the first lady in Merino."

"O-oh! Mrs. Sutherland's making up to old Mr. Jason," stated Rose Marie. "I heard Mrs. Felton tell Miss Smith so. May I tell Mother you will take me to church so's she can iron my very best dress?"

"Yes, you may do that. Then, sometime this afternoon, I'll want you to go along to one of the stores and buy me a nice new shirt and a collar and tie. Do you think your mother would lend me an iron? I hope that young Mr. Jason won't be jealous of me."

Rose Marie became firm.

"If he is he needn't take me to church ever again. Can I go and tell him now that I am going with you tomorrow?"

"Perhaps it might be as well," replied Bony gravely.

She got to her feet, started towards the front gate, then came back to the pram.

"Will you see that Thomas doesn't go and fall out while I'm away?" she requested, and, receiving his assurance, left him.

He watched her leave the compound, watched her as she passed along the outside of the front paling fence. When she returned at the expiration of fifteen minutes, she came across the compound at a skip and a jump, to tell him brightly that young Mr. Jason would not be jealous, and that now she must go and tell her mother about the ironing of the "very best" dress.

Bony was not expected to work on Saturday afternoon, and so, having written out his sartorial requirements, he gave Rose Marie money and dispatched her to do his shopping. Ten minutes after she had gone he also left the compound and strolled down along the street in the hot afternoon sunlight.

There were but few people in the shops and on the street. A sleepy Major Mitchell, tethered to one of the pepper trees by a length of fine chain, said sleepily, "Good day," to him.

Arriving outside the parsonage, his blue eyes became restless and searching. He ignored the small gate giving access to a cinder path leading directly to the front of the house set well back from the street. He saw the Rev. Llewellyn James reclining on a cane chair on the house veranda. He was reading a book whilst lying full length in his chair. Bony proceeded a little farther and entered the parsonage by the driveway gate, which was open. At its far end was a garage, through the open doors of which he could see the minister's dusty car.

As he walked up the driveway the garden was to his right. On his left was the large weatherboard church. Between himself and the garden was a border of shrubs, starved and growing on ground needing cultivation. Beyond that, the garden cried for loving hands to tend it.

It was Bony's intention, when nearing the house, to take the path leading through the shrubbery border to the steps of the front veranda. Because he walked silently, Mr. James did not hear him and was too engrossed in his book to see him. From this place Bony could observe the minister much better. He was lying with a cushion beneath his head, a large leather-covered tome lying opened on his stomach, and in his hands a paper-covered book which he was reading.

The interested Bony was about to leave the drive when he heard the sound of an axe being used somewhere at the rear of the house, and upon impulse he continued towards the garage and so skirted the north wall of the house till finally he entered a rear yard. There he saw a woman chopping wood at the wood heap over by the back fence.

She was a little woman, slight of figure, dressed neatly in a dark blue linen house frock. Her back was towards him. The sunlight fell fiercely upon her light brown hair, which was drawn back tightly into a bun. It also was reflected by the blade of the axe, which rose and fell, rose and fell upon a log of hard red box. When Bony coughed she turned her head, her hands still clasping the handle of the axe, now biting into the wood.

"Good afternoon! Are you wanting to see Mr. James?" she asked, her breath coming quickly.

"I have called to see him," Bony replied, smiling at her.

"You will find him lying on the front veranda. Poor man, he is not very strong, you know."

Soft grey eyes examined him. Once she had been fresh and pretty; now her complexion was ruined by the hot suns and the hotter kitchen stove. Perspiration dewed her forehead.

"That is unfortunate, and we should be glad that we are strong," Bony said. The smile continued to light his eyes, and before she realized it his hat had dropped from his hand and he had taken the axe from her hands and wrenched it from the log. "I am considered the best axeman in my family," he told her. "Charles, my eldest son, is much too cunning to take any interest in woodcutting, and James, my next boy, makes blind swipes and often splinters the handle. The word 'swipes,' by the way, is his, not mine. Now observe the champion axeman of the Robert Burns family."

Bony was not a champion axeman, which she quickly saw, but he could cut wood for a stove, and he didn't rest till he had six sections of the log lying at his feet. She was saying: "Oh, that will do. That will do very nicely, thank you. I wanted only a stick or two just now. The man is due to come this evening to chop for an hour."

"He might not turn up, marm," Bony told her. "Sometimes they don't," and he fell to work splitting the sections. Having done that, he knelt on one knee and began to pile the billets on the crook of an arm. When he rose, the pile was large and heavy.

"Where will you have the wood, marm?" he asked.

"Oh! I could take it to the kitchen. Thank you for having cut it."

"Where is the kitchen? Suppose you show me. If I have to drop this load through sheer weariness . . ."

"Oh, over here. Thank you so much."

She snatched up his felt hat and almost ran before him to the kitchen door, where she indicated a box to take the wood. She stood in the kitchen doorway looking at him whilst he dusted his hands and accepted from her his hat, her eyes large and a trifle misty, and on her face an expression of wistful appreciation. She said:

"When you have finished your interview with Mr. James, perhaps you would like to come back here for a cup of tea?"

"I would appreciate it, marm. Never at any time do I refuse a cup of tea. Thank you." And now, with the smile gone from his eyes, he bowed as no man ever had bowed to Lucy James.

Walking back down the driveway beside the house, he took the path to the front veranda steps, taking care to move soundlessly.

Mr. James was still interested in his paper-covered book, the title of which Bony could now see. Many other people, not necessarily ministers, were interested in *A Flirt in Florence*.

Purposely Bony kicked against the lowest step, and his head was bent when Mr. James swiftly lowered his book and looked sharply at his visitor. When Bony looked up and began mounting the steps, Mr. James had in his hands the leather-covered tome: *The Life and Epistles of St. Paul*. What had become of *A Flirt in Florence* Bony did not observe.

"What d'you want?" asked the startled minister.

"I called, Padre, to see if you've done anything about seeing Mr. Leylan for me," Bony said mildly and, on reaching the top step, sat down on the veranda floor.

Mr. James swung his legs off the chair and put down his big book. His light blue eyes were still uneasy, and anger gleamed from their depths.

"I am not sure, but I fancy that I am displeased by your apparent disrespect to a minister," he said brittlely. "Let me see now. Your name is . . ."

"Burns—Robert Burns," Bony announced.

"Ah, yes . . . Burns. I remember you. I did speak to Mr. Leylan about you. He said he would consider giving you a job. Should he do so, I trust you will work hard and honestly, and not make mock of my recommendation."

"I will do my best," he was assured gravely.

" 'Adversity is useful to us if we profit by it,' " Mr. James went on, his voice betraying the quotation. Bony could not resist the temptation, and so he also quoted:

" 'If all were prosperity, we all would be without character.' "

"Ah, yes . . . yes . . . to be sure."

Mr. James noted the brown hand dive into a trousers pocket, and he saw the hand withdrawn with tobacco and cigarette papers.

"I ask you not to smoke here," he said sternly. "I approve of neither tobacco nor drink. Remember that this is the parsonage. I will speak again to Mr. Leylan about you, as he is a great friend of mine. I will also have a word with Sergeant Marshall before you are finally freed. Is there anything else?"

Bony appeared to hesitate. Then:

"Yes, Padre. I'd like to come to church tomorrow evening. The sergeant says I may."

"You will be welcome. The service begins at seven," Mr. James said, although there was neither interest nor welcome in his voice. "You must leave me now. I have work to do. Good day!"

Bony rose languidly, and when he gained the path he turned round to say, "Good dayee, Padre!" and to see the minister standing foursquare on his feet at the top of the steps. He felt the light blue eyes boring into his back as he walked down the driveway to the street.

The impression he had received of the Rev. Llewellyn James was not of a man suffering from a weak heart or any other kind of physical weakness. He was smiling up to the instant that he remembered the little woman cutting wood in the hot sunlight, and then the smile vanished. He had not forgotten the offered cup of tea.

XIV. Bony Goes to Church

AT HALF PAST SIX O'CLOCK that same Saturday, Marshall entered Bony's cell to find the detective brushing his black, sleek hair.

"I am not going to do any more painting," announced Bony, continuing to regard himself in the mirror. "You promised to pay me my two bob per diem not later than five-thirty to give me a chance to spend it over at the pub before closing time."

Marshall could not forbear a grin. He said:

"I've been out to Wattle Creek Station on your official business."

"That doesn't quench my thirst with a nice cold pot of beer. Slaving for you all day, too. You never take me anywhere, you beast. I've a good mind to go home to Mother."

"Darling!" breathed the sergeant. "I've got a couple of bottles over in the office."

Bony sniffed, turned, and held out his hand.

"My wages, please."

"Bit of a snorter, aren't you, for a prisoner?" Marshall said, chuckling. "Two bottles waiting, and now wants two shillings. Here, take it. You're ruining that child of mine."

"Sez you. Now for that drink. Let's go."

On entering the station office, Bony closed the door and the sergeant poured the drinks. From a near-by room came the sound of exercises being played on a piano by not too facile fingers.

"Luck!" murmured Marshall.

"Luck! How did you get on?"

"I had a word or two with Perkins, the bookkeeper," began the sergeant. "Drew a blank. He was busy all that day the swagman was camped at the woolshed, and so he left the mailbox clearance a bit late. The mail car arrived before he had cleared and it was then a matter of grabbing the letters out of the box and bundling them with the office stuff, chucking the lot into a mailbag, sealing and handing to the driver."

"Oh! A pity."

"Yes. Anyway, Perkins didn't leave his office all that day excepting to go to lunch, and during the time he was in the office the swagman didn't post a letter in the station box, which was in his plain view beyond the open window.

"Had afternoon tea with the Leylans," Marshall went on. "Met a guest by the name of Lawton-Stanley. He's engaged to Miss Leylan. Good fellow all which ways. He's a bush evangelist and the real Mackie. Afterwards I asked Leylan point-blank where he was the night the swagman was done in, and he said he was up at Ivanhoe, slept at the hotel there, and didn't leave next day till after nine."

"Good work, even if the results are apparently poor," Bony said. "Now I want you to ring up Wattle Creek Station and contact that Lawton-Stanley. When you get him, just give me the telephone. Say nothing to the bookkeeper or to the evangelist that I want to speak."

Marshall contacted Perkins, and a few minutes elapsed before Lawton-Stanley reached the telephone.

"Are you alone?" Bony asked, deepening his voice.

"I am," came to his ear in the finely modulated voice of the man known to many hundreds of bushmen as a friend. "Who is speaking?"

"I am the dark man whom the fortuneteller told you would have a great influence in your life," replied Bony.

"What are you saying? Who are you? What do you want of me?" enquired Lawton-Stanley. Bony said, maintaining the deep voice:

"Please do not repeat my name. Go back into the dreadful past, and see there a home at Banyo, and Charles, my son, whose ambition it is to become a medicomissionary."

Lawton-Stanley broke into a roar of laughter which shocked Bony's eardrums.

"You villain!" he chortled. "Fancy you being down here. Where are you speaking from?"

"I am in Merino," replied Bony. "I understand that your fiancée and you are coming along to church tomorrow evening. Correct?"

"Yes. It is our intention."

"I shall be at church too," Bony said. "I shall be accompanied by a lady who is anxious to meet you. You will be charmed by her. My name is Robert Burns, nicknamed Bony, and you will remember that we last met on a Queensland cattle station. Clear?"

"Quite. You are always clear, most clear."

"I want you to be especially nice to my lady friend, and after service Mrs. Marshall will ask Miss Leylan and yourself home for supper. You will accept—without fail. Clear?"

"As a foggy night. Righto, Bobby! Gang your ain gait. Did you get over that drubbing I gave you before breakfast at Quinquarrie?"

"Without losing a breath. How did your black eye get along?"

"Nicely, thank you. How are you keeping?"

"Fine. I've fallen in love again."

"What, again!"

"Again. You'll meet her tomorrow evening. My lady friend's name is Rose Marie. Miss Leylan knows her quite well. Now good night, Padre, and all the best."

When Bony hung up he turned to Marshall, saying:

"Finest man in the back country. Fights like a threshing machine. Isn't really happy unless he puts on the gloves before breakfast. You any good?"

"Not according to Queensberry," replied Marshall, smiling. "Pretty good under Rafferty's rules, though."

"Won't do. Must be Queensberry. Lawton-Stanley bars knees and boots at his prebreakfast exercises. Now we shall have to be especially nice to your wife, for as yet she knows nothing of her invitation to Lawton-Stanley and Miss Leylan. How will your wife take it, do you think?"

"Pretty crook, probably," replied Marshall. "You'll be doing the talking. Come on. Dinner's ready."

"Oh, there you are!" exclaimed Mrs. Marshall when they entered the living room. "Dinner's waiting. I'll call Rose Marie."

"Er—one moment," Bony interposed blandly. "I have a confession to make . . . a moment of weakness. A great friend of mine is staying at Wattle Creek Station. He is the Rev. Lawton-Stanley, a bush evangelist known far and wide."

Mrs. Marshall's eyes grew big.

"I have seen him, but I've never actually met him," she said. "He's engaged to Edith Leylan, so I'm told."

"Yes, that is so. Er—as a matter of fact, they are both coming to church tomorrow evening, and I told him a moment ago on the phone that, after service, you would invite them both home to supper. I hope you won't let me down."

"Of course not. That will be lovely. I've always wanted to meet him. But . . . I think I'd better not go to service. There will be supper to prepare."

"I said that you would be going to the service," insisted Bony. "You see, Mrs. Marshall, I am taking Rose Marie, and in view of my present social status it would be proper if you chaperoned us."

Mrs. Marshall hesitated, smiled, and assented.

"It beats me," snorted her husband. "Easy victory! If it had been me there would have been yells and screams about not having had sufficient notice, and this and that."

His wife smiled at him affectionately and said:

"You'd better behave yourself, young man."

"I'm trying to in spite of my hunger."

"Well, then, sit down. I'll call Rose Marie."

"Let me," requested Bony, and with the freedom of a member of the household he passed to the "front room," where Rose

Marie was courageously working and wondering when on earth her mother would release her from durance vile.

"Oh!" she exclaimed when Bony came silently to stand at her side.

"You play very nicely," he told her. "I've been listening to you. Dinner is waiting, and here are my wages for today for you to put into your box. Is your dress all ready for church tomorrow?"

"Yes. Mother ironed it this afternoon. And your clothes too?"

"And have you decided what to say to Miss Leylan's sweetheart?"

"No . . . I haven't. What shall I say, Bony?"

"The first thing that enters your head."

For this Marshall family Bony had come to have an affectionate regard. Beneath his official exterior Marshall himself was a kindly man and generous in his outlook to everyone, a good husband to a woman who gave as well as accepted, and matched his sense of humour, and a father who had an enormous and secret pride in his daughter, in whom quaintness and precociousness were due to the undisputed place she occupied in their hearts. Mrs. Marshall was one of those rare women who seem incapable of finding any fault in any person. And in both her husband and Bonaparte she had good companions.

The sergeant chewed his food well and truly. Rose Marie copied her father in this as well as in nearly everything else. She never interrupted the conversation, choosing her moment to ask for something. Seated on a doubly cushioned chair, she appeared larger than she actually was.

The following evening, dressed in a grey frock and velours hat, she called on Bony to tell him it was time for church and that her mother was waiting.

"Do you think I look nice?" she asked him.

"I think you are adorable, Rose Marie, and I am sure that Mr. Lawton-Stanley will think so too. Do I look all right enough for church?"

"Of course," replied Rose Marie.

Together they crossed the open space to the front of the police station, where Mrs. Marshall waited. The sergeant accompanied them as far as the front gate, and Mrs. Marshall told him:

"Don't let the fire go out, Father, and don't stoke it up so that the house will be a furnace time we get back."

"I'll do my best," he promised, and stood watching them walking down the street, Bony on the outside and Rose Marie walking sedately between him and her mother. He reckoned he had known a number of good half-castes in his time, and a lot of white men too, but not a man approaching the one who was taking his wife and daughter to church.

There were some thirty people already within the building when Rose Marie led her mother and Bony into a pew. Bony recognized Mrs. Fanning with her husband, and Mrs. Sutherland with her two boys. Mrs. Sutherland rose and came to them to whisper a few words of welcome. Her girlish figure was moulded into a black gown, both gown and figure sufficient to make envious any girl of seventeen.

Soon after she had gone back to her pew, Mrs. James emerged from the vestry and went up to the pulpit with a sheaf of papers which she placed on the reading desk and weighted with a block of white marble. Her short-skirted costume seemed to emphasize the slenderness of her body, which, however, radiated energy in every quick and purposeful movement.

Rose Marie nudged Bony's elbow and he, looking down at her, followed the direction of her eyes and saw Edith Leylan and Lawton-Stanley walking down the far aisle to a large family pew. The girl walked easily. She was plainly but expensively dressed, and it did not appear strange to either Bony or Lawton-Stanley that many of the women present dressed with better taste than the average city women. Lawton-Stanley wore layman's clothes. He was six feet tall and his well-knit, lean body was perfectly balanced on his feet. His features were slightly sharp and on the bridge of his long, straight nose were rimless pince-nez. They could now see his face in profile, strong, open, and clean, and lighted by a lamp of inner joy.

Covertly Bony glanced down at Rose Marie, to observe her flushed cheek and one very wide and bright grey eye, and he whispered:

"What do you think?"

"He's just lovely," she replied.

Mrs. James, having prepared the pulpit, passed down the steps to the church floor, and then crossed to welcome Lawton-Stanley. Bony could see that she was being torn by two opposing forces, that opposed to her desire to welcome the bush evangelist being the great enemy Time. Three minutes later she emerged from a side door into the choir gallery, seated herself at the organ, and began to play. The gallery filled up with senior boys and girls of the Sunday school.

The Rev. Llewellyn James entered from the vestry. He was arrayed in his black crepe gown and moved with ponderousness in contrast to the lightness of his wife. When he mounted the pulpit steps he appeared to haul himself upward by a hand upon the single banister. The organist ceased playing. The minister stood up and removed the marble block from the sheaf of papers. He picked up the top one and announced the opening hymn without any warmth in his voice.

Mrs. James played the opening bars and led the choir. Bony could not hear her voice but he knew that she was singing with all her might. Her head was held well back, her face lifted so that she must have been looking high at the organ pipes and not at the music.

Although professionally interested in the minister, the service was not entirely to Bony's liking. It was a fault due less to the material than to the manner in which it was given.

It became plain that the Rev. Llewellyn James was an automaton. The entire service was set out for him on that sheaf of papers placed by his wife in the pulpit. The hymn numbers were there. The prayers were there for him to read. The passages of Scripture were marked ready for him in the Book. And from the sheaf of papers he read his sermon. His voice was strong and his enunciation good, but that was spoiled by the overlaying nasal whine and the ending of every sentence on too high a note, which became monotonous. He was lacking in spiritual warmth as was the block of marble on his desk.

After the service the Rev. Llewellyn James hurried from his pulpit to the vestibule to speak a few parting words with members of his congregation. His wife remained at the organ. Bony, with his two ladies, left before Edith Leylan and her escort, Mr. James shaking hands with Mrs. Marshall and giving Rose Marie a pat on the shoulder. He stared at Bony and said not a word.

"He might have spoken to you," Mrs. Marshall remarked as they walked towards the gate.

"I find it hard to blame him for being speechless," Bony said gravely. "After all, he has reason for being astonished at a known jailbird taking to his church the wife and daughter of Merino's senior police officer. Even to me, it doesn't all seem to square. Ah, here comes Lawton-Stanley."

The bush evangelist's expressive hands were held out to clasp Bony's shoulders. His hazel eyes were alight, and upon his fine face was an expression difficult to define.

"Bony!" he said slowly, and then went on at quicker tempo: "I never thought to see you in this part of the continent. You are looking well."

"I am feeling better than I did two minutes ago, Padre. Oh, good evening, Miss Leylan. You remember me, I hope. We met on the Walls of China."

"I remember you, of course," she said gaily. "But just fancy you two knowing each other."

"The padre knows everyone, including all blackguards. Please pardon me. Mrs. Marshall, allow me to present to you an old friend, the Rev. Lawton-Stanley."

Mrs. Marshall was delighted. She found herself wanting to talk, and Bony had gently to interpose himself.

"And this young lady is an especial and a very dear friend of mine. Rose Marie . . . permit me to present to you the Rev. Lawton-Stanley."

Lawton-Stanley did not stoop to conquer. He had done that even before he noticed the little girl. He stooped to take her hand and to smile into her face, and he said softly, as though she only was to hear:

"Rose Marie! I am happy to meet you, Rose Marie, happy indeed, to meet any of Bony's friends. You remind me of someone I cannot now recall. Did I hear you singing during the service?"

"I hope so. I tried to sing loud enough," she replied.

"I thought I heard you. Keep on singing, Rose Marie. Sing all the day through. Open your chest and sing hard. And then you will grow up to be a wonderful woman."

Rose Marie nodded, for she was unable to speak. She heard him chatting with her elders, heard her mother issue the invitation to supper, and heard the acceptance. And then she realized that she was walking alone with Miss Leylan's Frank, walking up the street behind her mother and Miss Leylan and Bony, and Miss Leylan's Frank was asking her all kinds of questions.

When she retired to go to bed, she gravely wished each one a good night, gathered into her arms Edith and Thomas, walked out through the doorway happily tired. By that time Bony had made himself known to Edith Leylan, and they had discussed the country within the Wattle Creek boundary east of the Walls of China; water holes, shapes and areas of paddocks, and the various classes of timber and feed. And then, when covert glances were being directed to the clock, Bony put a direct question to Lawton-Stanley:

"What is your opinion of Mr. James as a preacher?"

Lawton-Stanley turned a calm face and steady eyes towards his questioner and replied:

"I am inclined to think there is room for improvement."

"He interests me," Bony stated. "I find him quite a study. His heart is not in his work, and that would not be due entirely to a weak heart, which, I am led to believe, he finds a sore trial. Do you think it not impossible that he is an impostor?"

"Why do you consider such a thing?" countered the bush evangelist.

"From the time he entered the pulpit this evening to the time he vacated it," Bony said slowly, "Mr. James did not utter a single word from his own mind. Did you not observe how he read everything; everything from hymn announcements to the benediction?"

"Yes, I did note that."

Lawton-Stanley's face registered sadness. He appeared to be interested in the pattern of the carpet under his feet, and when Bony said nothing to change the subject he asked:

"Are you interested in James . . . professionally?"

Bony chuckled.

"I am interested in everybody, professionally," he said. "Now, after all this shying away, let me have your opinion of Mr. James."

Lawton-Stanley looked up and into the blue eyes of the half-caste, to see in them and on the dark face no trace of the chuckle. From that he understood that Bony had made no idle request. He

129

nodded his head slowly, as though reaching a decision was difficult. Then:

"My opinion of him hasn't altered from what it was seven or eight years ago when he and his wife and I were students in the same theological college," he said. "James just managed to scrape through and gain ordination. He probably wouldn't have survived to be ordained had it not been for Lucy Meredith. She was studying to become a deaconess, and she was brilliant. How James was ever recommended by his church minister and elders for admission to the college always has beaten me. All he ever wanted was an easy and respectable job, a job requiring no effort, or very little, for a small return.

"Anyway, Lucy Meredith married him, married a merely lazy dog wanting only ease, even ease with hunger. From the beginning of his call she always wrote all his sermons and prepared every part of his service."

"And chops the wood for the kitchen stove," added Edith Leylan. "I've seen her."

"And cleans his boots too," added Mrs. Marshall. "Rose Marie saw her at it one day."

"Do you think he has a weak heart?" Bony asked.

"I do not," firmly replied Lawton-Stanley. "He has never suffered from anything worse than muscular inactivity." They could see the pain on the evangelist's fine face. He added: "Would you mind if we do not discuss him further? You see, I don't like thinking ill of anyone."

"Very well, Padre," Bony assented quickly. "You can safely leave me to do all the ill thinking. I revel in it."

And no one noted the mirthless grin of joy on the large face of Merino's senior police officer.

XV. Bony's Philosophy of Crime

ON THE LAST DAY of Bony's incarceration he and Marshall were seated after lunch on the rear veranda of the station house. The sergeant had remarked on Bony's apparent inactivity as a detective whilst imprisoned, and he had expressed the hope that after this day his superior might get down to solid work. He had spoken in the casual fashion of the bushman, and Bony would be the last to take umbrage at what the big man said.

"It's like this, Marshall," he explained. "There is a much greater detective than I, one with whom I have allied myself to a very great degree. I refer to Providence.

"We are men who have arrived at the stage of life when our storehouse of experience is becoming full. We have learned many lessons, and we have come to understand many truths, among which is that Evil never triumphs. We may recall instances where Evil apparently has triumphed, but in those instances Time has not had sufficient scope to bring about Evil's defeat.

"It doesn't matter two hoots whether the form of the evil is a murder or an unjustly harsh act. Evil is always countered by God, or Good, or Providence, or whatever name you might choose to give it. You and I know, as well as other sensible and experienced men, that Evil never blesses, and the evildoer never prospers. I recognized that eternal law years ago . . . which is why I am an investigator of crime and not a supermaster of crime.

"Why should I rush about and demand of every Tom, Dick, and Harry the answer to this and that question? Why, when by merely keeping open my eyes and my ears and exercising ordinary common gumption the murderer of George Kendall and that swagman will surely reveal himself as the sting ray in my netful of fishes?"

Marshall sighed, loudly and long. Then he argued.

"Your general idea may be all right, Bony, but while you are waiting for Providence to lend a hand another poor devil may be murdered."

"I grant you the contention," agreed Bony, "but I doubt that still another murder would be prevented by rushing about and cross-questioning everyone in the district. Think now. Investigation of a common passion-and-bash murder is almost always elementary. But this Kendall affair is not a common passion-and-bash murder. I have never thought it, and do not now. Did I not tell you that this case on which we are engaged is in the Jack-the-Ripper class? The man we seek is cold and unimpassioned. He thinks and plans, and gives nothing away through loss of temper or the mastery of emotion.

"Now look at me. I am an emotional man. I have a soft heart. I am naturally a kindly man. If I permitted emotion and kindliness to control me I would never unearth a criminal. I never allow emotion or even humanitarian thoughts to sway me in the slightest whilst I am investigating a murder. I was not emotionally concerned because Kendall was murdered, and old Bennett probably frightened to death before he could be murdered, and that swagman strangled and hanged.

"Many young detectives, and older ones too, are too liable to the emotion of indignation because of a brutal killing. They accept such a crime as a personal matter and so permit their judgment to be clouded by animosity towards the killer.

"To me the three deaths here are pointers in a puzzle. I would be regretful if another person were murdered by the man we are after, but I would not be perturbed and would not accept it as a personal affront. I would not blame myself for not having caught the murderer before he committed the fresh crime. Not a bit of it. I proceed calmly and without undue haste, gathering clues and proofs with each successive murder, until I have enough to name the killer."

"Sounds all right," agreed the sergeant doubtfully.

"It *is* all right," Bony asserted. "I always win. People say what a jolly fine fellow Bony is, how sagacious. Actually all I do is to wait for Providence to toss the clues into my open hands. I do little but wait . . . and watch . . . and observe Providence doing the work for me. Evil is always vanquished. I find it quite simple."

Sergeant Marshall exploded.

"I'm damned if I know when you are being serious and when you are pulling my leg," he snorted.

Bony began to laugh, then checked himself.

"A lot of sense if not all sense," he admitted. "A case like this is not dissimilar to a sum in addition. We add something to something else, and that total we add to another something else. For instance we now know that Massey Leylan spent that night the swagman was killed at Ivanhoe and therefore could not have done the killing. To that is added the recently acquired information that the swagman's name is John Way, no known relatives.

We have gained a large number of facts with which to play and on which to base assumptions. As sure as the sun will set this evening, we shall one day be in possession of a sufficient number of facts to justify an arrest."

"Will you tell me something?" Marshall asked.

"I am at your service."

Marshall gulped. He wanted to tell Bony that he was a liar. He said tartly:

"I'd like to know why you want to know why the Rev. James keeps a horse?"

"That's an easy one," replied Bony. "As I told Lawton-Stanley yesterday evening, I am interested professionally in the Rev. James. He rides a horse. In spite of his allegedly weak heart, he rides a horse so hard that the animal becomes winded, and then he wipes the animal down with a piece of hessian sacking. First question: why does he ride a horse so hard? Second question: where did he obtain the piece of hessian sacking? Third question: what was he doing out eastward of the Walls of China early the morning after the swagman was killed, and in country from which the man with hessian sacking about his feet went to the hut and returned from the hut? We may assume that the Rev. James could leave Merino at night much more quietly on a horse than in his car, and that he could return more quietly in the early morning on a horse than in his car.

"When I visited the parsonage I saw no stable, and I am interested to hear from you that James does own a horse which he stables with another belonging to Fanning, the butcher. If enquiries produced the information that the reverend gentleman's horse was not in Fanning's stables during the night that Kendall was killed and the night that the swagman was killed, we would have added yet another interesting fact to our collection."

"Crumbs!" exclaimed Marshall.

"You will not give rein to your imagination, my dear Marshall," Bony said quietly. "Did I exert myself to find out that James rode his horse so hard as to wind it, and that he wiped it down with a piece of hessian? I did not. Providence gave to me those little facts. Every detective who ever was will admit that Providence is kind to him. Describe to me the position of that stable."

"It is well back from Fanning's shop and house," Marshall began. "The stable is in a yard of about an acre in area. The animals are fed in the stable and have their freedom to run in the yard. Fanning is able to get to his stable through a door in his rear fence."

"Good! Most interesting! It is a fact, then, that Mr. James, or anyone else for that matter, could take a horse from that yard at night and return it before morning without anyone being the wiser?"

"That's so," agreed Marshall.

"So that we were justified in not allowing rein to our imaginations, rushing to the conclusion that the Rev. James takes out his horse at night to do a little murdering. You see how we gather bits and pieces to fit into or to discard as useless from the framework in our puzzle. Some of us sometimes have all the pieces in our possession, but only clever people, like me, can fit all of them together. Now I must return to my painting. On several counts I am not a little saddened by the thought that this is my last day as your prisoner. However, I could raise myself on my toes sufficiently to punch your nose and get myself another ten days, couldn't I?"

"Better not try it," retorted Marshall. "I can hit hard—when I'm in the mood. And I'm in that mood now."

"Now! Now! Keep cheerful! Have patience. Have I not patiently served you for ten long days? See you later. Cheerio!"

Bony having left for his painting work, the sergeant heaved himself to his feet and waggled his head in mock despair. Then he lumbered through the kitchen and along the passage to his office.

Sergeant Marshall's prisoner would now not be able to complete the painting of the entire compound fence. That fronting the street had been done, the yellow colour outraging the colour sense of every inhabitant of Merino. The division fence between the police station and Mr. Jason's residence had been completed, and but a few yards remained to be done to complete the rear fence. On this remaining section Bony fell to work.

The early afternoon was hot and dry, with a light wind coming down from the north. The sky was stained with a white opalescence beneath the blue which promised wind, and this fact was registered by the mind of the half-caste, whose very being was sensitive to weather changes.

To Bony the day was a good one. He had done more preparatory work than Marshall knew. Marshall was depressed because H.Q. had reported that there were no fingerprints on the door handles removed from the hut at Sandy Flat. They had been wiped clean of all prints, for microscopic examination revealed traces of the rag or cloth over the surface. The report had the opposite effect on Bony. To him it enhanced the interest of the investigation, proving that the man he sought was leaving little to chance, and also providing additional proof, if such proof was needed, that he was a killer in the top class.

Marshall did not know that Bony had urged H.Q. to institute enquiries into the histories of the Jasons, Mr. James, Constable Gleeson, and several other men. People are not murdered without motive, and if the motive for such a crime is not passion, greed, jealousy, then it might well lie somewhere within the limits of insanity. And if that were so, the past might well provide the key piece to this puzzle of the present.

Shortly after five o'clock Bony was summoned to the front fence by a shrill whistle given by little Mr. Watson. Mr. Watson was without hat, coat, or waistcoat. He appeared to be worn by the heat, for even his grey moustache was less stiff than was usual.

"What about sinking a couple?" he suggested hopefully.

Bony smiled, saying:

"You are a man of ideas."

"It comes natural to me," Mr. Watson said modestly. "One idea will bring another, see? . . . Heat—a gargle. Cold—a blood warmer."

Bony vaulted the fence and joined the local newspaper correspondent.

"Get your story of the inquest away all right?" he asked when they were crossing the street to the hotel.

"Oh yes. Great story. It'll hit the top lines. The papers are sending out a couple of the boys. Merino's looking up, ain't it?"

Bony glanced at the whiskey-reddened face.

"It might look up even more someday soon," he predicted.

"I hope so. She's pretty dead most times. Wants a murder now and then to circulate the blood, sort of."

Mr. Watson led the way into the hotel bar, where they found the licensee in conversation with Mr. Jason and two other men who were strangers to Bony. The licensee left them to move along behind his counter to serve them, and Mr. Watson decided that a gin sling would be an appropriate gargle. With soft voice Mr. Watson said confidentially:

"Young Tom's been telling me that the old boy hasn't done a stroke of work since he held the inquest on that swagman. He's just living to get the papers reporting that inquest. They should be here tomorrow from Sydney."

"He'll be disappointed if you didn't give him a boost," remarked the licensee. "I wasn't there, but they tell me he carried out his coroner's job first-rate."

"He did so," agreed Mr. Watson. "Give the devil his due, I say. Old Jason done a good job, and he looks the part too, don't he?"

"Well, not just now, d'you think?" Bony argued.

"No, not now, but when he's on the bench," persisted Mr. Watson. "He knows his law, and he's very fair, and he can handle a court. Hush! He's coming along here."

The two men who were strangers to Bony left the bar, and Mr. Jason stalked the few yards to join the latest arrivals. Mr. Watson asked the funeral director and wheelwright to name his poison, and Mr. Jason called for a shandygaff.

"Good day, Burns!" he said to Bony. "Let me see now. This is your last day, isn't it?"

"That's so, Mr. Jason."

"No ill feeling, I hope?"

"None at all, Mr. Jason," Bony assured him. "You had a job to do, and you did it quite well. As a matter of fact, I have enjoyed the period in jail."

"I am glad to hear that."

The rich voice seemed oddly at variance with the dungaree overalls being worn by Merino's first citizen. Mr. Jason's white face and black moustache appeared at variance with those overalls too.

"What are your plans for the future?" he asked.

"Oh, I'm going to work for Mr. Leylan. Reporting to him in the morning. Mr. James got me a job with him."

"Hum! You will find him quite a good employer. His men

speak well of him." Mr. Jason produced his pipe and tobacco plug and knife. For the first time he smiled. Then: "There is one place on Wattle Creek Station I would not like to work from."

"Sandy Flat!" breathed Mr. Watson. "I wouldn't camp at that place for a hundred pounds."

"Nor me, either," interjected the licensee. "Not after what's happened down there."

Bony called for drinks.

"If Leylan wants me to go and live at Sandy Flat," he said, "I'll not be going. No, not after having seen all those blowflies that day me and Marshall found the man hanging from the roof."

Mr. Jason, having loaded the bowl of his pipe, applied a match to the weed, and Mr. Watson gently nudged Bony. The pipe seemed not to draw well, and Mr. Jason unscrewed the little cup beneath the bowl, emptied the fluid nicotine onto the floor, replaced the cup, and applied another match. When the smoke appeared to rise slowly above his head like a lifting halo, he said:

"I cannot at the moment recall a line written by Milton about the spirits of the departed. To me the spirits of the departed would be less uncomfortable than the dust down at Sandy Flat. I understand that even a gentle wind will raise the dust there to suffocating volume. Still, to a man having imagination dead quiet nights would be very trying."

"Any kind of nights at that place would be too trying for me," Bony asserted. "Suppose I'd better be off back to put the paint and things away for the last time and wash for dinner. See you all again sometime. Cheerio!"

XVI. Sand and Wind

IN THE LATE AFTERNOON of the following day Bony, now an employee of Massey Leylan, left Wattle Creek homestead for Sandy Flat. He rode a spirited grey gelding with whom he had till to make friends, whilst fresh in his mind were the well-wishes and the condolences of Sam the Blackmailer, and those employed about the homestead. He had been assured by everyone that "not for a million quid" would they camp at the hut at Sandy Flat for a single night.

On leaving the homestead, instead of following the road to Merino till the right-hand turn was reached, he rode close beside the Walls of China, which rose on his left side in steep ramparts and slopes of sand supporting never a blade of grass nor a shoot of scrub. The wind came from his right, the west, fairly steadily and at an estimated velocity of fifteen miles an hour. It carried towards the Walls the sand grains flung upward by the hoofs of his horse and it blurred with white mist the curving lines of the summits upon which rested the blue sky. The sun was hot and good to feel on bare arms and neck and right cheek, and now and then Bony expanded his chest and breathed deeply. He was inclined to sing, for his spirit was uplifted.

This was his country. The vast, almost mountainous range of snow-white sand to his left, and the red bush-covered land rising gently on his right to the far distant horizon beyond and higher than Merino, was his city. The endless white sand flats separated by water gutters which rarely knew water were his streets. The very ground itself was his newspaper, supplied to him freshly clean and new after every moderately windy day.

Over the broad sand flats he rode a horse anxious to gallop, anxious to be free, to stretch the muscles of its legs and whistle the wind through distended pink nostrils. Well, during the immediate days ahead, the horse should have its wish, for there were hundreds of square miles of land to be surveyed, land over which a man had twice passed to and from the sinister hut at Sandy Flat.

The west wind carried to him the hum of the truck engine on its way to the hut to deposit his swag and rations and meat. Not long afterwards he saw it again, returning to the homestead, and he smiled, tight-lipped, at the mental picture of the driver wasting not a moment to do his errand and leave a place of such ill repute.

He came to the eastern fence of the half-mile-square horse paddock, a fence which hugged the foot of the Walls, and when he reached the southern corner he rode for three hundred yards to pass the hut and to examine the water troughs. The truck's wheel tracks were plain, as were the tracks of the driver from truck to hut and back. Yet even so soon, the wind was filling in those tracks. A few sheep were drinking at one of the troughs; several others were lying down far out and chewing the cud. The ground indicated that comparatively few stock were watering here, that the water holes in the paddocks were still serving the majority.

He gave his horse a drink and then rode again past the hut to the gate of the horse paddock, went through it, loosed the horse, and hung saddle and bridle over a rail sheltered by a small roof of iron. The horse galloped away, and Bony walked back to the hut. By the sun it was then a few minutes after five o'clock.

In place of the door handles sent down to the fingerprint section a length of fencing wire had been passed through the hole and knotted, its outer end angled to slip down over a nail driven into the doorframe. This primitive door catch Bony lifted up and then pushed inward the door, smiling grimly at the unwarranted precaution so soon after the visit of the truck driver. He even peered through the space between door and frame to ascertain if anyone stood behind the door with a strip of hessian sacking ready in his hands. On the table were the rations, a tucker box and meat in a calico bag, and his strapped swag.

Having raised the drop window in the back wall, he took two petrol-tin buckets to fill at a tap beneath the reservoir tank. The outside indicator showed that the tank was four-fifths filled, and so there was no necessity to release the mill. On getting back to the hut with his water supply, he made a fire on the open hearth and slung over it a filled billycan of water for tea. In the tucker box was fresh bread and cooked meat, so no cooking had to be done this evening. Then the jam tins, in which stood the legs of the meat safe in the small cane-grass hutment, had to be filled with water to defeat the ants, which in these parts defied even the shifting sand. After that he unrolled his swag on the bunk and prepared his bed for the night.

The sun could be seen framed within the trap window. It was huge and blood-red, and the light it shed into the hut splashed crimson upon the bunk, the table, and the floor near the door. The air was cooling, but the flies remained "sticky," and even when the sun did vanish beneath the tree-bordered horizon they remained active, loath to leave Bony's arms and face.

The wind was not as strong now, but it promised to blow

throughout the night and the following day, and when he had washed the dishes after his meal and stood on the doorstep smoking a cigarette, he saw that the truck's wheel tracks were almost obliterated. His own—excepting those against the doorstep—were wholly so.

As the twilight deepened he sat on the doorstep and smoked, the nature lover in him entranced by the slowly changing colours of the Walls of China.

The setting sun had stained the faces of the slopes with coral pink, and the gullies with soft purple, and, when it had set, the pink and the purple changed to old ivory. Now again it was changing, this time to the colour of new silver barred with the black velvet of the deeper gullies between the rising slopes. Presently the living colours appeared to be drained of colour and warmth, leaving but a chalky white smeared with bars of ink. And above that chalky whiteness the pale green of the sky was being washed out by the indigo blue of advancing night.

The wind's plaintive moan at the corners of the hut failed to drown from his ears its hissing over the sand ribbles all about. Unaccountably a cold arrow sped up the flesh covering his spine and made him glance over his shoulder at the dark interior of the hut limited by the oblong opening of the drop window. The same swift glance noted the crossbeam from which had dangled a dead man.

"There are times," he mused aloud, "when my mother in me makes me too sensitive. I can smell the blood of men, and I can feel their spirits near me. Now, now, Detective Inspector Bonaparte, stand no nonsense from Bony."

He stood up, stretched himself, turned into the hut, and relit the fire to brew some coffee. By its light he let down the drop window and fastened it. The lamp he did not light. He returned to the doorstep, wishing that the night was past. The crackling of the fire he found a comfort.

Now the Walls of China were masked in black without a single eyehole. They presented a complete void above which floated the stars. The wind continued to moan at the hut corners and to play over the sand ribbles, its noise sufficient to drown the sound of the bush banshee's footsteps or the hessian-blanketed steps of the man who had strangled the swagman and then hanged hi body. The banshee never made a mistake once it got on the tracks of a blackfellow caught away from his own campfire at night, but surely the man with sacking about his feet must make a mistake sooner or later!

When the billycan on the fire began to sing its boiling song Bony rose once again and made coffee, which he took to his door-step with pannikin and sugar. Soon afterwards invisible wings fluttered above the hut roof, and again the icy arrow sped up his spine to chill the hair of his head. A thin sigh escaped his lips when from the roof of the cane-grass meat house came the "mo-poke, mo-poke" of the night bird.

The sky above the Walls was becoming diffused with a peculiar sheen and the stars were losing their brilliance. He sighed with relief. Far away to the south appeared a chain of strange clouds —the taller summits bathed in the light of the rising moon.

The moon was high above the Walls of China when Bony rose and, entering the hut, rerolled his swag and took it over to lay out upon the sandy floor of the meat house. He took his tucker box and rations, which he placed within the safe. He lay upon his bed and smoked his last cigarette for the evening, and some-how he found the air sweeter to breathe.

He was awakened by a rhythmic clanging sound. He sat up abruptly, listening, straining his ears. He knew what that noise was. The windmill was in action.

XVII.   Adventure by Moonlight

SPLINTERS OF MOONLIGHT lay upon the floor of the cane-grass meat house. The wire-netted door was wide open, and beyond it could be seen a section of white sand beneath the star-filled sky. The wind still blew, whispering secrets into the clefts of the sand ribbles, and hissing with the soft music of bursting sea suds through the tough grass of the hutment. Discordantly, without rhythm but with an inevitable regularity, there came to Bony's straining ears the "clang . . . clang . . . clang" of the windmill in action.

141

Surely he had not released the mill to take the wind! For an instant he checked upon himself, knowing then that he had not even interfered with the mill. It was not an old mill. The original paint was still in good condition. When he had visited the tank to draw water for his own use the tail fan was swung into line with the wind. That position of the tail was maintained by a strong wire fastened near the ground to a lever bar, which in its turn was kept in position by an iron pin. For the mill to gain freedom, that iron pin would have had to be withdrawn or, alternatively, the wire would have had to break.

The remote chance of the wire breaking was debated by Bony whilst he pulled on his riding boots. The chance *was* remote, for the mill was not old and that wire was not likely to be worn in any place.

There could be no legitimate reason for anyone to release the mill. The reservoir tank was almost full and there was hardly any stock as yet coming to drink here. Leylan and all his hands at the homestead knew that he, Bony, was camping here this night, and it could not be imagined that any of the hands would be sent to release the mill after ten o'clock, the hour that Bony had retired. From the position of the moon, it was now verging upon two o'clock.

The banshee? Oh rot! Cut out that stuff, Bony!

Detective Inspector Napoleon Bonaparte moved toward the open netted door on his hands and knees. When he emerged into the moonlight he almost faced the front of the hut. For nearly a minute he regarded that sinister dwelling, noting how deserted it looked and that the door was fastened shut. He tried to recall if he had closed it. Unsuccessful, he began to crawl round the circular cane-grass meat house, keeping tight against the wall, until he reached the narrow segment of black shadow on its south-eastern side. In this shadow he stood up, pressing with his back against the wall and wishing that it had been made of brick, not grass.

The scene presented to him was almost as clear as at high noon. The Walls of China rose tier upon tier in snowy whiteness. To the south was the reservoir tank on its tall stand. He could see the black shadow about its wooden supports, and he could see the moonlit sandscape beyond and between the supports. The mill towered higher than the reservoir tank, its iron stand laying a maze of narrow shadows below it. The "wheel" of wind vanes was revolving fast. Almost facing Bony, the light of the moon blended the vanes into a solid disk of bright silver. And outward from the mill above the covered well radiated the three long lines of troughing, black upon the brilliantly lit white sand.

Nothing moved in all that far-flung waste of white sand save the wind vanes of the mill. The sheep that had come to drink at sunset had gone away out into the feed.

The control wire must have broken.

Unhurriedly, almost casually, Bony visually examined every object made by man and set down there on the white sand. There were no shadows cast by Nature's handiwork. There was no living thing beneath the mill, and after a full minute he was convinced that nothing alive lurked in the shadow cast by the reservoir tank. A man could remain concealed by lying down beyond any one of the trough lines, but to do that he must continue to lie full length.

Yes, that control wire must have broken this very night through a million-to-one chance. And yet . . .

For the third time during his stay at Sandy Flat the icy arrow sped up the flesh covering his spine and became lodged in his scalp. Somewhere in Bony's sensitive being a warning chord was being struck.

All was not right with the place, despite the power of the moonlight and the paucity of objects casting shadows to conceal danger. The entire picture was illumined clearly enough, and the shadow-casting objects easily totalled. The mill, the reservoir stand and tank, the three lines of troughing, the hut, and the meat house against which he was leaning made but seven objects set upon a ruffled sheet of white cloth. Yet the number seemed to be wrong, either one too many or too few compared with the number which had been impressed upon his mind whilst he sat on the hut doorstep the previous evening and smoked cigarettes. The westering moon shed its glare full upon the vast face of the Walls of China. Upon it there were no shadows.

The minutes were ticked off the sheet of Time by the moon's inevitable passage down the pale blue bowl of the sky, and still Bony continued to remain passive, leaning back against the cane-grass meat house, now and then changing his weight from foot to foot. That inherited sense of unseen danger remained strongly in him. There *was* something wrong about the place, a something which had not been wrong with it when he made up his bunk in the meat house and fell asleep.

The vanes of the mill followed each other round and round to fashion an opalescent disk, raising and depressing the long iron rod connected to the pump deep within the well. Why should anyone release the mill in the middle of the night when water was not necessary? Well, one objective could be to awaken him, to take him to the mill to shut it off and so make a target of him with a rifle. Why that? The killer of Kendall and the swagman, the man whom he was seeking, might have learned who and what he was, and might be lying down on the far side of one of the trough lines, waiting for him.

Then abruptly Bony froze.

The wooden floor of the stand upon which the tank rested was larger than the tank itself, and coming round into Bony's view on the edge of the tank flooring was the dark figure of a man. He was holding to the top edge of the open tank as he stepped round the edge of the flooring, to reach the iron ladder leading to the ground. He was halfway down that ladder when Bony left the shadow of the meat house.

Determined to identify this man who released windmills in the middle of the night, Bony's objective was to get as close as possible to him before he reached the bottom of the ladder down which he came with his face to it. The sand smothered all sound of Bony's racing feet, and when he was still twenty yards from the tank stand the man stepped down from the bottom rung.

Bony fell forward, scooping a small rampart of sand before him as he did so. In those swift seconds whilst the man was bringing his second foot to the ground and then turned to face towards the mill, Bony's body was concealed by the sand rampart he had flung up.

The man did not turn fully towards where Bony lay, but began to walk towards the mill. Each of his feet was bound loosely with hessian sacking, and the heart of the foxing half-caste exulted and sent the blood pounding through his arteries. He desired mightily to rush forward and arrest this climber of tank stands, this mover over sand with hessian-covered feet, and it was one of the rare occasions that he lamented an objection to carrying a gun, without which to attempt the arrest of a man so suspect would be folly.

Recognition, possible in the moonlight, was out of the question, for about the fellow's head was a cloth hood.

He walked to the mill, where he pulled down the lever bar of the control wire and shut off the mill, and, having done that, he left the mill, stepped over a trough line, and set off southward, keeping roughly parallel with the Walls of China.

Bony permitted him to proceed for a hundred yards before he rose to his feet and followed, determined to keep him in sight and to follow him to his abode, confident that he did not carry a rifle, and mindful that shooting with revolver or automatic pistol is at such a range extremely erratic.

The man went through two wire fences; and through those fences went his tracker. Thence onward to the south, hugging the great sand range, illumined by the full moonlight, onward for half a mile when the quarry abruptly stopped and looked back.

Bony had not time to go to ground, but he did have time to freeze into a tree stump, one knee bent and one unraised bent arm, his face partially hidden by the angle of his head, in which position he was just able to watch the man ahead. His quarry was standing quite still as though trying to recall if he had passed a tree stump.

It became obvious that he was uncertain about it. To make sure, he began to retrace his steps, and he had not covered twenty yards towards the motionless detective when Bony saw in the hand of the crooked right arm the glint of metal, a weapon held ready for action.

The aspect of that hooded man whose feet were submerged in flapping strips of sacking was a little unnerving. He came towards Bony like a soundless wraith accompanied by an equally soundless shadow lying from him towards the Walls. The "tree stump" came alive and moved backwards. The man appeared to hesitate, then came on till, eventually, he stopped. Bony stopped . . . and waited. The distance between them was less than ninety yards.

Bony was in command of the situation. He could follow at a distance dictated by himself. If the other man returned in an effort to checkmate him, he could retreat and continue to maintain

145

what was reasonable to think was a safe pistol-shooting distance.

The hooded man made another move, coming forward swiftly, and, as quickly, Bony went back towards the mill. Again the hooded man stopped and again Bony stopped. Across the intervening white sand they stared, to one the necessity to throw off his tracker, to the other the determination to continue tracking his quarry. And not far off the new day.

Movement in the hooded man ceased after his two arms seemed to cross in front of his body. Bony instantly broke into movement, for the meaning of those crossed arms was that the pistol hand was brought to rest on the left forearm to gain steadiness. The pistol snapped and the bullet whined past Bony's left side. The weapon was an automatic, possibly a .38, and if accuracy at approximately one hundred yards is most difficult, the distance was certainly not beyond the range of the discharged bullet.

Bony's movements became a crouching dance, and he danced back and back from the hooded man, who was now coming on once more. Again he stopped, rested the weapon on his forearm, and fired.

The noise was carried by the westerly wind towards and over the Walls of China, and he knew that there was no possibility of anyone in Merino hearing the shooting, even if anyone in the township was astir so early in the morning. Nevertheless, he desisted from further shooting and stopped once again.

Bony decided to increase the safety limit before he also stopped.

"Now you're biting your fingernails, aren't you, my friend?" he said conversationally. He knew that his voice could not reach the other, but he went on: "You are finding yourself in a bit of a hole, eh? You cannot very well chase me around the country, and you cannot have me chasing you around, either. You have to get out of that rig before daylight when someone mounted on a horse might observe with interest this little comedy of 'I chase you and you chase me.' And to add to the complications is the fact that, despite your footwear, I still can track you . . . should I lose sight of you . . . which I won't."

Abruptly the quarry turned and again proceeded to walk southward, moving very fast over the white sand; and, maintaining the distance between them, Bony followed.

So far the situation was quite satisfactory to Bony. The moon would not set until after day broke. There would be no period of darkness to give his quarry the chance of slipping away or of hiding up and taking a better-aimed shot at him. Well, well, was he, Bony, not correct when he told Sergeant Marshall that Providence was always kind to detectives? Kind especially to patient detectives!

There now appeared even greater purpose in the quarry's walking. He was moving diagonally away from the sand range, and if he should continue along that line for two miles he would then reach the timber edge. That was probably not his objective, for had it been he would have turned due west to reach the timber in less than half a mile. And then, suddenly, he vanished into the ground.

Again Bony halted. He could not see it, but he knew that his man had jumped down into a dry water channel coming down from the west to end at the Walls.

Now what? The fellow could adopt one of at least two movements. He could remain in that gutter and defend himself from physical arrest, or he could sneak along the gutter till he reached the timber country, where he would have a much better chance to evade his tracker.

But would he? Come on, Bony, use your brain. He could not stay in that gutter forever because if he did his tracker would also keep his position. He couldn't wait even till after day broke, for, like Cinderella, he must get home before daylight revealed his garb to all and sundry. He must be making for the timber. Well, in that case, why not walk to it in the open? Did he want to gain time? Time for what? Ah . . . time to reach a horse, and, once astride a horse, he could ride his tracker down and shoot him at close range.

The initiative had passed from Bony.

Bony could not be caught out on that open country. Even against a man on a horse, he would be far safer within the timber, for trees balk a horse as well as providing a degree of shelter from pistol bullets. He began to race for the timber.

It was half a mile distant, the white sheet of the sand ending abruptly against its black border. Only half a mile! But the soft sand cloyed his feet and before he had covered half the distance he began to experience the sensation of a man in a nightmare.

Then out into the open sprang the hooded man, running fast despite the hessian about his feet, running parallel with the gutter towards the timber line. His tall and robust figure appeared to move without effort, and Bony began to deplore his cigarette-smoking habit. His quarry had appeared at least two hundred yards ahead of him, and now seemed to be increasing the lead.

Yes, there it was. Bony could now see the horse neck-roped to a tree. It was standing motionless, watching the men approach, standing in the shadow cast by the leafy cabbage tree. Useless now to continue in the direct line to the timber, following as he was the hooded man, who would certainly first reach the horse, and, having reached it, mount and come riding back to meet him on the open ground.

Bony veered northwest. The timber still offered him better protection than the gutter, deep and angled though that would be. He clenched his teeth for an instant when he saw the hooded man gain the shadow of the tree beneath which stood the horse. Then he opened his mouth wide to gulp in air and steady his heaving lungs.

Providence had been kind, indeed, and now she was teasing him, teaching him more respect for her, teaching him not so easily to accept her for granted. He was two hundred yards from the timber edge when the hooded man came out from the tree shadow on the horse, plunging into a gallop, riding straight towards him.

Bony halted. He had to conserve his strength. To run was to use up what was left to him. With breath rasping through his mouth and nostrils, he bent forward, arching his body, his hands resting on the ground. With all the might of his mind exerting control over his body, he waited.

The moon was just above the rider's left shoulder. The man's hood was almost in alignment with the horse's head. He held the reins in his left hand, in his right was the pistol. For the waiting Bony, much depended on the training received by the horse.

As is normal on such occasions of mental stress, time ceased to have meaning. The very condition of mental stress cleared Bony's brain. He was no longer conscious of bodily fatigue, no longer conscious of his rapid breathing, and no longer was there any effort required to remain still, to wait. The instinct of self-preservation was now in full control of him.

148

He could see the rider's purpose. The hooded man was not going to be foolish enough to ride him down, followed by the probability of his horse tumbling and throwing him. It showed that he hadn't that confidence in the horse, or in himself as a horseman. He intended to ride past on Bony's right and attempt to shoot him. And he held the reins only in his left hand.

The very manner in which he held those reins gave Bony hope. And the very manner in which the fellow rode the horse increased hope. Still Bony waited, crouched forward upon his hands. He waited till the horse was but ten feet from him, headed to pass him, when he sprang upward, jumped high with arms flung wide, and shouted at the top of his voice.

The horse flung up its head in swift fright, and with it missed the head of its rider by a fraction. It swerved far to the rider's left, almost unseating him, so that he had to bring the pistol hand up and across the other to bear upon the reins. Now the horse was past Bony, and now the rider was engaged in mastering it as it continued to gallop down the slope towards the foot of the distant Walls of China.

And Bony continued his race towards the timber, refreshed by the short space of waiting. He had two hundred yards to cover.

He had halved the distance when, looking back, he saw that the hooded man had mastered the horse and was turning it to ride back to get him before he could cover the last hundred yards. He had reduced that last hundred to fifty yards when he was forced to halt and again meet the charge.

This time he did not wait. Horse and man were fifty feet from him when he began to run towards them, crouching low and zigzagging. The manoeuvre nettled the rider, who came on direct and opened fire.

Where the bullet went Bony could never subsequently make up his mind. It was instantly evident that the horse was not accustomed to a pistol being fired close to its ear, for the shock of the explosion so astonished it that it faltered in its stride, almost tripped, and almost sent its rider over its head.

That was when Bony was approximately twenty feet from the horse's bridle bit, and during a split second he debated whether to rush forward and grab that bit and toss the rider off, or to continue his progress to the timber. He decided on the latter course, and made for it.

He had almost reached the nearest tree when the report of the pistol followed the impact of the bullet into the trunk of a tree to his right. Again the pistol cracked. The bullet must have gone high, for he did not hear its whine.

No lover ever caressed his loved one with such fervour as Bony laid hands upon the trunk of that tree he reached, a nice substantial mulga tree of about a foot in diameter and as hard as teak. There he halted himself, swung round to its far side, and with astonishment saw the hooded man riding south as hard as he could press his mount.

When he recovered normal breathing the hooded man and horse had disappeared along the timber line, and Bony's strained face was subsiding to normal.

"Ran out of ammunition. . . . That's a monty, as son Charles would say," he said aloud. "But what a nice, determined gentleman! Now what will he do? What will he be planning to do whilst I make and smoke a cigarette, just to calm my nerves? Why, he will be wanting to get home as soon as possible for two quite simple reasons. One, to shed his ballroom clothes for his workaday clothes among the cinders, and two, to get his horse over the ground as soon as possible in order to give that damned wind every chance of smothering his tracks so that he can't be tracked to his home. And it is going to be nearly two hours yet before full daylight. Dear me, how this case is busting open! Charles again. I *must* be careful of my language."

Leaning back against the tree trunk, he felt elated whilst he smoked. This case was breaking his way at last, even though fresh questions rose like an army of enemies from the Walls of China. What had that man been doing on the reservoir tank stand? He had been there for some time certainly, because he must have been there all the time Bony had been standing with his back to the cane-grass meat house, and that had been for at least forty minutes.

Examination of the ground about the tank stand and mill, as well as the mill and tank stand itself, might solve that question and provide, possibly, other information. The wind was going to obliterate the faint tracks left by the hessian-covered feet, and it might well cover the horse's tracks on the white sand and red sand which came down to border it. And, further, with the dawn, the wind would probably increase in velocity.

That the fellow had ridden off to the southward did not indicate that he had come from the south. He left with the knowledge that he had been observed, and he would ride in order to frustrate that observation.

Well, Bony could do little until day came, for the moon even now was against tracking the horse, its light too oblique. He could wait there for daylight and then do all possible to track the horse, or he could return to the hut, boil the billy for a badly needed pint of coffee, and then go out to the horse paddock and catch and saddle his own station horse. Or . . . But wait . . .

Tossing aside the cigarette end, he rose and began a long easy trotting run to the township. He covered the distance in three quarters of an hour, reaching a position due south of the parsonage when the dawn was barring with white the sky above the Walls of China. Maintaining that easy lope, and conscious of the risk he was taking of being shot at, he skirted wide southward of the township till he came to the wire fence surrounding the butcher's horse yard and stables.

He was climbing through the fence when he heard a horse shake itself inside the enclosure. He found that horse, felt it with his hands all hot and sweat-grimed. It had but recently been freed from saddle and bridle. The blaze on its forehead proved that it was the horse owned by the Rev. Llewellyn James.

XVIII. *Lawton-Stanley Talks*

THE REV. LAWTON-STANLEY was a great man as well as a fine Christian. He was a lover of all men and women, and he appeared to be utterly blind to their faults. His popularity among outback folk rested entirely upon his ready sympathy and his remarkable simplicity. He told everyone he wanted to be a friend to everyone who wanted a friend, and the number of people

151

in the interior of Australia who wanted him for a friend was remarkable.

There was no "side" about Lawton-Stanley, and no narrowness of outlook. He composed love letters for young men and letters of conciliation to the wives of older men separated from them. Never did he leave a homestead without taking the mail for lonely stockmen stationed on the track ahead. He could talk horses with the best, and he could talk on any cultural subject to the many hungry for culture. When a man swore in his presence he smiled and fined the culprit a shilling, which went towards the fund for the purchase of Bibles. A lot of money passed into that fund, too.

Day was breaking when Bony slapped the side of the canvas hood covering the evangelist's truck and softly called for the "padre." The padre was sound asleep in blankets laid upon a straw mattress that in turn was laid on the floor of the truck, and when he awoke to recognize Bony's voice he directed his visitor how to enter his house on wheels and switched on the tiny bedside electric light.

"A little early," he said, faint surprise in his voice. "Anything wrong?"

"Nothing serious," replied Bony, sitting down on a petrol case and producing tobacco and papers. "Just a little problem which I find I must discuss with you. Sorry to wake you so early. Mind if I start up that primus stove and make a pot of tea?"

"Do. Pump 'er up. Water in that drum with the tap. Spirit in the bottle over there. Make plenty. I like three cups."

"Bad for the wind—so much tea before breakfast," Bony asserted smilingly, and began work on the stove.

"Not nearly so bad as those terrific cigarettes you smoke. It's a marvel that you have any wind at all."

"The wind I have got is a marvel even to myself," admitted Bony. "I can sprint a bit even at my age. Hope this thing won't explode."

"You sprint!" scoffed Lawton-Stanley. "Why, I could give you fifty yards in a hundred right now."

"You could give me ninety yards in a hundred right now, Padre, but I am not taking them. No, not this morning, or even tomorrow morning. I have had a guts full of sprinting quite recently. By the way, is 'guts' a swear word?"

"No. Possibly a little more forceful than elegant. Get to work again on that stove."

A few minutes later the tea was made and set before the padre, who remained in bed, and who noted with interest that his visitor drank two cups of the scalding-hot beverage in quick succession.

"Ah!" sighed Bony. "That's better. Now for a smoke and then my little problem. You ever smoked?"

"Never."

"Don't ever. Smoking costs a lot of money—when your eldest son is loafing about a university and also smokes. I'd give a fiver to any of your numerous funds if only I could see the Rev. James smoking a clay pipe."

"Is he still occupying your mind?"

"Now and then," admitted Bony, draining his third cup of tea and pouring himself the fourth. "He is my current problem. You will remember that, when we spent the evening with the sergeant and his wife, I referred Mr. Llewellyn James to you. As the subject appeared a little distasteful to you, I didn't press it, but I am going to now in order to avoid what might be a bad mistake."

"Oh! Enlighten me further. If you want help, professionally, you will get it."

"Thanks. Well, now. Doubtless you are *au fait* with the series of crimes committed recently in this district. I am here to find the sting ray, and the sting ray is one of approximately twenty-eight men living in this district."

"And you think that friend James is the sting ray?"

"I am as uncertain about him as I am about a dozen others," Bony answered. "I have to work on the assumption that all men are guilty until proved to be innocent . . . the reversal of British justice. Among the killers I have brought to book there is, at date, not one minister of religion. Still, one never knows what the future will bring to my gallery. Parsons have committed murders, you know. Tell me all you know of our friend's history. What you said the other night indicated that you know something of it."

Lawton-Stanley regarded the strong face of the half-caste whom he knew was his mental equal. Beyond the canvas walls of his "home" the roosters were crowing and the magpies were chortling. A calf separated from its mother was bellowing in the near-by yard. The wind irritated the canvas curtain, shutting off the truck's cabin. It was becoming light outside.

"It's going to be rather difficult," said the evangelist, "and I think that I would decline to discuss James with a lesser man than you. Even you, I fear, may not understand my difficulty!"

Bony smiled, saying:

"I shall understand. I am the most understanding man in all your wide circle of friends."

"I agree with you that that is probable. Well, here goes. Eight years back, James and his wife and I were in the same theological college, Mrs. James then intending to become a church deaconess. Let me think, now, about ages. I would be twenty-seven, James was twenty-four, and Lucy Meredith would then be twenty-three.

"Here is a fact which is distasteful to me to talk about to a layman. The majority of men who enter a theological college with the ambition of becoming ordained are men having in their hearts a love for the work in which they want to engage. But there is a minority who enter college and seek ordination because they desire a respectable, secure, and, they think, an easy life's work. They have no more aptitude for the work than I have for your work. James belonged to the minority in our college.

"His father is a minister, and a fine one, too. The son is one of those fortunate beings able to 'swot' well, but he seemed always too tired to 'swot' enough to pass his examinations with distinction. I don't think anyone really liked him."

"Did he then have that nasal whine?" Bony enquired.

"He adopted it during his second year. Our principal frowned upon that kind of thing, but James persisted. As I have said, no one really liked him—that is, none of the men. A real Christian will speak straight out from his heart, not down through his adenoids.

"James made no friendships, and of course, in a place like that, no enemies. And then during our fourth year that extraordinary attraction of opposites became manifested.

"Lucy Meredith was, and still is, one of the loveliest women, spiritually, who ever lived." The speaker paused and sighed. "I am unable to talk to you, Bony, as I could if you were not such a wretched pagan."

Bony smiled, saying softly:

"A pagan can recognize, and appreciate, a lovely personality in woman. I've seen in Mrs. James all that you have. Proceed, ease."

"I have thought it probable that Lucy Meredith first became racted to James because of his self-sought isolation. The fellow s a brain and he might have played upon her unbounded sym- thy. Anyhow, she married him. They were married the day lowing the passing-out ceremony, and there was not a joyful art among those who were present."

"And he was appointed to a church?"

"Yes, to a church in a Melbourne suburb. They were married that he could accept the call."

"Ah! A round peg in a square hole, eh?" remarked Bony. When he was at that church, his first, did his wife prepare all his vice?"

"No, I think not. Towards the end of his ministry there, I un- rstand that she prepared his sermons because the elders ex- essed dissatisfaction. Anyway, the appointment was terminated, d after a period of comparative idleness he accepted the call to s church in Merino."

"When the wife prepared all the service, eh?"

"That is so," agreed Lawton-Stanley sadly.

"What was his health like . . . at college?"

"He complained often about his heart."

"What was the medical verdict about that, do you know?"

"I never heard that he consulted a doctor."

"Any vices?"

"If he had he kept them mighty secret." Lawton-Stanley was out to say something further but desisted. Bony waited. Then prompted his host, and the bush evangelist said: "James is just turally a vampire man."

"Oh, indeed! Interesting! Does he crawl out of his coffin after down to . . . ?"

"You know what I mean, Bony. You know as well as I do that ere are men and women, and they are not rare, either, who st on the spiritual strength of others. That type invariably rries the gentle, forbearing, and retiring partner. They main- n the domination. The victims become so dominated that they re not even try to flutter to maintain independence of soul. The

155

dominant partner is invariably an invalid whose aches and pain are all that matters in the home. They must ever come first. The must be waited on hand and foot. They must be served by su missive victims. Read *The Barretts of Wimpole Street.*"

"I have done so, but I know your vampire people without ha ing read that book. Lots of men have been hanged and impri oned for life for having murdered their vampire wives. Qui decent and respectable men, too. I am glad, Padre, that we agre that James is just a vampire man. That is a good name, too, a though there is another which would the better fit Mr. Llewelly James. I won't use it . . . in your presence. Did you know h family at all well?"

"Yes," admitted Lawton-Stanley.

"Any insanity?"

"Yes. The mother's brother was a certified lunatic."

Bony rubbed his hands, saying:

"Ah . . . hum! You know, I always have had the idea that th murderer in these parts is not quite normal."

"Is any murderer normal?"

"Normal!" Bony echoed. "Of course they are normal. They ar just as normal as the petty thief. It is only now and then that on comes across the abnormal. In this case of mine there is a stron suspicion of abnormality, resting on the cunning with which th crimes have been committed and the apparent absence of mo tive."

"Why do you suspect James?" asked Lawton-Stanley.

"I didn't say that I suspected him."

"No. But you do. Come, tell your old pal."

Bony smiled.

"None of your vampiring with me, now," he implored. "Prom ise not to tell?"

"Certainly."

"Cross your fingers and promise properly," Bony commande and chuckled when the evangelist gravely obeyed. "You don't loo like Rose Marie, Padre, but that is her definition of a promis signed, sealed, and delivered. I understand from Mrs. James, an others, that the parson suffers from a weak heart, so that he ha to be careful not to exert himself. Under no circumstances may chop a little wood or do a little digging in the garden. He al suffers from a debilitated brain, to the extent that he cannot concentrate sufficiently to prepare a sermon. But, Padre, he can ride a horse at such a pace as to drench it with perspiration and to wind it, and he can concentrate sufficiently to read light literature, such as *A Flirt in Florence*. Ever read that novel?"

"I never read any novels."

"Oh, come now! You mustn't be so wowserish, Padre! A nice tale of juicy doings in Florence would so improve your mind. No, James doesn't square with life. You don't like James, and I'm blessed if I do either. But we must not permit our prejudices to cloud our judgment. Now I'll be off. There is a lot of work in front of me. I'll leave the cups and things to you. Never forget that you crossed your fingers. Thank you so much for the tea."

"You haven't told me yet why you suspect the fellow," objected Lawton-Stanley.

"Oh, I have," Bony countered smilingly. "See you again shortly. And look here—if you could persuade Mr. Llewellyn James to take a little morning exercise with the gloves, please, Padre, please plant a good 'un on his nose for me."

Full daylight greeted the detective when he emerged from the evangelist's truck, his expression of lightness changed to one of stern concentration. It was still too early for even the early risers to be about the street. The sun was not yet risen.

On leaving the truck, he walked along the sidewalk towards the police station, and, as was his habit, his eyes mechanically registered the prints of human feet upon the ground. The street at this end was not swept clean by the shop people and the sand lay fairly thick.

He was not positively sure of the fact, but the ground all round the truck was covered with the faint remnants of so many tracks as to lead him to believe that the bush evangelist had held a service the previous evening. The truck was parked several yards westward of the garage, and when Bony came into the wind shelter provided by the garage he found the tracks on the sidewalk much clearer. He recognized the tracks of young Jason going in and out, and he recalled that that young man was to supply the evangelist with additional electric power. Passing along the street were the tracks made by Mrs. Marshall and Rose Marie, who at a later hour were followed by Constable Gleeson. They were a

157

few of the tracks he recognized. Then, when he drew opposite the gate giving entry to Mr. Jason's private residence, he saw that Mr. Jason himself had stepped off the roadway and had crossed all the other tracks to reach his house. Adjacent to the police station fence the wind had smoothed away all impressions made upon the ground the previous night.

On passing the police station, Bony crossed the street and slowly walked back to the hotel, rounded that building to reach the back of it, and then skirted the rear of the hotel, another building, the rear of Mr. Fanning's shop and house, and so reached the butcher's stables within the yard.

The two horses came trotting towards him, whinnying a request for chaff, and he went through the wire fence and made friends with them, murmuring in a language which they appeared to understand. He gave especial attention to the horse with the white blaze on its forehead, and noted the imprint on the ground made by each of its hoofs.

Approximately in the centre of the yard stood the ramshackle stables, and after him entered the horses, looking for breakfast. He found chaff in an inner compartment and fed a little of it to them. And then he examined two saddles placed on pegs driven into a roof support.

The saddle carried by the horse owned by James was easily marked by the colour of the hairs upon its felt saddlecloth. The stirrup irons were crossed over the saddle, which could have been done when the saddle was placed on its peg. But likely enough the hooded man, who last had used that saddle, had ridden without using the stirrups, for into them he could not thrust his hessian-covered feet. That would account for his poor riding when attempting to shoot Bony, which had given the detective hope that he could be outwitted, as, in fact, he had been.

On leaving the stables, Bony walked to the gate in the yard fence. This gate was opposite the wooden door in the corrugated iron fence at the rear of the butcher's premises. Here the tracks made by the parson's horse when led into the enclosure an hour or two previously were almost obliterated by the wind. The depressions were more than half filled in, and there was no possibility of the wind having spared those extremely faint depressions left by hessian-covered human feet.

He crossed the sandy ground to the door in the butcher's rear fence, where in this shelter he saw the tracks of boots made by a man entering those premises. They were still fairly clear-cut, but the man who made them had not come from the horse yard but from the rear yard of the hotel.

On either side of the butcher's premises was a vacant allotment, unfenced and eaten bare of vegetation by the town goats. They were merely bare, sandy patches of ground open wide to the wind that by now would have smoothed out any tracks made by human footwear.

Bony returned to the horse-yard gate and there leaned against one of the posts whilst rolling a cigarette. Assuming that it had been the parson who had visited the mill at Sandy Flat and had ridden back at top speed to get away from his tracker, as well as to reach his home before the day broke, he would be anxious to reach the hard roadway of the street, where he could walk without leaving tracks after removing the hessian from his feet. To accomplish this, he needs must cross from the horse-yard gate to one of those empty allotments, cross that to the sidewalk, and cross the sidewalk to reach the macadamized road.

Still assuming that it was James, the parson would cross the allotment on the east side of the butcher's premises, which would be the side nearest the parsonage. Bony endeavoured to project himself into the mind of the Rev. Llewellyn James.

On leaving the gate, he crossed to the allotment eastward of Mr. Fanning's house and shop. He passed over the length of that allotment, and so came to the sidewalk bordering the road. The surface of the sidewalk here was covered with a thin layer of sand.

Opposite the centre of the allotment frontage grew one of the street-bordering pepper trees. It was a fine specimen which would certainly give a black shadow on a moonlit night. There, beneath this leafy tree, seated on the curb, the hooded man might well have removed the hessian from about his feet, and then have gone on to his home in day shoes, or even with his feet bare.

The rising sun was gilding the summit of the Walls of China when Bony came to lean against that pepper tree, as though he had done little else all his life but lean against something. The wind had smoothed all tracks from the thin covering of sand upon the sidewalk. It had piled into little mounds in the dry gutter sand which had been carried across the road, and here and there in the gutter were little piles of the dead needle-pointed leaves of many pepper trees.

Two such piles of leaves were not so symmetrical as those created by the wind. They were flattened and spread out. Bony went down on hands and knees to bring his eyes closer to those two piles of leaves separated by about ten inches of fine sand. With a twig he teased the massed leaves further apart and found three strands of jute fibres. He found more. Two yards farther down the gutter he found a strip of hessian measuring approximately one inch in width and ten inches in length.

He sat on the curb with this strip of hessian stretched between the forefinger and thumb of each hand. The sun was now peeping above the Walls of China, and its rays came along the street, striking upon his hands and the hessian strip held taut.

The material was not clean. There was in it a stiffening substance, and there was on its surface and within the folds of the edges many brown hairs. Bony sniffed at the material. He smelled the sweat of a horse. The brown hairs were similar to those of the horse owned by the Rev. James.

So there, where those two small wind-created heaps of dead leaves had been depressed, was where the hooded man had sat with his heels resting upon them whilst he removed the hessian from his feet. He had then stood up and walked along the macadamized roadway, leaving in the moonlit night that strip of hessian, sweat-stiffened and impregnated with the hairs of the animal he had ridden.

That was all Bony did find, and that was no mean achievement.

Rising to his feet, he walked slowly down the street at the edge of the sidewalk. His eagle gaze scrutinized the surface of the sidewalk on his right and the gutter on his left. He found nothing. He went on past the entrance to the parsonage, past the entrance to the parsonage garage, on and past the church. He retraced his steps. For a moment he halted at the driveway, and for another he loitered outside the parsonage gate. Beyond that gate he saw the imprints of tennis shoes on the sheltered path. Between the gate and the roadway the sidewalk was blown clear of sand, and its hard surface registered no imprints. The tennis shoes had been worn by the minister, and the imprints might have been one hour or ten hours old.

The wind's velocity was increasing with the rising of the sun, as Bony sauntered back up the street. A town dog came out of a gate to wrinkle its nose at him in friendly fashion, and to it Bony said:

"We don't mind now how hard the wind blows. It has done all it could to frustrate me. Now you had better go home again, because I am going to call on Sergeant Marshall."

XIX. Another Murder?

At half-past six the clock on the table at the sergeant's bedside began its uproar, and a large red hand automatically reached for it and snapped off the ringing. For a few minutes the sergeant lay fighting sleep and uttering a series of moans and grunts meant to inform his wife of the martyrdom imposed upon him by the necessity of rising to light the kitchen fire so that he might have the smallest kettle boiling for tea when she appeared in the kitchen. Then, without bothering to slip on a dressing gown, he rolled out of bed and thudded in bare feet along the passage. Inside the kitchen doorway he halted abruptly.

"Well, I'm——"

"Don't say it," Bony pleaded, a hand raised towards Marshall, who, in pyjamas with a wide pink stripe overlaid on a blue background, scarcely looked his usual, dignified self. "If you say it, it will cost you a shilling. I am collecting for Lawton-Stanley. I've had my breakfast and the water is boiling for your early cup of tea."

Marshall surveyed the table. Used eating utensils were pushed back to become a border to notebooks and a writing pad and pencils. It was obvious that Bony had occupied the kitchen for some time, and here he was now as well groomed as ever.

"Never heard you come in. Never heard a sound," Marshall said.

"I can be silent when I want to," stated Bony airily. "I borrowed your razor and a comb and towel. Now I'll make the tea, and you can take a cup in to your wife. I've had breakfast, and before yours is ready I can tell you a thing or two which will interest you. There is a deal of work ahead for both of us."

"Yep! Looks like it, too," Marshall averred, and watched Bony brew tea in the proper manner. "Thought I locked the doors and the windows out here."

"You did, but I unlocked the scullery window. Count twenty, and then I'll pour the tea. Hand me that tray."

"What for?"

"That on it you might carry a cup of tea to your wife without shaking half of it into the saucer. Let me see. Ah yes, I remember. In this tin. A biscuit on a plate to accompany the tea."

"You aim to give her breakfast in bed?" demanded Marshall.

"No. Only morning tea. Sometimes, when I am home, which is seldom, I prepare morning tea for my wife, so you see I know how it's done . . . like this."

The tea and biscuits on the tray were presented to the astonished sergeant. He said:

"D'you know what my missus will say when she sees this?"

Bony chuckled, and his blue eyes beamed.

" 'Thank you, dear?' "

"She's going to say," Marshall said grimly, " 'You must be sickening for something. Where's the pain?' "

"Don't believe anything of the kind. Now get going. I'll load another tray which we can take to the office."

Evidently not feeling very happy about it, Marshall departed, and when he returned he muttered:

"She said—she said, 'Give my thanks to Bony.' Seems to have guessed you were here."

"Well, well. Let it be a lesson to you. Now to your office."

Marshall glanced down at his pyjama-covered stomach and grinned. He tried to walk with dignity, failed, and ambled heavily after Bony, who carried the tray. He closed the office door and Bony poured tea, then sat in the official chair and gathered together the notebooks and papers he had brought from the kitchen. The sergeant sat down on the visitor's chair and sipped his tea whilst watching this most extraordinary man manufacture his extraordinary cigarettes. And then Bony was regarding him seriously, and he could see on Bony's face the evidence of fatigue.

"We progress, Sergeant," Bony said, as though occupancy of

the official chair had removed the previous bonhomie. "Events during the last few hours have established that the killer of Kendall and that swagman lives here in Merino. I told you, didn't I, that Providence is always kind to detectives?"

He related all that had occurred from the moment he had arrived at the hut at Sandy Flat to the finding of the strip of hessian in the Merino gutter, and Sergeant Marshall became so engrossed that when the story was finished the tea in his cup was cold.

"I must get back to Sandy Flat as soon as possible," Bony went on. "The wind would have smoothed away all tracks before daybreak, but that reservoir tank and mill might provide a clue as to what the fellow was doing there. Before I left town I thought of calling on Mr. James. Then I thought of asking you to do so. Finally I decided to go slow with Mr. James. We can't afford to make a mistake with a parson. They can muster a lot of influence and kick up a deal of fuss should a poor detective make a mistake concerning them. If James is actually our man, and I am by no means certain that he is, we mustn't jump on him till we are all set. And so far, we are not properly set to do any jumping on anyone."

"Did that chap look anything like the parson in build and gait?" Marshall asked.

"We can't rely on the manner of his walk. Remember he was wearing swathes of hessian about his feet and would then walk not unlike a man wearing snowshoes. In build he was similar to James. That is all I can say. His clothes were much more loose-fitting than those normally worn by the minister."

Marshall pursed his lips. He said:

"I suppose a parson is as likely to be a killer as a butcher or a bricklayer?"

"Quite. Criminal history contains many. In this particular case, however, we are in danger of allowing our personal antipathy to cloud judgment. Our greatest difficulty is the absence of motive behind the killing of Kendall, and if the murder of the swagman was not the result of attempted blackmail, then we do not know the motive for that killing, either. It doesn't follow because we know of no motive that there was no motive.

"Because we don't know the motive, we can assume that there was none, and on this assumption we may further assume that the killer is insane. Only an insane person would kill without a motive . . . or for the sheer lust of killing, which is in itself a motive

"You should read 'The Rape of Lucrece,' a poem written by
Shakespeare. Old Shakespeare was a good criminologist. In that
poem he describes the growth of an idea of the crime in the
criminal's mind before the crime was committed. Very often the
crime of murder is the effect of thought extended over a length
period. In other words, the actual act of the crime is the effect of
long and careful planning, following an idea which has become
an obsession.

"If we assume that Kendall's death was due to insane blood
lust, we may be sure that the satiation of that lust was not accomplished on the spur of the moment. We may assume that, even
were we ignorant of what we do know of the murderer's efforts to
escape detection.

"There is in this district no one sufficiently insane to kill without a motive. However, there may be one or even two people in
this small community sufficiently insane to kill from the motive of
satiating the blood lust. And, believe me, Marshall, the lust to kill
is in itself a terrible thing. It is more terrible than killing for revenge or for gain, for it makes of a man a human tiger, a ravening
human tiger whose thirst for blood is never quenched.

"This type of killer is invariably supercunning, and also invariably supervain. His vanity is enormous, so much so that when
he is brought to trial he craves to read the newspaper reports and
to wallow in the temporary fame he has achieved. Do you think
the Rev. Mr. James is a supervain man?"

"No. He has never struck me that way," Marshall replied.

"Mr. James is a loafer, and he is cunning enough to be a quite
successful vampire man," Bony continued. "He is a supercilious
and intelligent man, and I should say that his mental make-up
comprises twenty per cent cunning, thirty per cent sheer stupidity,
thirty per cent tiredness, and but twenty per cent vanity. If we
assume that the murder of Kendall was the result of the lust to
kill, we must go cold on the idea that James is the killer, despite
all the circumstances against him.

"There is also further evidence tending to remove James from
the suspicion of having killed Kendall. We have through the

effluxion of time made a great advance on Redman's investigation. We know that the man who killed Kendall was not one of Kendall's class, working all over the state and seldom remaining in any particular place for long. Kendall's murderer never left this district, because he was here when the swagman was killed, and he was here last night.

"He lives here in Merino. It might be, of course, that the killing had its genesis many years ago in some other place, and that after years of separation killer and victim happened to come together again here in Merino. If we accept that hypothesis, our friend James is ruled out still further. Kendall, remember, was a bushman and James was a city man. Kendall was just a rough, roaming man; James is the son of a minister of religion, and his life has been lived in the religious confines of home, church, and college.

"It is possible, of course, that Kendall accidentally discovered a criminal weakness in James, or another here in Merino, and attempted blackmail, and was murdered because of it."

"That seems likely, come to think of it," Marshall put in.

"Yes, I agree. But I warn you again not to allow your imagination to be fed by personal dislike. There is something else in this investigation which has inserted itself into my mind even against a degree of mental resistance. That thing is . . . windmills. You are justified in wanting to ask what windmills have to do with this killing of Kendall. It is what I would like to know.

"Kendall was killed on a night when the moon was at full and when the wind was blowing at an estimated velocity of twelve miles an hour. Last night the moon was at full and the wind blew. There was no wind that night the swagman was killed, and we must not forget that the time of that death was dictated by the swagman himself . . . or we have reason to think so.

"The moon at full may have an effect upon insane persons, but I think we can rule this out of our probings, although we must keep in view the fact that the light of the moon might be the factor behind these murders.

"Why did the fellow with sacking about his feet and a hood over his head ride to within a few miles of Sandy Flat, tether his horse and walk to the windmill, release the mill to the wind, climb up the ladder to the floor of the reservoir tank, stay there for at least forty minutes, and then come down to the ground and brake off the mill, and finally set off back to his horse? When we can answer those questions we shall know the motive for the murders."

Bony automatically rolled yet another cigarette with fingers that were steady and sure. Marshall poured himself a second cup of tea. It was almost cold. He heard Bony say softly:

"Windmills! Windmills have an important place in this puzzle, but where they fit in beats me so far. Er—I think I shall have to do something which is distasteful to me. It is not the first time in my career that passion for investigating crime has warred with my instincts as a gentleman—the meaning of the word 'gentleman' being in its widest sense. Were it not for the fact that our killer might kill again before we can unearth him, I would not even contemplate doing this thing which I find distasteful.

"Well, now, here it is. There is here in Merino a person who could tell us something about windmills, or, for us, could add a significant something to this subject of windmills. That person, however, is under a bond of silence. With her fingers crossed she promised someone not to tell something about windmills. At the time I took but little notice of it, but it has grown to importance since last night."

Sergeant Marshall sat bolt upright.

"You are not referring to our Florence, are you?" he demanded.

Through a haze of tobacco smoke Bony regarded the sergeant.

"I happened to tell Rose Marie that Lawton-Stanley's father was a maker of windmills in Brisbane," he explained slowly. "She was keenly looking forward to meeting Miss Leylan's fiancé, and she became upset by the thought that Lawton-Stanley would want to sell his father's windmills in Merino. When I pressed her to tell me why she was afraid of such a thing as that, she told me that she had promised not to tell—with her fingers crossed."

"Oh, that be blowed!" exploded Marshall. "I'll soon get that out of her."

"One moment, Marshall. That might seem an easy road, but it is one which I will not take until every other avenue is explored. Rose Marie is a sweet child, and when she makes a promise she stands by it if the promise is made when her fingers are crossed. Neither you nor I are going to force her to break that promise because there are all too few people in the world today who place any value whatsoever on their given word."

"But, as you just mentioned, another poor devil might well be murdered if we don't nail the killer pretty soon," objected the sergeant.

"Nevertheless," Bony persisted, "we will allow ourselves to persuade her to tell us what she knows by putting to her such questions, and in such a manner, that she will not know she is telling us what she promised with her fingers crossed not to tell. I think I can manage to do that. She is your daughter but she is not to be forced to break a promise so solemnly made. I hope that you agree with me?"

Marshall nodded, and his affirmative reply was spoken softly:

"She's a great kid," he said, and in his mind ran another thought: "And you're a fine man." Bony was saying:

"It is a little early, even now, to wake Rose Marie, but I should get back to Sandy Flat. I'd like to talk to her before I leave. You go and ask her to come here to me. Tell her that Bony wants to see her. And you stay out and get dressed. You're a disgrace, in pyjamas at seven-thirty in the morning."

Marshall heaved himself to his bare feet and passed out of the office to pad along the passage to the rear of the house. Bony swung round in his chair. Through the window he could see the front fence, the pepper trees, and a portion of the roof of the butcher's shop all painted with the light of the risen sun. As though in the background of his mind, he heard Marshall padding about somewhere in the rear of the house. He heard Mrs. Marshall's voice raised in surprise. Then he heard her husband's voice outside the station house, shouting the name "Florence." He continued to sit there in the sergeant's chair revolving in his mind the questions he would craftily ask the child.

Several minutes passed, and then he heard Marshall's heavy feet again in the house, and his voice loud, in keeping with the raised voice of his wife. The big man came running along the passage and entered the office as though he sprang across the threshold. His eyes were big, and his mouth was stretched in a frightful grin. He strode to the table desk and, glaring down at Bony, shouted:

"She's gone. Our Florence has vanished. She knew too much

about windmills, and that killing swine has taken her. Her bed's cold. She's been gone for hours."

XX. Bony Holds Audience

"WELL, what have *you* got to say, Inspector Napoleon Bonaparte?" Sergeant Marshall demanded in a tone of voice which, had Bony heard it from another policeman, would have astounded him. "You've been dawdling on this case, waiting for time or Providence or something to drop the clues into your open hands. Evil never triumphs, eh? You never rush about like Tom, Dick, or Harry Redman, do you? You take everything calmly, and just wait and wait and wait, until another poor devil is murdered and the killer can hand you another clue or two. You never allow emotion or even humanitarian thoughts to sway you when you're on an investigation, do you? You proceed calmly and without undue haste, don't you? You don't care two hoots if a dozen persons are murdered, do you? Not even when a little girl is murdered for knowing something about windmills? Why the hell didn't you tell me that Florence knew something about something vital to that killing swine? I'd have got it out of her—quick."

With singular deliberateness Bony stood up, stood up to meet the blazing brown eyes of Sergeant Marshall, still incongruously dressed in pyjamas. Feeling in his own body had drained away so that he was conscious of having no physical feeling at all, save a sensation of terrible cold in his brain.

"You are right, Marshall, and you are wrong," he said. "As a father you are right: as a policeman you are wrong. Take a holt on yourself. What's Gleeson's telephone number?"

"He's out in the yard, searching the outbuildings. But what's the use? They'll find her body. Oh, they'll find that. I'm going to have a word or two with that snivelling parson. I'll fix him for a start."

Abruptly the big man stood away from the table desk and strode to the window. He stood there staring with unseeing eyes, his hands clasped behind him, ceaselessly gripping each other in

rn. The agony of the man's mind was visible in those large, red,
nd capable hands. When Bony spoke his voice was intentionally
rsh.

"*You* will leave the parson to me, and you will continue to fol-
w *my* instructions. You don't know nearly so much as I know
out this investigation. *You* will now conduct me to the bedroom
cupied by your daughter, and then *you* will get dressed and
rt work."

Marshall swung round. He opened his mouth to say some-
ing, snapped it shut, and walked to the door. Bony followed
m along the passage to a room opening off it just before the
tchen was reached.

The room was small and crammed with the evidence of parents'
ve. A rocking horse stood in one corner. Pictures of Mickey
ouse and Donald Duck adorned the walls. On a table stood a
rge doll's house, and beside it was the small pram in which, care-
lly "tucked in," were Thomas and Edith.

Over the foot of the bed the clothes were tossed in disarray. On
chair beside the bed the child's school clothes were laid, neatly
lded, and upon them was a plate on which a peeled orange had
aited for the child to eat on awakening.

"Go and dress," Bony snapped.

"I'll see you——"

"Sergeant Marshall, go and dress and then report back to me."
ony glared upward into the furious brown eyes. "Take a holt on
urself. Until we find Rose Marie is dead, I for one will believe
e still lives."

The anger began to fade out of the brown eyes, and into them
ept a new expression, one of painful surprise, for Marshall
und himself looking upon the Mr. Hyde of kindly Napoleon
onaparte. He was gazing into eyes which appeared to glow with
bluish fluorescence, and underneath those eyes was a mouth,
less and filled with clay-white fangs. The usual carefree and
bonair expression had vanished, giving place to one of ferocious
te. And that new face which he had never seen before gave him
mfort, for what he saw in it matched all that was in his own
art. The hope that sprang to life within him made him turn
pidly and depart to his dressing.

Bony strode to the open window. It faced to the north. Beyond it, some twenty feet away, was the paling fence bordering the north side of the station compound. He bent forward and thrust his head beyond the sill and noticed the fine red sand being whisked over the hard ground by the wind. He said something for which Lawton-Stanley would have fined him a full twenty shillings.

From the window he returned to the bed, where he stood for a few moments quite motionless. The mattress still contained the depression made by the child's sleeping body. The depression made by her head was still upon the pillow. Then, abruptly, he leaned over the bed and sniffed with his nose but a fraction above the linen cover.

There was a square of carpet between the bed and window, and this he picked up and held to the light, squinting his eyes to stare all over it, square inch by square inch. The carpet he rolled and pushed beneath the bed. He closed and fastened the window, and then left the room, closing and locking the door and placing the key in his pocket.

Mrs. Marshall was sitting on a chair beside the kitchen table. He went to her, brought his head down to the level of hers, and said:

"I do not believe that Rose Marie is dead until it is proved. You must not think of it, for you have work to do. We all have, every one of us. Slip out and tell the Rev. Lawton-Stanley that I want him, urgently. Will you do that?"

Slowly she turned her head and stared at him with tear-dimmed eyes. She nodded in assent. Her gaze fell away from his eyes and rested upon his brown hand laid lightly upon her forearm.

"I love Rose Marie too," he told her.

Abruptly he turned and walked swiftly to the door, to the passage and back to the office. He noted the time by the clock. It was twenty minutes to eight. He took up the telephone.

"Hullo!" said a dreamy feminine voice.

"Dr. Scott, please."

"Number, please?" came the dreamy voice.

"This is Detective Inspector Napoleon Bonaparte speaking from the police station. I want Dr. Scott. You know the number. If not, look it up."

"The number is Merino 14," came the now pert voice.

"Ring me when you get the doctor."

As Marshall had done, Bony strode to the window. He saw Mrs. Marshall reach the gate and turn westward towards where the evangelist's truck was parked. A doubt cast a shadow over his mind. Had he been in error, had he always been wrong in accepting the death of human beings by violence in the cold academic manner of the scientist, and not with the righteous indignation of a warm human being? Murders he had always accepted as food for his mind, the victims meaning nothing to him save as the foundation upon which to raise the scaffold to hang the killer. As Marshall had justly pointed out, an additional killing or two meant little whilst his Providence dropped clues into his hands. Had he dawdled? Had he failed in his duty to humanity? Had he permitted his pride to overrule his own humanity?

Had he . . . ? Oh hell! It was a different proposition when the probable victim of murder was a little child whom he had come to love, a winsome little girl whom young Jason had named Rose Marie. He had scoffed at the Redmans for permitting their emotions to trouble them, had boasted of his own scientific coldness. Had he dawdled . . . had he . . . had Marshall been right . . . as a policeman?

The telephone bell shrieked at him.

"Dr. Scott here," the staccato voice announced.

"Good. Bonaparte speaking. Will you come right along to the police station?"

"Certainly. Has the child been found? Housekeeper just told me about it."

"No. I want your assistance—urgently."

"Be there in a minute."

Bony cut the connection and then rang the exchange.

"Is the postmaster on the phone?" he asked the girl.

"Yes. His number is——"

"I want him. Get him."

"You might be a little civil, Inspector," she said.

"I am. Your ears would burn were I uncivil. Get the postmaster quick. I'm in a hurry."

He slammed down the receiver, then spun about to see standing in the office doorway little Mr. Watson and two men standing behind him.

"Morning!" said Mr. Watson smilingly. "You cleaning up here Where's the sergeant?"

"Out. What d'you want?"

"Oh, just a friendly call on Marshall. These gentlemen a city colleagues up here to get a little news about the murders. it possible that Marshall's child has been kidnapped, d'you think

"Nonsense. She has walked out in her sleep. Proved slee walker."

"Interesting," remarked one of Mr. Watson's companions.

"Yes, isn't it!" Mr. Watson agreed. "Let me introduce yo This is a friend of mine, Mr. Burns—Bony to his friends."

"Eh!" ejaculated the other of his companions. "My hat."

"Yes. I am Inspector Bonaparte. I have no news for you gentl men this morning. When I have I shall be happy to impart it you. Call again at six o'clock this evening."

He returned to the shrieking telephone. On lifting the receive he heard Marshall's voice out in the passage, and, placing a ha over the instrument, he called to the sergeant:

"Show these gentlemen out, Marshall. I am expecting Lawto Stanley and Dr. Scott."

One red hand at the extremity of a large uniformed ar seemed to encircle the three newsmen and draw them out throu the doorway. Then the door was slammed shut.

"Lovell here, the postmaster." The voice coming along the wi was quiet and level.

"Ah . . . morning, Mr. Lovell. I am Inspector Bonaparte spea ing from the police station, and I rang to ask you a favour. It that you come along here as quickly as possible. I haven't met yo but I understand that you are a family man, and I am sure y would be only too glad to render all assistance in a most urge matter."

"Certainly. I'll be right along."

Three seconds after he had disconnected, the sergeant a Lawton-Stanley entered the office, followed by the hesitant M Marshall.

"Got rid of those newsmen?"

Marshall nodded. To the evangelist Bony said:

"You have heard that Rose Marie has disappeared. You c do a big part in the search for her. I know you will do it. Liste

Marshall and Gleeson and I are policemen, and we are controlled by far too much damned red tape. Sorry! Here's your shilling." As he went on speaking he pulled coins from his pocket, selected a shilling piece, and placed it on the table before Lawton-Stanley, who, without comment, placed it in his collecting box, the pocket of his open-necked shirt.

"As I have pointed out, we policemen are bound hand and foot. We cannot enter houses and shops and search without a warrant. But you can, Padre. You can gather a band of men and women and go from house to house to make search for Rose Marie. No householder will object to such action by you. It is useless to search for tracks outside or on the street. So go out and rouse the people to hunt for Rose Marie. Turn every house and shop inside out. Game?"

"Of course," replied Lawton-Stanley. "We'll go along one side of the street and up the other."

"Good! And include the church and the parsonage."

The evangelist nodded, turned, and went out with Mrs. Marshall. They could hear him talking softly to her in the passage Then Dr. Scott came in . . . like a little dust storm.

"Morning!" he snapped, his white hair all ruffled. "Bit early. I haven't had breakfast yet."

"I want you to go along to Rose Marie's bedroom, Doctor, and there take a sniff at the child's pillow. When I did so I fancied I could smell chloroform. Then, under the bed, you will find a strip of carpet, rolled up. Take that back to your laboratory and, with your microscope, establish the foreign matter adhering to it. I think it is jute fibres. Anyway, I must know just what that foreign matter is. Will you do that for me?"

"Of course I will. Damn the breakfast! I'll do that immediately and come back with my report."

"Good! You may be disturbed by the evangelist and his search party, but you won't mind that, will you?"

"Mind it!" echoed the doctor. "What the heck does Lawton-Stanley want to search my house for?"

"To find Rose Marie. They are going to search every house in the town."

"Oh, all right! I won't bellow."

As he had entered, so Dr. Scott left, followed by Marshall. In less than two minutes the doctor returned to the office to tell Bony that he was sure the smell of chloroform still clung to the child's pillow. Marshall let him out and then rejoined Bony.

"Sorry I spoke like I did," he said gruffly, without looking at the inspector.

Across Bony's face flashed a smile. It vanished as quickly as it had appeared.

"That's nothing to worry about, Marshall," he said softly. "I felt no better about it than you did, and do. When it is all cleared up you will acquit me. I am now expecting the postmaster. After he arrives I want you to go along to the garage and ask young Jason to come in for a moment or two. As you well know, young Jason was very friendly with Rose Marie. He may be able to give us a lead. Treat him very gently."

"Yes, he might give us a lead," Marshall agreed. "He's a queer fellow, but all the kids like him. He might give us a lead as you suggest. Ah . . . there's Lovell coming in now."

The postmaster's pale face was adorned with a thin moustache. His shoulders were slightly stooped. The sergeant placed a chair for him at the table opposite Bony and withdrew.

"So you are a police inspector," Lovell said, brows raised. "What can I do for you?"

"A lot for me and more for Rose Marie," Bony told him. "The child was kidnapped sometime during last night, and I am going to confide in you this much. I believe that she was taken by the man who killed Kendall and that swagman." Bony leaned well back in his chair and stared hard at Mr. Lovell. "I am professionally interested in certain parties here in Merino, and some time ago I wrote to Sydney asking for enquiries to be made concerning their origins and histories. Being a civil servant, as I am, you will appreciate that no sense of urgency will be experienced by the officers in Sydney. You will appreciate the urgency animating us here in Merino, and you will appreciate the urgency with which I want to contact Sydney."

"That's so, Inspector. Rule of thumb, you know, and all that. Still, as a general rule, it's better to be slow and sure."

"I agree there with you. Now . . . will you take over that telephone exchange yourself and do all possible to clear the lines to police headquarters, Sydney, as quickly as possible?"

"Yes."

"I am going to ask headquarters to speak on matters which normally would be contained in a sealed envelope, and, therefore, would you remain in that exchange until I am done?"

"Of course."

"Thank you. How is the line to Sydney normally? Dull?"

"Not good. But I can get help at various offices en route."

"Fine. Thank you, Mr. Lovell. Will you get going?"

The postmaster pushed back the chair and got to his feet.

"Anything else I can do?" he asked. "I've got a kid of Rose Marie's age."

"Well, now," said Bony slowly, placing the tips of his fingers together beneath the point of his chin. "You could take a faint interest in the conversations of other telephone users this morning, and make a mental note of anything which might have a bearing on the disappearance of Rose Marie. But haste in contacting Sydney is of first importance."

"I'll bet I'll get Sydney within an hour. So long. And when I do, I'll lock the exchange door and shut fast the window."

It was a quarter to nine o'clock. Left alone, Bony sat still and stared at the police notices on the back of the door which Lovell had closed behind him. From outside came the voice of the wind which since sunup had risen to become half a gale. Bony's mind became less taut, more fluid. He thought of young Jason and of Mr. James. Then again of the postmaster. What had Lovell said just before he went? Something about shutting a door. Yes, that was it. Shutting a door. Who else said something about shutting a door?

Into Bony's mind appeared, as on a screen, the hut at Sandy Flat, the hut as he had last seen it in the moonlight. The door of the hut was shut, and he remembered that he had debated then whether he had closed it. Closed it! No, he hadn't closed that door when he left the place for the cane-grass meat house, because his arms were loaded with his swag and things. And that door would not have been closed by the wind. It would not just catch shut because there were no door lock or handles. There was merely a bent piece of wire to keep that door shut. Bony leapt from his chair. Within three seconds he was out in the street.

XXI. Mrs. Sutherland Is Thrilled

IT WAS NOT by chance that Mrs. Sutherland arrived in town so early that morning. She was to meet a sister who was coming from Mildura by the mail which reached Merino at eleven o'clock, and she found that she had certain shopping to do, so decided to do the shopping before rather than after the arrival of the visitor.

The track from her homestead joined the main road just below the church and, on arriving at the lower end of the macadamized street, she was astonished to see the activity of the inhabitants. Her destination was the hotel yard, where she always parked her car, and halfway up the street she saw the Rev. Lawton-Stanley emerge from a shop followed by more than a dozen men and boys. They all trooped into a house next door to the shop. She saw another party of men swarming about a house which stood back from the street beyond an empty allotment, whilst others stood in groups here and there, engaged in excited conversation.

Mr. Watson, who was accompanied by two strangers, waved to her. The Rev. Llewellyn James, who was talking to Mr. Fanning, the butcher, raised his felt hat to her, but on neither his face nor on Mr. Watson's face was there a welcoming smile. And then, as though he materialized out of space, the man she knew as Robert Burns was standing on the running board of her moving car.

"I want you to take me at once out to Sandy Flat," he told her.

Instinctively she accelerated, then put the brake on, hard. The car stopped midway between the hotel and Mr. Jason's garage. Bony dashed round to the front of the car and climbed into the seat beside her. Mrs. Sutherland giggled.

"What *is* this, a getaway from the police or attempted elopement?" she demanded. "Get out of my car. I don't budge till you do."

"Neither, Mrs. Sutherland. Your car is the only one on the street at the moment, and I've got to get to Sandy Flat without loss of time. Come on now. Be a sport and take me there. I can tell you all about it on the way."

Mrs. Sutherland was first and foremost a romantic. To back up her romanticism there was a strong vein of humour. And, in addition, there was a fine confidence that she could take care of herself. Besides, this Burns man was a good-looking fellow, and he had nice eyes even though they were somewhat small and fierce this bright morning.

She pressed the self-starter, geared in, and drove the car in a small circle to begin the journey to Sandy Flat just as Sergeant Marshall and young Jason emerged from the garage.

"Thanks, Mrs. Sutherland. Drive like . . . hell," Bony said.

"You are not escaping from jail, are you? I thought you were out," she remarked without visible concern. "What's it all about?"

People stared at the old car as it sped down the street, the hardest woman in all the district holding with sun-blackened hands to the driving wheel. No one of them was more astonished than Sergeant Marshall.

Bony told her who and what he was, and gave in very broad outline the purpose of his visit to Merino. He spoke with unmasked truth in his voice. And then he told her how Rose Marie had been taken from her bed, and what he suspected was the reason, and whom he suspected of kidnapping her.

"You don't know who has done these murders?" she asked, the veneer of frivolousness stripped from her.

"No . . . not yet . . . but I'm getting warm. Can't you drive faster?"

"Perhaps I could," she agreed, and pressed the accelerator down to the floorboard. "You know, I always felt you were not an ordinary stockman. I was only saying so to Mr. Jason the other evening. He comes out some evenings to listen to my playing. Says that no one troubles to play the piano now the wireless is all the boom."

"Strange man," remarked Bony. "I understand that he's been an actor. He can certainly quote Shakespeare. When was he out at your home last?"

"Ah, that's telling." She cut off the giggle before it got fully under way. "Let me think. Oh yes. It was last Saturday week.

177

You needn't be jealous, Inspector. You will be welcome any evening. My sister is due today from Melbourne. She plays the violin rather well."

"I may accept your invitation. Thank you. Better stop before the gate. There is a lot of barbed wire about it."

When he did not trouble to shut the gate after the car had been driven beyond it, and had regained his seat beside her, she said:

"What about shutting the gate?"

"Drive on, Mrs. Sutherland. Minutes may count vitally. The gate can wait."

"Oh, all right! What do you expect to find down here at Sandy Flat? The murderer?"

"No, Rose Marie."

The wind was racing the car. The dust was being swept along with it. The woman's hands were glued to the steering wheel and she risked sand-skidding. Ahead, the Walls of China were light brown and indistinct. She said:

"D'you think he will have killed her?"

"I am hoping not. It's why I asked you to bring me, and did not wait to suggest to Sergeant Marshall that he bring me. Better drive slower when we reach the white ground. A few seconds will make no difference."

They passed out from the tree line to the white sandy waste footing the Walls. Ahead, the dark blurs of the hut and the reservoir tank appeared very small. Mrs. Sutherland was driving well over thirty miles an hour when twenty was the safety limit. Her arms and hands were stronger than the apricot silk blouse with its unfashionably long sleeves revealed. The engine was labouring when she drove the car in a circling movement to stop outside the hut and facing the road back.

"Stay here, please," Bony commanded.

He got out and stood for a few moments staring through the sand murk at the hut, at the door closely secured. He wasted no time on the ground, for he knew how clean that page of the Book of the Bush had been whipped by the wind. Then he walked to the hut door.

The doorstep was covered with sand, like fine drift snow. The temporary wire catch was dropped down over the nail. He released it and pushed inward the door. Then he turned and beckoned to Mrs. Sutherland.

When she entered the hut he was raising the drop window in the far wall. He from the window and she from the door stood without movement regarding the little body on the bunk. Simultaneously they advanced to the bunkside. Then Bony was on his knees. And then she heard him cry, loudly, so loudly that the moaning hiss of the wind was subdued:

"She's alive!"

Clad only in her pyjamas, Rose Marie was lying on her back. On her face the sand dust lay thickly, and Bony gently blew it off her brow and her closed eyelids.

"Is she asleep?" asked Mrs. Sutherland. "Move away so that I can take her up."

"Wait! I don't think she's asleep." Bony softly patted a limp hand. "Rose Marie! Wake up! Mrs. Sutherland and your friend Bony are here to take you home." Gently he raised her head. Mrs. Sutherland uttered a cry. There was blood on the back of the child's head. It had dripped through the wire netting of the bare bunk to the floor beneath.

"Bashed on the head with a blunt instrument, eh!" Bony said, his voice a snarl. He moved each of her legs, and then each of her arms. "Doesn't seem to be any other injury. I'll carry her to the car and take her back to town. Never mind the door. You get into the car first and take her from me. I'll drive."

Mrs. Sutherland climbed into the seat Bony had occupied, and he passed the limp little figure into her waiting arms. The wind tormented the canvas hood and carried the hissing sand past and under the machine. Presently they reached the gate, and without stopping to close it Bony drove on to the main road and up the long incline. They were well past the cemetery when the child said loudly:

"Annabella! Annabella!"

"Who is Annabella?" Bony asked of Mrs. Sutherland.

"I don't know—unless it's Annabella Watson, Mr. Watson's mother."

Bony made no further comment, and a moment later Rose Marie said in a singsong tone of voice:

"Annabella Miller, what are you doing with that caterpillar?"

179

"The child's delirious," Mrs. Sutherland said. "Poor little mite. She's repeating a rhyme learned at school or from the wireless."

"Annabella Miller," now whispered Rose Marie, "what are you doing with that caterpillar?"

Presently they reached the street, passed the church, and were between the skirting pepper trees.

"I am going to drive into Dr. Scott's yard," Bony announced. "His drive gate is always open."

"Very well. If the doctor will care for her, I'll stay and do the nursing. I was a nurse once."

They arrived at the doctor's residence and Bony drove into the driveway and stopped the car outside the veranda steps leading to the front door. He got to the ground and took the child from Mrs. Sutherland and carried her into the house through a side door which happened to be open. An elderly woman met them, and Bony called for the doctor. The elderly woman shouted: "Doctor! You're wanted, quick!" Then she added quietly, "Come this way . . . to the doctor's surgery."

Bony followed her into a large room, a combination of surgery, library, and laboratory. She smoothed a mattress on a trestle bed and shook the pillow, and Bony laid the child down. The doctor came in, exclaimed sharply, bent over the still form. Bony sat down in a great easy chair. Quite suddenly he felt very tired.

He heard the doctor call for hot water and the elderly woman hurried from the room. He saw Mrs. Sutherland draw near to the trestle bed a trolly loaded with instruments. She selected a pair of scissors and placed them in the doctor's outstretched hand. The elderly woman came back, carrying a can from which issued steam. The two women stood by the little doctor, who was bending over the child.

Bony knew that should Rose Marie die the edifice of the philosophy responsible for his success in crime detection would fall, possibly without replacement by any other. The mood of self-condemnation was heavy upon him.

Lawton-Stanley came in. He glanced at the three about the bed. On seeing Bony, he crossed to him and sat on the arm of the chair.

"Someone saw you carry the child in," he said. "Thank God she's alive. Hurt much?"

Bony nodded.

"We found her at Sandy Flat," he explained. "Will you go and tell the Marshalls? Tell everyone to keep out. If you see Gleeson, ask him to come here and keep everyone out."

Lawton-Stanley rose to his feet. "Can I give the Marshalls any hope, d'you think?"

"I don't know."

The evangelist departed. Bony continued to sit in the great chair, the thought in his brain that the death of the child would affect him as much and as vitally as it would the sergeant and his wife.

Presently the doctor came to him and sat on the chair arm as the minister had done.

"Bad," he said. "Fracture at the base of the skull. May pull through. Be a long time, and she will require very close attention. I am going to keep her here. Mrs. Sutherland will do the nursing. Where was she?"

"In the hut at Sandy Flat."

"Ah! Any connection with those other murders?"

"Yes. The murderer may very well make another attempt to kill her. The house will be guarded day and night, never fear, until I get him. That won't be long now. Lawton-Stanley was here. I asked him to fetch the parents."

The doctor pursed his lips. His grey eyes were hard and small.

"There were jute fibres on that piece of carpet," he said slowly. "They came from a sack of some kind. I put a quantity of them into this envelope."

Bony indicated thanks with a movement of his head. Mrs. Marshall appeared in the doorway, her husband behind her. The doctor went to them, spoke rapidly and firmly, and conducted them to the trestle bed. After a little while the sergeant came over to Bony.

"Not as bad as I thought, although bad enough," he said.

"Nothing is ever as bad as imagination can paint it," Bony told him, rising. "Ready for duty?"

"More than ready."

"Come on, then."

Gleeson was standing at the end of the front veranda, in which place he could stop people from reaching either the front or the side doors. To him Bony rapidly outlined the circumstances, and warned him that the person who had abducted the child and had attempted to kill her might very well try again. He was to remain there until relieved.

Together Marshall and he strode up the street to the police station.

"No talking just now, Marshall," he said firmly. "You go and get your car out. We must get back to Sandy Flat. While you're getting the car I'll ring your headquarters and ask for assistance."

On reaching the station office, Bony rang the telephone exchange. He was answered by the postmaster.

"No, I haven't raised Sydney yet," Lovell told him. "Very sorry, but there seems to be trouble somewhere along the line. There is a heavy official envelope, registered, just in. Addressed to Sergeant Marshall. Posted at Sydney."

"Ah! That's good. We may not have to bother with Sydney after all. I'll come across with Marshall in a minute. Thank you, Mr. Lovell. . . . Yes, the child was found. She's been knocked about badly. Dr. Scott has her. . . . Oh yes! Yes, the doctor has hope."

XXII.   The Windmill at Work

WHEN BONY and Sergeant Marshall left Merino in the latter's car for Sandy Flat it was not possible to see the Walls of China, nor even to locate the cemetery halfway down the long slope. The wind was blowing strongly from a little north of west, sweeping over the world of scrub tree and shrub in prolonged gusts reaching a velocity up to forty miles an hour. It raised the sandy dust high so that the sun's orb was the colour of an unwashed dinner plate.

"I contacted your district headquarters and spoke to your senior officer," Bony told Marshall. "He's sending two constables by car."

"Say anything about . . . Florence?"

"Yes. And I asked him to be kind enough to let me finish the job. Said he would be only too pleased. Quite a nice fellow."

"Haven't found him particularly nice. Always expects too much too soon."

"They all do, Marshall," Bony stated emphatically.

Neither spoke again for a minute, then Marshall urged pleadingly:

"Break it out, Bony. Did you expect to find my girl at Sandy Flat?"

"Yes, I did. You know, last night when I was awakened by the mill in action, I crawled on hands and knees to the door of the meat house and then faced the hut. For a little while I stopped still, staring at the place. I saw that the door was shut, and I wondered for a moment if I had closed that door or not. The importance of the question was submerged by the greater question whether the mill had broken loose or had been deliberately released to draw me outside so that I could be shot.

"Then, when the postmaster was with me in the office and he was about to leave, he mentioned that he would lock the door of the exchange room when I was speaking to Sydney. That remark stuck in my mind after he had left and produced the association of ideas, sending my mind back to the period when I wondered if I had or had not shut the hut door. Then I remembered quite clearly that I had not done so when I left it for the meat house.

"That being so, the man who wore hessian on his feet and a hood over his head must have done so. He must have done so whilst I slept. And why had he gone into the hut . . . if not to leave Rose Marie inside? Acting on that supposition, I chose to requisition Mrs. Sutherland and her car in preference to calling on you to take me down there."

"I still don't understand why the swine took her there. Do you?" asked Marshall.

"Not yet. I have a glimmering of an idea, though."

"Have you got any idea where windmills come into the picture?"

"Only a glimmering of one."

"Well, what are the glimmerings?"

Marshall spoke sharply, still suffering from strain.

"There are several nebulous theories floating around inside my cranium, Marshall. They are all so silly that I am unable to voice them. How did you get on with young Jason?"

"Oh! When I arrived at the garage young Jason was shutting up. On seeing me, he rushed to me and poured out a flood of questions concerning Florence's disappearance. When was she first missed? How long had she been out of the house? Did I think she walked out or did I think she was carried out? He was properly upset. Seemed a damn sight more upset than I was.

"I asked him where the old man was, and he said he was still at the house. Hadn't made an appearance. Expected he was washing up the breakfast things, as he always did. He himself was shutting up the place so that he could join in the search for my girl."

"Did you see him when we left the doctor's house? I didn't."

"No."

They came to the gate left open by Bony on the previous trip, and this time Bony alighted and closed it before they proceeded now on station property.

"What did you do with young Jason after you saw me clear out with Mrs. Sutherland?" he asked when again beside Marshall.

"Well, I had told him that, having been friendly with Florence and all the other kids, he might be able to help us, and we were on the way to the office when we saw you getting off with Mrs. Sutherland. That stonkered me somewhat, so I told him we'd both join in the search till you came back."

"You told him, then, that I am a police officer?"

"Yes. You had yourself been broadcasting the fact, and so I told him that you were in charge of the investigation, and he had no need to be hostile to you because of Redman's dealing with him. I wanted to keep him easy, you see."

"Ah, well! We can collect him when we get back. And after we've had a yarn with him we'll invite the Rev. Llewellyn James to call on us."

"Can I be present?"

"If you promise to behave yourself."

"Rats!"

"Pardon my levity at such a time, Marshall," Bony said quietly. "But we have to treat James with velvet gloves on our hands, as it were, with perhaps a horseshoe inside them. Pull up outside the hut door. We'll have a look inside for a start."

On getting out of the car, Bony peered through the now white sand mist. He could see the dim shapes of the reservoir tank and the mill head but not the mill stand. The Walls of China were completely dissolved in the whirling flurry. The very ground seemed to be a moving white fog.

Inside the hut the wind tore through the lifted drop window and out through the open door. Bony was thankful to observe that the mark of blood beneath the bunk was obliterated by the white sand brought inside by the wind. There was nothing to find, nothing to help. He closed the window, shutting out the wind, and in the comparative quiet he said:

"I'd like to know why the killer brought Rose Marie to this place. Why here, instead of dumping her anywhere in the scrub? He thought he had killed her when he dropped her on the bunk, otherwise he would have come back to the hut after climbing from the tank stand. And why climb up to that tank stand? I'll go up there and try to work it out."

They left the hut, Marshall fastening the door. Bony walked across to the meat house, glanced inside to see his swag and tucker box as he had left them. The wind assisted them over to the tank stand.

"Look out that you're not blown off," advised the sergeant.

"The sand's soft if I am. Phew! What a place to be on such a day!"

Bony climbed the iron ladder and, when standing on the edge of the flooring, was just able to reach up and grasp the edge of the open tank, precisely as he had observed the hooded man do. Foot by foot he went round the tank, now and then glancing back to note the position of the hut and meat house. Eventually meat house and hut were blocked from his view by the curving bulge of the tank. He proceeded another two yards and then stopped.

There was nothing amiss with the tank itself. There was here no easier access to the top of the tank, presuming that the hooded man had reached this side of it to put something into it. There was nothing out of place with the flooring of the stand. Why should he have come here? Why should he have stayed here for at least forty minutes—the period that Bony had watched from the shadow of the meat house?

With both hands gripping the top edge of the tank, Bony hauled himself up so that he was able to peer over its edge. There was nothing additional to what he expected to see—the wind-disturbed surface of clear water. Despite the wind's action on the surface, he could see down to the bottom of the tank. There was nothing inside the tank save the water.

Having lowered himself again to the flooring, he turned his body so that he came to stand with his back to the tank. All that he could see then was the mill, the head of it a little higher than himself. The three lines of troughing extended outward into the white murk.

Marshall came and stood looking up at him.

"Release the mill!" Bony shouted down.

The mill sprang into action immediately the draw pin was removed from the lever bar, and so vigorous was its action that Marshall had to adjust the bar to prevent the vanes from meeting the wind full-faced. Water began to pour into the tank at Bony's back.

The direction of the wind had not altered since the previous night, and although Marshall had partially braked the mill, the angle of the vane wheel to Bony was not markedly different from what it had been when the hooded man stood in that place. For several minutes Bony watched the working mill. He was oblivious to the wind and the discomfort of the flying sand mist. He could hear beneath the howl of the wind about the tank the "clang . . . clang . . . clang" of the labouring mill.

Was that harsh, monotonous sound of pulling iron music in the ears of the hooded man? Were the swiftly moving vanes, even then gleaming dully in an almost solid disk, the reason why the hooded man had stood so long where he was standing? There was no sand mist last night to obscure the moon's silvery light. Did that revolving wheel have a hypnotic influence? If so, what had that to do with the killing of Kendall, and what with the attempted murder of little Rose Marie?

To Bony the light of day appeared to increase. He glanced up to the sun, only to observe that its pastiness was the same. He began the journey back to the ladder. He might easily have slipped and broken a leg, for his mind was not on the job of getting to the ground.

"Well, what d'you know?" enquired Marshall when Bony joined him.

186

"I cannot find anything up there," replied Bony. "Better shut off the mill, and then we'll get back to town."

Before reaching the station gate on the main road they met a car. Both vehicles came to a standstill, as the passing was in a difficult place. The driver of the other car backed for several yards and again stopped. Marshall was now able to steer off the track to pass the other car, and when opposite, he and Bony saw that the driver was Mr. Watson, and his passengers were the two pressmen.

"Nice day for an outing," shouted the sergeant.

On again, then to the station gate and the main road. Marshall tried several times to start the conversation but Bony relapsed into a silence from which he could not be roused. All the way up the incline to the town he sat slumped into his seat, gazing with unseeing eyes through the windscreen.

"You might like to stop at the doctor's place and ask about Rose Marie," he suggested when they had passed the church. "I'll walk on from there. If your wife is with the child, tell her not to worry about us. We can make ourselves some tea and get our own lunch. Better arrange with Gleeson, too, to relieve him while he has his lunch."

"Thanks. I'd like to know how she is."

"Of course. Don't hurry."

He entered the police station by the back door, which had been left unlocked, and in the kitchen noted that the time was twenty minutes to one. The fire was out, and he set it going to boil water. That done, he passed along to the office and lifted the telephone. The postmaster replied.

"You still on duty?" asked Bony.

"Yes. I thought I might be more useful here. Quite unofficial, you understand, and all that kind of thing, but a long press message was handed in about an hour ago. A lot concerns you. If you care to come over, you could see the original."

"Thanks! I will. Get me now Wattle Creek Station, please."

The bookkeeper answered and Bony asked for Mr. Leylan. A minute later he heard the squatter's voice, and announced himself.

"Between ourselves, I have quite a lot of work to do here in town," he explained. "I left Sandy Flat per boot, in a hurry, and

187

I am wondering how the horse will get on for water in the night paddock."

"You will not be going back there tonight?"

"I may. I have been thinking of asking you to send someone out there to give the animal water, and then put him back into the night paddock in case I should want him before tomorrow night."

"Oh yes. I can do that. How's the investigation going?"

"Slowly. A fresh development occurred last night," replied Bony, and then described what had happened to Rose Marie. He heard Leylan exclaim whilst he related the story, out of which he left his own adventure with the hooded man.

"That place seems to be cursed," asserted the squatter. "What's the attraction there for a man to commit his murders?"

"I wish I knew," answered Bony. "Tell me now, have you ever found on visiting the place that the water in the reservoir tank has been overflowing?"

"Well, yes. It's peculiar that you asked me that," Leylan said. "Several times over the last couple of years, when I've gone there, I noticed a good deal of water soaked into the ground beneath the tank. Once I made a careful survey of the tank itself to see if it was leaking."

"You didn't attach any significance to it?" pressed Bony.

"No. You see, when there isn't a man living there, I send a rider out just to see that the tank is full, and to brake the mill to fill it slowly if it isn't. The fact of the water overflowing I put down to bad judgment on the part of the man sent out."

"Hum! Thank you. Quite an interesting little point. Well, we Miss Leylan home today? . . . She is! Say we'll ring her a little later to tell her how the child is progressing. Yes, Scott has hope. Good-bye."

Bony had made tea and set the table for lunch when Marsh came in.

"No change," he said. "Still unconscious. The wife's watching her. Mrs. Sutherland has gone home for some clothes and to take her sister, who arrived on the mail car."

"Did you see Scott?"

"No. He had to go out."

Bony poured the tea, and the sergeant carved from a leg of mutton. They ate in silence for some time. Then:

"I have glanced through the contents of that registered envelope you received this morning from Sydney," Bony said. "The reports give an amount of information on the Jasons, Gleeson, Dr. Scott, and Way, dealing with their lives and reputations before they came to Merino. Nothing was known at date concerning the other people included in my list. I haven't got much out of the information sent, for which I am truly thankful."

"Oh! Why?"

"Because I want to finalize this case off my own bat, and if headquarters had supplied a missing link or two of my chain, you and I would receive less credit than is properly ours. Way did time in 1931 for sheep stealing . . . and that's about all."

Having eaten, Marshall went off to relieve Gleeson for lunch, and Bony walked out to the post office, where in the little room devoted to the telephone exchange he read through the original press message from one of Mr. Watson's colleagues. Much had been made of the fact that Detective Inspector Napoleon Bonaparte was in charge of the investigation into two murders and the attempted murder of the daughter of Merino's senior police officer.

"The sender knows quite a lot about me, doesn't he?" Bony observed to Mr. Lovell. "The padre gets a good notice too. Just too bad. Honestly, I hate publicity. Have you ever heard your children recite a rhyme running: 'Annabella Miller, what are you doing with that caterpillar?' "

"Yes, often."

"Little Rose Marie spoke it quite distinctly when we were bringing her to town, and when she was lying unconscious in Mrs. Sutherland's arms. I was merely wondering if there was any significance in it. How long have you been in Merino?"

"Too damn long. Eight years," replied Lovell.

Bony smiled.

"If you want a change, write a thousand-word letter to the postmaster general and tell him what you think about his rotten politics and his rotten post offices, and his rotten wireless voice. You'll be shifted quickly enough. Sound advice . . . if you want a transfer to a better town. I must be going. Thanks ever so much for your co-operation. Receipt of that registered envelope saved a lot of bother."

On leaving the post office, Bony walked slowly back to the police station. He was about to turn in at the gate, when he saw young Jason standing outside the garage doorway. He beckoned to him, and when the young man arrived at the gate he found Bony waiting for him at the open front door.

XXIII.   Two Particular Fish

"Sɪᴛ ᴅᴏᴡɴ, Mr. Jason," Bony said, waving to the chair set opposite the official chair at the table desk. He pushed tobacco pouch and papers across the desk towards young Jason, who nodded and began the task of making a cigarette without removing his gaze from the man he had learned today was a detective inspector.

"If you think I did it, have another think," he said, his voice low and menacing. "I could have done in Kendall, but I could not have done in Rose Marie."

"Oh! Why?"

Bony gazed into dark eyes now regarding him with a fixed stare. The greasy cap had been dropped on the floor beside him, and the almost black hair, parted low on the left side, was well brushed. But the eyes were not level and the mouth was not straight, and the left shoulder was lower than the right. The hands manufacturing the cigarette were large and strong. They were capable hands, very capable.

"You wouldn't understand if I told you, so I'm not telling you . . . why."

Bony lit a cigarette. Then he said briskly:

"All right. Now listen to me. There is someone here in Merino who took Rose Marie from her bed last night, carried her away, then hit her on the back of her head with a blunt instrument, took her to Sandy Flat, and dropped her unconscious body on the bunk inside the hut. You say that you didn't do it, and I have not even hinted that you did, and so may I presume that you will assist me to find out who did that foul deed?"

"It depends," came the surly answer.

190

"Depends! Depends on what?"

"Nothing."

There was no expression in Bony's eyes as for a half a minute he regarded this unfortunate young man. Then he said:

"When Mrs. Sutherland and I were bringing Rose Marie back to town she became semiconscious and she said several times: 'Annabella Miller, what are you doing with that caterpillar?' Did you teach her that little line?"

The surliness fled from the dark eyes and was replaced by an expression of wistfulness.

"Did she really say that?" young Jason asked quickly.

"She did. One of your own little rhymes?"

"No. But she learnt it off me."

Bony nodded. The wistful expression was yielded again to the hard stare. The cigarette, now alight, was rolled from one corner of the crooked mouth to the other. It was obvious to Bony that the brain behind the high and broad forehead was exceedingly active.

"What does Dr. Scott think about her?"

"It depends," replied Bony.

"Depends!" echoed young Jason. "What d'you mean?"

"It depends on you whether I answer your question or not. I am willing to play ball if you are."

"Oh! So that's it, is it?"

"That's how it is," agreed Bony, adding quietly: "You've always liked little Rose Marie, haven't you? As a matter of fact, although I am a detective, I also love little Rose Marie, so that if you and I do not agree on anything of value, we agree on that. I have reasons to think that you did not abduct the child and attempt to kill her, and also I have reasons to think that you may be able to assist me in locating who did."

"That talk's all very fine," young Jason sneered. "We get that in the newspapers almost any day. 'Unknown man who witnessed the accident is asked to call at the detective office as it is thought he may be able to assist in identifying the body.' I had quite enough of it when that Sergeant Redman was here. Why, he said right out that I had a motive for killing Kendall."

"I know that. . . . And had I been here, it is likely that he would have said the same about me." Bony paused, then: "Now I am going to tell you something. It is one of my reasons why I don't think you attempted to kill Rose Marie. You once had a brown and white dog. You were fond of that dog. More than once I have seen you whistle it to you and pat it. It was obvious that that dog loved you. And I know that you didn't poison it. A man doesn't poison his own dog . . . not with strychnine. If he wishes to destroy it he shoots it."

Whilst he spoke Bony watched the anger grow big in the dark eyes.

"So the dog was poisoned, was he? How do you know that?"

"I found him . . . on the Walls of China."

"On the Walls of China?" echoed young Jason. "Why, he wouldn't have gone all the way out there. He never left town. He was never a hunter. That dog never hunted anything, not even a town cat."

"Yet I found him dead on the Walls of China," Bony asserted. "I backtracked him and saw where he had had the fits from the place where he had picked up the bait. And the strange thing about it is that the station people all state quite definitely that no poison baits had been dropped anywhere on the Walls of China."

The middle-aged half-caste and the unfortunate white man stared at each other.

"I don't get it," said young Jason.

"Do you ever ride a horse?"

"No. . . . Why?"

"Do you ever go for long walks in the surrounding bush?"

"What the hell would I want to go and do that for?"

"Because it has occurred to me that the dog might have been following someone . . . when it picked up the bait."

Young Jason nodded his head very slowly while he said, also slowly:

"Yes . . . that . . . might . . . have been . . . how it happened. He was following someone."

"Who do you think he would follow, away out on the Walls of China?"

"Who? How the devil do I know that? He might have followed—he might have followed anyone."

The pause did not go unnoticed by Bony. Then the young man asked a shrewd question:

"If you backtracked the dog to where he picked up the bait you would know if he was following anyone because if he had been you would have seen the bloke's tracks too."

"No, I saw no boot marks anywhere in the vicinity," Bony said truthfully.

"Then why suggest that the dog was following somebody?"

"I don't know. I merely put the idea forward because it seems so strange for a town dog to be so far away, and then to be poisoned under circumstances indicating that it was deliberately done."

"When did you find the dog?" asked young Jason, and the manner in which he was now cross-examining Bony secretly amused the detective, amused him in that sardonic manner which contains no genuine mirth.

"About the time you missed him," Bony replied. "Tell me, why you are so interested in windmills?"

"Windmills!" young Jason almost shouted. Then in a softer voice he went on: "I'm not interested in windmills, only when I've got to do repairs to the mill up at the town dam. And I've been mucking about with that mill, which was wore out years ago, so much that I'm sick and tired of even thinking about it. Who said I was interested in windmills?"

"No one actually told me that you are so interested, but you made Rose Marie promise, with her fingers crossed, to say nothing on the subject, about which she had evidently learned something."

"She didn't tell you?"

"No. Didn't I say she had promised not to, with her fingers crossed?"

Over the ugly face spread a grin.

"I can explain that easily enough," young Jason said. "One day when I had to go up to repair the town mill I took Rose Marie with me. Most of the trouble with that mill is making new parts to fit because new parts for it can't be bought. The part I took there that day when Rose Marie went with me wouldn't fit properly and I sort of lost me temper and swore pretty crook, forgetting that the kid was close handy. Then, another time when I was forging a part in the garage, something went wrong and I let me tongue loose, and looked up and saw the kid in the door-

193

way, and she said: 'Why do you always say those nasty words about making windmill parts?' And I told her I wouldn't never again if she promised not to talk about windmills and me, and she promised and I promised with our fingers crossed."

"This subject of windmills did not concern a third party?"

"No, of course not. What has all this to do with Rose Marie being knocked about?"

"I don't rightly know," confessed Bony. "I was hoping that you might be able to help me. Do you know of anyone in Merino who is a little cranky on windmills, say cranky on inventing improvements?"

"No. I'm the only cranky bloke on windmills hereabout. I hate 'em. If I had my way I'd blow 'em all up. They're always giving trouble. A motor engine is something what's got feelings and what a man can do something to to make 'em run smooth and well. But windmills!"

Bony permitted himself to smile, saying:

"There is something in what you say about motors and windmills. A perfectly running motor engine sings a song of its own, doesn't it? I suppose you can tell merely by listening to a running engine whether it has developed a fault or not?"

"I can. I can tell long before the fault will bring a breakdown," replied the young man, pride in his voice, and even the evidence of affection for which he was probably being starved. "In fact I've stood outside big city garages and guessed correctly the make of a car from its running engine. Each of 'em has a different voice."

"You like the Buick best?"

"Yes. Their 1936 engine was the greatest engine ever built."

The momentary enthusiasm for motor engines subsided, and there returned to the dark eyes and the pathetic face the customary surliness. Bony was not unsatisfied with this interview, but yet he was not fully satisfied with it. There still remained the fence erected between them by this young man who now made that fence even more impassable.

"Windmills and motor engines!" he scoffed. "What's it all to do with Rose Marie? That's what I want to know. You've got me here and have been pumping me with your fool questions, and presently you'll be telling me that I took her away and bashed her." His voice rose when, now on his feet, he stood glaring at Bony. "You think you know a lot, don't you? You think you're pretty clever, eh? You don't know that I've had to be clever all me life, but I have. Everyone laughs or sneers at poor young Jason, but the kids don't. They will, of course, when they grow up, but while they're kids they don't; in a sort of way they belong to me. And if I find out who bashed little Rose Marie—well, it is going to be just too bad."

"You can leave him to the law," Bony said.

"Leave him to the law!" snarled young Jason. "Leave him to the law! What then? For the law to give him six months, or find he's not quite right in his head, or to say that the poor feller isn't a bad sort of bloke and can't help himself. Murder and rape ain't considered much in this country . . . when it's kids what are murdered. But if a bloke accidentally kills a bank manager when he's robbing a bank—ah, that's a different thing, and they swing him for sure."

The rage subsided so quickly that Bony had the thought that the young man was acting. Had not the father been an actor? And that listening to running motor engines! Might not the man on the tank stand have been listening to the whirring of the mill fan wheel, a sound to be heard under the "clang . . . clang . . . clang" of the working pump rod? What, indeed, had Rose Marie, probably accidentally, learned about windmills in connection with his young Jason? The yarn about the swearing did not sound true. He decided to dismiss him.

"Well, we don't appear to be getting anywhere," Bony said, rising to his feet. "I am sorry that you will not co-operate. Good day!"

Young Jason stooped, snatched up his cap, and stood up. He reached the door, where he turned to regard Bony with that former flash of wistfulness in his eyes.

"Tell us how the kid's getting on, Inspector," he urged. "They won't tell me nothing up at the doctor's place."

"You don't deserve any consideration," Bony said. "But I'll tell you what I do know about Rose Marie. The scalp at the back of her head was badly lacerated, and she was unconscious when found. As I told you, she regained partial consciousness when in the car, but she has again been unconscious since then. Dr. Scott thinks she will recover, but she will require careful nursing. You wouldn't like to tell me, I suppose, who your dog was in the habit of following?"

"No, 'cos I don't know. That hound would follow anybody. Anything else?"

"Not for the moment."

Young Jason lurched out through the doorway to the passage. Bony heard him open the front door, heard the door slammed, and then pursed his lips and manufactured another of his fearful cigarettes. He was writing notes when Marshall returned from relieving Gleeson.

"Well?" Bony asked him, brows raised.

"Florence? Oh, there's no change yet. She's still unconscious. Scott was back when I left."

"I've had young Jason in here. Unbalanced fellow, and most unhelpful. He was interested in hearing about his dog being poisoned. That was about all. Like to be present when we overhaul the Rev. James?"

"Very much," replied Marshall grimly.

Bony lifted the telephone and asked to be connected with the parsonage. Then he heard the soft voice of Mrs. James.

"Good afternoon, Mrs. James," he said in his best manner. "I am Detective Inspector Napoleon Bonaparte. We have met, you know. My name then was Robert Burns . . . with apologies to all Scotchmen."

"Yes, Inspector. My husband was telling me at lunch how my Mr. Burns was actually a detective officer," she cried. "You must forgive me, but I came to call you *my* Mr. Burns after you so kindly cut the wood. I hope you will come and see me soon so that I can thank you properly. I have only just come back from making a call on Dr. Scott about poor little Rose Marie."

"Yes, it is all very dreadful, Mrs. James, and we can only hope for the child is in excellent hands. Er—what I rang up for was to speak to your husband. I shall certainly accept your invitation to call on you. Thank you very much. Is Mr. James at home?"

"He is, but is taking his afternoon rest. Poor man, he feels that he really must relax for a couple of hours after lunch."

"Hum! I regret having to disturb him, but time, and all that you know. Would you ask him to come to the phone?"

"All right . . . if you insist. It is important, I suppose?"

Bony laughed, and during the chuckling told her that he was an important person, and that he never did anything unimportantly. He was kept waiting fully three minutes before he heard the nasal whine.

"The Rev. Mr. James. You called for me?"

"Ah, yes! Good afternoon, Padre," purred Bony. "I am wondering if you would find it convenient to come along to the station office. I think that you may be able to give me a little assistance in this matter on which I am engaged."

Mr. James did not sound in good temper.

"Well, I suppose I could if it is really essential. But I am seldom fit for anything after lunch, you know. My heart disciplines me. Would not this evening do?"

"I regret that this evening I shall be busy elsewhere. I will not keep you long."

"But couldn't you call on me here?" argued Mr. James. "I am not fully dressed."

"I have only just promised your wife to make a social call in the immediate future," Bony said with ice in his voice. "Although I do regret disturbing you, I must urge you to call on me here as quickly as possible. I could, of course, get Sergeant Marshall to drive in his car to fetch you."

"Oh no! Oh no! That's not necessary," Mr. James said hastily. "I'll be there in a few minutes."

"Thank you, Padre. I shall be waiting."

Bony sighed as he replaced the instrument. He gazed over the desk to Marshall, and the sergeant exploded.

"Bit hoity-toity, eh?"

"Just a little," admitted Bony, and then passed the top of his tongue from one side of his upper lip to the other. "If you are going to stay, we'll want another chair. When the reverend gentleman arrives let him see you seated at Gleeson's table."

Mr. James did not arrive till fifteen minutes had passed. Bony did not get up to greet him. He smiled and waved to the chair opposite him, and Mr. James sat himself down without a word.

"Well now, Padre," Bony began, "as you must be aware, I have been investigating several crimes that have taken place in this district, the latest being the abduction and attempted murder of

Rose Marie. You have been in Merino for several years, and without doubt you know everyone, their habits and failings, and the rest. You being one of the leaders, if not the actual leader, of this small community, I was wondering if you could offer a suggestion or two which might prove of assistance to us. You own a horse, I understand."

"I do," answered Mr. James.

"You keep it in the stables belonging to Mr. Fanning, do you not?"

"That is so."

The light blue eyes were hardening.

"When did you ride it last?"

"The day before yesterday. I rode over to visit Mrs. Sutherland."

"You have a car. Why did you not drive over?"

"For two reasons. The track is rough in places, and I wanted a little gentle exercise. I find that riding a horse at a walk is beneficial to my health."

"Ah, yes, to be sure," murmured Bony. "Quite so! Quite so! Have you had the horse long?"

"A couple of years. I purchased it——"

"No matter, Padre. Rather a pity you are unable to enjoy a good old gallop now and then." Bony smiled reminiscently, and Sergeant Marshall, who was sitting behind the minister and thus could observe Bony's face, began to feel disappointment. The kid gloves were on, but there was no indication that within them was a horseshoe or two.

"Nothing like a good hard gallop," Bony went on. "Most especially on a frosty morning. How many times, on average, do you ride in a week?"

"Oh, I should think about three times. I ride mostly to visit my parishioners. The district is very large, as doubtless you know."

"Of course! Of course! You were out riding on December fifth. Where did you ride to that day—last Thursday?"

"Last Thursday? Er—let me think."

"It was that day the man was found hanged at Sandy Flat, you remember?"

Sergeant Marshall was now feeling a little better. The Rev. Mr. James leaned well back in his chair and took firm hold with both hands of the handle of his walking stick. The nasal whine was a little more emphatic when he said slowly:

"You know, Inspector, I think I am beginning to dislike the trend of your questioning. What on earth can my horse riding have to do with these dreadful murders? I am a minister of the Church. I am well known and respected."

"Of that I haven't the slightest doubt, Padre," Bony assured him. "But just visualize my difficulties. We investigating officers have to put into position many pieces of a puzzle. It is quite often that persons who haven't the remotest connection with the crime being investigated sometimes are able to show the officer where a particular piece of the puzzle belongs. I remember . . . but no matter."

Mr. James relaxed. Bony lit another cigarette. What he had remembered was the rebuke he had received when he had thought to smoke on the parsonage veranda. With seeming inadvertence, the smoke of this cigarette travelled to and about Mr. James's head.

"You were out riding on December fifth, that day the body of the hanged man was found," he proceeded. "Did you happen to come across anything unusual that day?"

"No. I cannot say that I did."

"You remember now where you rode that day?"

"Er—yes. I remember now. It was over the Walls of China and beyond them."

The pale blue eyes failed to hide the gleam of annoyance at having slipped into this little trap. Calmly, even conversationally, Bony went on:

"You tell me that you ride a horse only at a walking pace because of your weak heart, Padre," he said. "What caused you to ride your horse so furiously on the morning of December fifth that you winded it? Shall be obliged if you will kindly inform me of the reason for endangering your weak heart."

The Rev. James stood up. The large and flaccid face began to work with barely controlled anger.

"I shall not oblige you," he almost shouted. "I find your questions impertinent and your attitude insulting. I resent your probings into my private affairs."

"Now, now!" murmured Bony. "Don't let us cross swords. I

am sure you will forgive me when I recall to your mind that my work is to locate a criminal. I am equally sure that, as a minister, you would be only too ready to assist me. Pray sit down."

"I shall not. I am going to leave at once."

Mr. James turned towards the door, saw Sergeant Marshall, and exclaimed:

"Ah! I call on you, Sergeant Marshall, to bear witness to what this extraordinary person has been saying to me."

"That's all right, sir," responded Marshall cheerfully. "I've been taking it all down in writing."

"You have what? Oh!"

"By the way," interrupted the suave Bony. "What is the title of the latest novel you are reading?"

Mr. James swung about and glared at the questioner. Conversationally Bony continued:

"I hope you enjoyed the one entitled *A Flirt in Florence*. I have been informed that it is quite a juicy romance and was once a best seller. Haven't read it myself, because I am always so busy on cleaner murder mysteries. Do you think the members of your congregation would admire your taste in literature? Won't you sit down again?"

"I read that book for a purpose, for the purpose of being able to preach a sermon on the salacious muck being imported into this country," asserted Mr. James, who punctuated his vowels by vigorous thumping of the floor with his stick.

"Indeed! Oh, that explains a lot," commented Bony, adding: "Still you will admit that very many lewd minds would not accept that explanation. Do sit down."

Mr. James sat down, and Bony went on remorselessly:

"You were riding eastward of the Walls of China on the morning of December fifth. What time did you leave town?"

"Oh, I should say it was about ten o'clock," replied Mr. James resignedly.

"You winded your horse by hard galloping and were met by Miss Leylan a little after one o'clock. Where did you obtain the piece of hessian sacking with which you wiped down the animal?"

"I picked it up. It was lying near where I dismounted."

"Indeed!"

"I tell you that I picked it up. Anything more before I go?"

"Oh yes. Where did you ride to last night?"

"Last night?" echoed Mr. James. "I wasn't out last night. My wife can vouch for that."

"What time did you go to bed?"

"About eleven-thirty. We attended Lawton-Stanley's meeting."

"Do you and your wife occupy the same room?"

"This, sir, is becoming outrageous," snorted the minister.

"But, my dear Padre," Bony murmured soothingly. "Recall. You state that your wife can vouch for you that you were not out last night, and I am given to understand that you do not occupy the same room. My question was to verify that. As you do not occupy the same room, how can your wife vouch for the truth of your statement? How could she know whether or not you left the house after both of you had retired for the night?"

"If you think——"

"I don't think what you think I am thinking, Padre."

"Stop the padre-ing for goodness' sake," shouted Mr. James.

"Certainly. Merely a habit of mine," Bony said calmly. "Let me tell you a little of what I know. I know that your horse was taken from Mr. Fanning's yard very late last night and was brought back shortly before day broke this morning."

The light blue eyes were a little less indignant.

"Someone else must have taken him out. I didn't," asserted Mr. James.

"Then do you let it out? Or lend it out?"

"Let it out! Lend it out!"

"Yes. Do you hire it out to anyone? Or do you lend it to anyone?"

"No, of course not. If my horse was out of its stable last night it was taken without my permission."

"Ah!" Bony almost whispered. Then he smiled in quite friendly fashion. "Yes, that'll be it. Someone must have borrowed the horse. You will have to buy a chain and padlock and secure the yard gate. Why do you pose as a man having a weak heart?"

"I don't pose. I have had a weak heart from an early age."

"Have you sought medical advice?"

"No. I am not a wealthy man. The living here is very poor."

Bony placed the tips of his fingers against the point of his chin.

"You know, Mr. James, all men walk differently," he said. "I have made a lifelong study of tracks left on the ground by human beings. One day I am going to write a treatise on the subject. Long study has proved to me quite clearly that in addition to men walking differently, sick men always walk differently from healthy men. A sick man always places his feet evenly on the ground, for subconsciously he hasn't that confidence in his own strength that the healthy man has. It is possible, of course, to read character from the palm of the hands, but it is very much easier to read character from the footprints left on the ground. You have not a weak heart, Mr. James. There is nothing weak about you. Try more exercise, especially before breakfast. I suggest ten minutes with the gloves with Lawton-Stanley. Good afternoon. I may ask you to call again. Meanwhile please do try to remember to whom you lent your horse last night."

Bony rose to his feet and escorted the minister to the outer door. Sergeant Marshall heard him say in stuttering anger:

"I shall make a very strong written protest to the chief commissioner. Your attitude is absolutely astonishing."

Then Marshall heard Bony's suave counter:

"Do, Mr. James. Allow me to assure you that my commissioner really and truly likes to receive protests about me. It provides him with the golden chance of saying just what he thinks about me. *Good* afternoon."

On re-entering the office, Bony was met by a Sergeant Marshall gone off his head. The sergeant's huge arms were wrapped about his slight body and Bony was danced around whilst the sergeant's gruff voice repeated and repeated:

"You beaut! You little beaut!"

XXIV. The Sting Ray

ON REACHING MERINO shortly after four o'clock, the two constables sent by district headquarters were given a late lunch by Mrs. Marshall, who had relinquished her nursing duties to the trained Mrs. Sutherland. At five o'clock they reported to Sergeant Marshall, who was alone in the station office.

"The wife fix you up all right?" he enquired in his official manner. On being assured that "the wife" had certainly done that, he sent one of them to relieve Gleeson at Dr. Scott's home. When Gleeson returned he asked:

"Seen anything of the inspector?"

"Yes, Sergeant. He's been with the doctor for an hour. Then he went over to the parsonage, and after he left there he came up the street and went into Fanning's shop."

"Hum! Seems to be busy. You go out and ask the wife for a cup of tea. May want you to stay on duty. Hear how Florence was when you left?"

"Still unconscious."

Marshall sighed, and Gleeson turned about in his stiff military manner and departed. The second constable from headquarters was seated at Gleeson's desk reading a newspaper, and to him the sergeant said:

"At any time now Inspector Bonaparte will come in. I'm telling you because to look at him you wouldn't think he was an inspector. I didn't when I first saw him. He's middle-aged and of medium build—a half-caste but not the kind we see knocking about the bush. You'll know that when he looks at you."

"All right, Sergeant."

Marshall returned to the work of compiling a report. The constable returned to his newspaper. Through the open window came the familiar sounds of this bush township towards evening, the sounds of lethargic human activity beneath the piping of birds and the drowsy humming of nearer blowflies. The wind had gone down and was coming coolly from the south. In his secret heart Marshall was wishing for the old-time conditions of normal life when there were no worries additional to maintaining local order and being scrupulously careful with reports. How *could* he concentrate on this one?

Gleeson came back and sat bolt upright in the chair opposite him. He sat as though he were having his photograph taken. The sergeant glanced up at him, then back at his writing. But some now writing was impossible. He liked Gleeson. Men cannot work together in harness for years without getting to know each other.

A bit of a crank on efficiency and abiding by rules and regulations, but a sound man at heart. A good one, too, to have with one in a brawl.

A footstep sounded on the front porch. Marshall wanted to say "Thank heaven" or something like that. Gleeson stood up and crossed to the other constable, who also stood up to attention when Bony came in.

"Ah! Here we are, Sergeant," he said briskly, adding: "Hope you haven't been thinking I got bushed or actually had eloped with Mrs. Sutherland. Thank you."

He seated himself in the chair vacated by Marshall.

"Have been wondering where you had got to, sir," Marshall told him without smiling.

"I've been doing a little visiting, Sergeant. Interviewed the parson and paid my respects to his wife. Had a chat with Mr Fanning and went into a huddle with Dr. Scott. And now, think, we are all set."

"Meaning, sir?" asked Marshall, his eyes abruptly big.

Bony smiled, and Marshall was never to forget his face in that moment. In the dark blue eyes lurked that expression he had seen when, on the threshold of his daughter's room, he was told to go and dress. In the smile he saw the triumph of the aborigine about to throw his spear at the kangaroo he has been stalking for hour

"Constable Gleeson!" he said sharply.

"Sir!" replied Gleeson, and strode to the desk, where he stood like a child's toy soldier.

"I want you to go along and ask the elder Jason to step in here for a moment."

"Very well, sir."

"Er—you will see to it that he arrives."

"Very well, sir."

Gleeson turned about.

"Oh! Gleeson!"

"Yes sir!" Gleeson turned back and faced the man sitting in the place so familiarly occupied by Marshall.

"It might be as well to take a gun," Bony advised, and the a was sucked between Marshall's teeth with a soft hiss.

"Very well, sir."

Bony, the sergeant, and the constable watched Gleeson stri

over to the big safe, in the lock of which was the key. They watched him swing open the door and take from the interior a heavy revolver in its leather holster attached to a black leather belt. They watched Gleeson buckle the belt round his hard, slim waist, saw him take up his hat, and watched him leave the room. They heard the sharp but light step of this mounted constable in the passage without, and then on the porch. After that, in the comparative silence, they listened. Then Bony spoke, softly:

"I think we can leave that little duty safely to Constable Gleeson," he said. "However, you, Constable, go to the front gate to be on hand if Gleeson whistles for assistance, or if there is any shooting."

The constable left at the double. Marshall came nearer the seated Bony.

"Is Jason the man?"

"Jason is the man," replied Bony. "Providence did drop several important clues into my waiting hand, but today I have really exerted myself. When we have lodged Jason in safe custody we are going to open a bottle of beer—perhaps two bottles."

"When did——"

"No more just now. I'll talk it all over with your tame justice and deputy coroner when he arrives. Give me ten days in the jug, would he?" And Bony flashed his normal, sunny smile. That passed away before another mood, and he said: "The law is a terrible thing, Marshall. Think now! We have just given an order to a constable to gather into the law's grip one little human being. From now onward police and legal officers will be preparing to fight to uphold the law of the country, and others will be preparing to defend the man from the law's grip. And so the fight will go on and on over one human being who has been caught in the cogs of a machine. You and I are merely the teeth in one of the cogs of a machine which is greater than all the generations of man who have constructed it. And the man caught in the machine is no longer a man: he is merely a piece of living clay, to be fought over and disposed of as other men will."

"Are you going to charge him now?" enquired Marshall.

"Yes. Ah . . . here they come. Keep an eye on him. He might hurt something."

A short procession entered the office. It was led by the constable from divisional headquarters. After him came Mr. Jason, followed by Gleeson.

"Good evening, Mr. Jason. Come and sit down," Bony said pleasantly, and the tall, lean, and not undistinguished man advanced and sat down in the chair opposite Bony. Gleeson came forward, too, to stand immediately behind the funeral director. The other constable stood near the door.

Jason had discarded his working overalls and was wearing an old brown lounge suit. Bony was reminded of when this man sat on the seat of justice rather than when he leaned against a bar counter and exhaled tobacco smoke for long duration. Mr. Jason turned in his chair to look at Gleeson, the constable at the door, at Marshall, who sat at the end of the table desk and thus was able to guard the window. In his full and rich voice he asked:

"What is the meaning of all this?"

The long thin nose was the only feature that held colour. Against the white cheeks and chin the full moustache lay like a black mark. The dark eyes were big beneath the raised brows.

"I may be wrong, Mr. Jason, but I think it was a gentleman named Sam Weller who used to say: 'Cut the cackle and get to the hosses,'" Bony replied. "Sound advice. I am going to charge you with the wilful murder of George Kendall on the night o October eleventh."

"You astonish me," said Mr. Jason calmly. "I presume that yo have good and sufficient reasons for such action. I would like t hear them."

"Yes, Jason, I will outline them to you, although it is not m practice so to do," Bony assented. "You are a man of above ave age intelligence, and also one with me in appreciation of the dra matic. Gleeson, will you please search Mr. Jason."

"Stand up! Hands above your head!" snapped Gleeson. M Jason obeyed. The constable by the door came swiftly forward stand behind Mr. Jason. With the artistry of a conjuror Gleeso produced a wallet from an inside pocket, pipe and tobacco ar knife from a side pocket, and an automatic pistol which seeme to come from a hip pocket. The weapon was deftly passed to th constable behind Mr. Jason, and the other articles were placed the table before Bony. Jason was then ordered to sit down. remained unruffled and calm.

"The pistol is not registered," he said. "A technical fault."

"To one having your knowledge of the law, Jason, you will agree that it is not inconsequential . . . now," Bony told him. He pushed across the desk the tobacco, pipe, and clasp knife, and added his own box of matches. Gleeson frowned heavily. Bony continued: "You might like to smoke, as my recital of facts will occupy a little time."

"I thank you."

A silence fell within the office as Jason carved chips from the tobacco plug. When he had cut sufficient from it he laid down the knife and, whilst he was shredding the chips in the palms of his hands, Gleeson's hard hand slid by him and picked up the knife. That action made Jason smile, coldly. He filled his pipe, made sure that the little nicotine-catching cup at the bottom of the bowl was secure, and laid a lighted match against the tobacco.

As he was known to do in the hotel, so now did he draw and draw vigorously, inhale and inhale, until it seemed impossible that he could breathe. Twice Bony had observed him doing that locally famous act, and on each of those occasions Jason had been very angry. Jason was angry now, but he did not show it. The pipe held in his right hand, his hands came to rest upon the desk. He regarded Bony with his face void of expression.

"Well now, to make a beginning," Bony said. "You were born and educated at Bathurst, and there you served your apprenticeship to your father, who was an undertaker and wheelwright. Your only brother eventually set up in business as a chemist in Sydney.

"You became well known, first in Bathurst and subsequently in Sydney, as an actor, and the reason why you did not take up acting as a profession was because of your father's dislike of the stage. When he died the theatre was almost submerged by the moving pictures, and you, having inherited his business, carried on the business until you failed. Your wife then being dead, you came with your son to set up in business here in Merino.

"Here in Merino, cut off from all association with the stage and with people having literary tastes, you began to brood upon the ill fortune which had overtaken you. When you were insulted in the hotel by Kendall about your passion for acting, I discarded that as a motive for killing him. It was, however, contributory to the motive, which has been the most baffling feature in this case."

The tobacco smoke which Jason had inhaled was now beginning to trickle through his pursed lips. His face was still devoid of expression, and his hands resting upon the desk were perfectly immobile.

"The motive should be interesting, if not original," he said. "Please proceed."

He passed the matches to Bony when that lover of the drama took a cigarette from the little pile he had made whilst waiting for Gleeson to return with his prisoner. Bony lit a cigarette and noted the thin stream of smoke continuing to issue from Mr. Jason's lips. Then he went on:

"You see, Jason, there is a case on record similar to your own, and this previous case is noted in a volume on medical jurisprudence in Dr. Scott's library. In 1843 in England an inquisition was held on a young man who had a strong propensity for watching windmills—you know, the old-fashioned windmills having large latticework sails for arms. He wished to be tied to one of the arms and so go round and round and round. He would actually sit for days watching a windmill.

"You became a windmill watcher through first staring at the cooling fan of motor engines in your garage. It became an obsession with you, and your son discovered it and did what he could to wean you from a practice which would have ugly results to yourself. I myself once heard him shout at you to get away from the engine I saw you watching.

"Within a radius of three miles of Merino there are three modern windmills. They are: the one at the town dam, the one at the homestead of Mrs. Sutherland, and the third at Sandy Flat. You could not watch any one of those mills during daylight hours, firstly because your son would stop you, and secondly because you knew that others would be bound to observe you. But you could watch a mill in action on a moonlit night.

"The town dam mill was barred to you because an employee of the Shire Council lives in a hut there, and, moreover, this man in the habit of returning to his hut at all hours of the night from Merino.

"The best mill of the three for your purpose was at Sandy Flat. There a station employee rarely lived. And so you often visited

Sandy Flat and released the mill, then climbed to the tank stand to be as near as possible to the fan wheel so that you could watch it whirling round and round in the moonlight.

"Sandy Flat, however, is three miles away, and so you hit on the idea of riding there and back on a horse, a car or truck being out of the question by reason of its engine noise. You could not very well keep a horse yourself, because your son would get to know the purpose of it, and so you approached the Rev. Llewellyn James and you told him a story of romance.

"You told him that you wished to pay court to Mrs. Sutherland and that you feared the reaction this would have upon your son. You suggested to the reverend gentleman that he should have a horse to use in his parish work as a change from the somewhat old car provided by his parishioners. You offered to buy a good horse for him, and to pay the feed bills and the stabling charges provided that he would permit you to use the horse at night to pay secret court to Mrs. Sutherland. Mr. James demurred. He didn't like the idea of riding a horse as a car demanded less exertion. So you offered to pay him a pound a week honorarium if he would assist you in your ambitions of the heart. Mr. James accepted and finally grew to like horse riding.

"And so, Jason, you would leave home late at night, take the horse from Mr. Fanning's yard, having also taken Mr. Fanning into your confidence, and ride out to Sandy Flat, where you would release the mill regardless of whether the tank was full of water or not."

Mr. Jason listened with that stony calmness he had exhibited when on the bench.

"Watching windmills is not an illegal act, Jason, but one cannot approve, however, of your action in putting into the minds of two men the thought that Mrs. Sutherland was receiving secret court from you. That is of no concern to the police, but it most certainly should have been the concern of the Rev. Mr. James. The little scene between him and you at the graveside of the swagman put me slightly out of gear, as your son might well say.

"The employment by Mr. Leylan of a stockman at Sandy Flat stopped your visits to the mill there, and there was no other that you could visit with safety on moonlit nights. Kendall, the man employed at Sandy Flat, appeared to be satisfied with his home, and that urge in your mind to watch the revolving fans of a windmill became steadily stronger and stronger—until finally you decided that Kendall would have to be removed.

"It is, of course, impossible for me to follow the process of your planning to remove Kendall, but it is fairly certain that an objective of even greater importance than killing Kendall was to give the hut an evil reputation so that Kendall would have no successor. The killing would have to be done inside the hut, or in its vicinity, not here in Merino or elsewhere in the bush.

"Your greatest obstacle lay in the natural conditions at Sandy Flat. All about the place, outward from it for a mean distance of half a mile, the ground was covered with fine sand. There were no patches of wire grass, no claypans, over which you could pass without leaving tracks for even the police to see if the wind did not erase them. How to achieve that passing over such ground without leaving tracks? As Longfellow wrote, how 'Dance on the sands, and yet no footing seen'?"

Into the dark eyes gazing so steadily and so solemnly at Bony flashed an expression of pain, and for the first time Mr. Jason interrupted:

"It was not Longfellow who wrote that line, but Shakespeare," he said.

Bony bowed his head, saying:

"Thank you for correcting me, Jason. No doubt that line was in your mind when you planned to murder George Kendall. Anyway, you found that by wrapping strips of hessian about your feet your footmarks were made infinitely more difficult to discern.

"You may correct me again later on, but it appears that the time Kendall was killed was not quite of your own choosing. You knew that Kendall came to town on the evening of the social dance, and that he had booked in for the night at the hotel. Here was an opportunity for windmill gazing. Late that evening you rode from Merino on the horse presumably belonging to Mr. James. You tethered the horse well back in the scrub and walked in your hessian-covered feet to the mill, and when your passion had been satiated you walked back to your horse.

"You may correct me on this point, too, later. When you got back to your horse you found Kendall quietly waiting for the horse's rider, quite probably thinking that the rider of that tethered horse was engaged in a spot of sheep stealing. You were discovered.

"The wind was blowing strongly enough to wipe out the faint imprints made by your hessian-covered feet, and you knew that a windy night was essential. And so you killed Kendall with a billet of scrub wood, and you carried his body to the hut.

"Then you discovered that the body had bled during its journey on your back, and, properly to stage the killing inside the hut, you killed one of the ration sheep in the near-by pen, drained its blood into a basin, and then spattered the sheep's blood over the floor about the dead man's head."

Mr. Jason's hands moved slightly after a period of passivity.

"In such a case as you present, Inspector, I would not impose a fine of five shillings," he said. "It is based entirely on assumption prompted by imagination."

Bony's brows rose a fraction, and he said, with no trace of triumph or exultation in his voice:

"Indeed, it is not so, Jason. You were seen to carry the body into the hut. You were seen to kill the ration sheep and drain its blood into a basin which you took into the hut. You were seen to skin and dress the sheep's carcass and to hang it in the meat safe so that the police would assume the killing of the sheep had been done by Kendall before he left for Merino."

Mr. Jason leaned forward over the desk and stared at Bony.

"Who saw me?" he demanded, and over the face of Constable Gleeson spread a mirthless grin.

"Why, the man you strangled with a strip of hessian," Bony replied with feigned astonishment that such a question should be asked. "Unfortunately for you, that man was a genuine sundowner, not an ordinary stockman looking for work. Put yourself in his place. From some point of concealment, probably on the far side of the meat house, he saw you coming with Kendall slung over your shoulder. He watched you go to the pen and kill the sheep and bring back its blood in a basin. He saw you enter the hut with the basin of blood, saw you come out again, saw you go back to the pen, and then saw you come to the meat house carrying the skinned carcass of the sheep. He noted the hessian covering about your feet. It was quite simple for him to put two and two together.

"After you had gone, did he walk to Merino and report the matter to the police? No. Did he travel to a station homestead and report there? Of course not. That class of men hate the police and would not be drawn into a murder case on any account. He argued thus, however. He argued that it might be many days before the body was discovered, and during that period one of his own class might happen along and blunder into the scene of the murder. And so, in loyalty to his own class, he drew on the door of the hut a warning to keep away."

Bony paused for Mr. Jason to comment, and when Jason remained silent he said:

"That sundowner didn't hate the practice of blackmail like he hated the police. He wrote to you and arranged that you hand him money or place money for him to obtain, perhaps, underneath the hut. You forestalled him by reaching the hut before he did, carefully wiping out your own faint tracks with a flail, and when he entered the hut you—but you know all that happened, for it was related to you when you held the inquest. Matches? Certainly. The pistol which the constable has just removed from your person you obtained from the body of the man you strangled and then hanged."

"How do you know that?" Jason asked, and exhaled the last of the smoke.

"The sundowner was known to have an automatic pistol in his possession when he was at Ned's Swamp Station homestead," Bony lied. "Tell me, why did you visit old Bennett the night he died?"

Jason smiled that cold and humourless smile. His voice lost none of its richness when he said:

"As you seem possessed of such imagination, albeit uncontrolled, why not try to guess?"

"Very well, I will," Bony agreed. "Old Bennett had learned from his daughter or his son-in-law that you had an arrangement with them and Mr. James to take the minister's horse at night to visit Mrs. Sutherland. Old Bennett chided you about it in the hotel, and you decided to—er—bump him off."

Jason placed the stem of his pipe between his white teeth and slowly nodded his head, saying:

"You are even good at guessing, Inspector. Is there anything else?"

"Having killed the swagman, why did you hang the body?" Bony asked.

"I did it to make it appear that Way hanged himself in remorse for having murdered Kendall. That would have cleaned up the Kendall case and stopped men from living in that hut for a long time to come. Again, anything else?"

Mr. Jason might well have been terminating an interview.

"Yes. You might tell me why you wanted to kill Rose Marie."

"I did not want to kill the child," replied Mr. Jason. "I didn't want to kill old Bennett. But I saw clearly that I would have to. Old Bennett dropped dead when he saw me outside the door, and so saved me the trouble. I overheard Rose Marie tell you beyond my garden fence that she had promised my son not to tell of something she had found out about me watching windmills. I couldn't trust to a child's promise, and so I decided I would have to kill her."

Mr. Jason lit his pipe and gravely handed the matches back to Bony. No longer was his face expressionless. There was a faint colour in his cheeks, and his eyes became quick in movement.

"As it has all turned out," he said, "I am glad that I did not kill the child as I intended, and I hope she will recover. If I had had a daughter like her . . . but no matter. You see in me, Inspector, a man whom life has thwarted. My father thwarted my ambition to become a great Shakespearean actor. My wife was an ambitionless creature, and she thwarted my desire for a son who might have become what I wanted to be. She bore . . . you know. And then when I came to see glorious visions in revolving fans my son attempted to thwart me there."

"What did you see in the windmill vanes?" interjected Bony.

Jason's face actually glowed. His eyes became glittering orbs. The cold pipe became clenched in his two hands. And as though he were facing the footlights, he said:

"It was like looking through a doorframe beyond which was a scene of wondrous delight. I used to step through the doorframe, and I would find myself being interviewed by newspapermen, or gazing at great and colourful signs announcing that the Great Jason was to play Hamlet or Othello. All the visions I had had in the past came to reality when I stepped into the windmill vanes. I lived as I had always dreamed of living. I didn't really live at other times. And I shall never again enter the spinning, shimmering vanes . . . no, never again . . . for the grave awaits . . . for me . . . even for you."

"Where did you obtain the chloroform?" asked Bony.

"From my brother in Sydney," was the answer spoken under the stress of emotion which was swiftly mounting in intensity. Into the dark eyes swept remorse, and when Jason spoke again the rich intonation was absent. "I ought not to have said that. I got it when I was down in Melbourne some time back."

"And the strychnine with which you poisoned your son's dog?"

"Oh, that! One can buy pounds of it in any store, and cyanide, too. The sale of such poisons should have been stopped years ago. I wrote to the Premier about it, but no notice was taken." Once more the eyes of Mr. Jason burned, and he went on: "I have done a little good in my life . . . not much. I could have done far more had not life thwarted me. And now . . . the end."

Mr. Jason slowly rose to his feet, and Gleeson's hands rose in readiness and Gleeson's eyes bored into the back of the prisoner's head. Mr. Jason came to stand at his full height. The pipe was held in his two hands. He stared above the seated Bony and Marshall, stared out through the window. His voice was deep and clear when he cried:

" 'Though death be poor, it ends a mortal woe.' . . . 'He that dies pays all debts.' . . . 'Death is a black camel which kneels at the gates for all.' "

The fingers of the right hand, which had been placed upon the bowl of the pipe, flashed to his mouth. In them was the little cup which collected the nicotine at the bottom of the bowl.

Gleeson was too late. His arms swept about Jason's body, imprisoning the man's right arm and the hand which had conveyed the cup to his mouth. Jason spat out the cup, which fell upon the desk.

" 'The tongues of dying men enforce attention like deep harmony,' " he quoted. "I am no gallows meat, nor will I rot among a community of lunatics. I . . ."

His dark eyes blazed like black opals. His back became arched against Gleeson's chest. And then, like a lamp going out, the warmth faded from his eyes, and Gleeson laid down the body.

XXV. Bony Concludes His Investigation

BONY RANG for Dr. Scott.

He had not risen from his seat, and he toyed with the telephone whilst the doctor was being called. Sergeant Marshall was standing looking down at the two constables who were kneeling beside the late Mr. Jason, J. P., Deputy District Coroner. When Bony heard Scott's voice he asked the doctor to come immediately, and when he had replaced the instrument he said:

"How many are thwarted by life? All of us would be were we not strong enough to fight it." He sighed, and then said: "Well, well!"

Gleeson stood up. His face was impassive, but his eyes blazed.

"I'm sorry, sir, for being too late to grab him."

"Seeing that you were standing behind him, Gleeson, I think you did very well," Bony told him. "We had the pistol. We had the tobacco knife. No one of us could have known that he would secrete poison in the nicotine cup of his old pipe. If anyone is to blame it is I, for allowing him to smoke when being examined."

No one spoke till the doctor came tearing in. The little man's gaze swept over them, then down to the body on the floor. As the constable had done, he fell upon his knees, was there for a few seconds, then rose to his feet.

"Dead!" he snapped out. "Poisoned. What's it all about?"

"Sit down, Doctor," Bony invited him, and, when Scott sat down in the chair recently occupied by Mr. Jason: "Jason is the man I have been after. I allowed him to smoke his pipe while I was interrogating him. Here you will see a tiny metal cup which is screwed to the bottom of the bowl to catch the nicotine drained from the bowl. It is evident that the dead man suspected that his time was short; for, you see, he stopped up the small hole in the bowl of the pipe and filled the cup with powdered cyanide."

The doctor accepted the little cup from Bony, looked into it. It had been cleaned and dried thoroughly, and, although it had been in Jason's mouth, the interior was still dry and still contained a little of the poison.

"Quite a natty idea," Scott said. "Would hold more than sufficient cyanide to kill a dozen men. Jason had quite a collection of pipes. Saw it when I was attending him some time ago. This, and another he had, were small replicas of the big German affairs. And so he did all the murders, eh? And you had him nailed?"

"Yes, we had got him all tied up," Bony admitted.

"There's no 'we' about it, Doctor," Marshall cut in. "Mr. Bonaparte did the job well and truly."

Scott stood up.

"Well, I can do nothing here," he said cheerfully. "Hope you'll drop in before you go and tell me the story, Inspector. Your girl's going along nicely, Marshall. Came to half an hour ago. She's sleeping now, nice and cool and natural. No, no! I will permit no visitors till tomorrow. 'Bye!"

He left as he entered.

The constable on duty at Dr. Scott's house was brought back to the station. Mrs. Marshall gave him and the second constable dinner, and afterwards they brought the headquarters car to the back door. The body of Mr. Jason was carried through the house and placed in the car, which was driven out of Merino by the two constables. When Marshall and Bony sat down to dinner the day had passed.

"I do wish the doctor would let me see Rose Marie," Mrs. Marshall said wistfully.

"Well, he said you couldn't," growled her husband.

"Perhaps he might if I asked him," Bony added. "I would ask him if you promise not to stay long . . . both of you."

"There you go—always backing her up," complained the sergeant.

"Well, wouldn't you like to see Rose Marie?"

"Of course. But the doctor said no, and he meant it by the way he said it."

"When people say no, I always get the itch to make them say yes," Bony told him, looking him straight in the eyes. "I exert myself especially when my wife says no, and most especially when

216

my chief commissioner says no. And no man in all the world says no more emphatically than does Colonel Spendor."

It was nine o'clock when Bony rang Dr. Scott.

"How is Rose Marie?" he asked.

"Still sleeping beautifully."

"Good! Marshall and his wife would like to take a peep at her before they retire for the night."

"No. Won't have it."

"They promise just to creep in and look at her. They won't——"

"Damn it, Inspector, didn't I say no?"

"Yes, something like that," Bony agreed. "But what about cutting out the 'Inspector' and calling me Bony? All my pals do."

"Well, I've no objection. What about coming along and telling me the story? I'm all on fire to hear it."

"No. Won't have it," Bony shouted. "I'm leaving tomorrow too."

"Well, you said you would," argued Scott.

"No. Won't have it," repeated Bony.

"Oh, all right! You win. Tell the Marshalls to come along within half an hour. You come with 'em and give the yarn about old Jason."

"That's better," Bony murmured. "I will see you tomorrow morning without fail. Got work still to do. Good night!"

"Will he let us?" asked Mrs. Marshall from the doorway.

"Of course he will. You can both go right along."

Mrs. Marshall's eyes grew misty.

"Thanks, Bony. You're a terrible good sort," she told him.

After they had left he wrote a note to Sergeant Marshall which he left on the blotter. A minute later he was knocking on the door of Jason's house.

"Oh, it's you, is it?" snarled young Jason. "What d'you want now?"

"Just to talk to you. I've news of Rose Marie."

"Oh! Good news? Come in."

Bony was conducted along the passage to the living room. It was large and well windowed and cool. To the right of the fireplace dozens of pipes were suspended from nails driven into the wall.

217

"Well! What's the news?" young Jason demanded.

"Can I sit down?"

"Yes."

"In the first place, Tom, I have something to tell you about your father."

"I know all about that," snarled the young man, his eyes directed fiercely to his visitor. "I got it all out of him, every bit of it. I—I wanted to kill him . . . but he's my old man, after all. I've known he was going balmy . . . and he is balmy, too. I told him that the game was up. I knew from what you said, and from you telling me about my dog being poisoned, that he had done the murders and why. But they won't hang him, will they? He's as ratty as a stirred-up snake—looking at windmills and motor fans and things."

"Had he been like that long?"

"It was over two years back when I tumbled. But what about Rose Marie?"

"Just a minute. Your father admitted many things when he found that the case against him was fairly complete. At the end he took poison."

Bony gently related what had happened. Young Jason's pathetic face lost its antagonism. He sniffed several times, and without looking at Bony he said:

"I'm glad he beat you policemen. He was a decent old stick at heart. Cranky on acting, of course. Then he had me, and I'm nothing out of the box. Funny . . . I'll be planting him with the old hearse he was so proud of."

Bony spoke softly:

"I didn't think you would like that, so I had him taken by the constables to divisional headquarters. He won't be buried here at Merino. And now for Rose Marie. She has regained consciousness and the doctor gave her a sleeping draught. She will wake to-morrow in her right mind, and time only will be necessary to bring her back to health and strength."

The young man's eyes gleamed.

"Honest!" he said.

Bony nodded.

"I'd like to see her, but they won't let me," asserted the young man, the snarl coming back into his voice.

"Not tonight they won't," Bony said decisively. "But tomorrow in the morning they will. If you like to, you may go with me, because I want to see the child before I leave Merino."

"You'll take me, honest?"

Bony nodded, then he rose to his feet and went round the table to sit upon its edge and to regard the misshapen face with his kindly eyes. He said:

"I am going to ask you to do me a favour. It is growing late, and my swag and things are down at Sandy Flat. Would you put me up for the night? Anywhere would do, you know. And I'd like a feed too."

Young Jason actually smiled.

"Too right, you can stay," he told Bony. "I'm a bit fed up tonight, what with one thing and another. And the place will be sort of empty with the old man not hanging around. I could cook you some bacon and eggs, and make a pot of coffee."

There was eagerness in his voice. Bony rubbed his hands and smiled too.

"That'll do me," he said. "Let's get to it. I'm hungry . . . and very tired."

In answer to a telephone call the following morning at noon young Jason closed the garage, scrubbed his hands, arms, and face, brushed his hair, ignored his grease-covered cap, and hurried to meet Bony, waiting for him at the police station gate. Five minutes later Dr. Scott was leaning over a bed and saying to Rose Marie:

"There are two visitors to see you. Do you think we might let them in?"

The dark grey eyes in the pale, oval face widened a fraction.

"Are they my Thomas and Edith?"

"No. Would you like to guess?" asked the little doctor.

"I don't know. It can't be Mummy and Daddy. I don't know." The voice was so tired and the eyes were not the eyes of the Rose Marie who had peeped through the door grating into Bony's cell. The doctor persisted.

"Well, I am going to tell you. One of them is Bony. And the other—why, the other is young Mr. Jason."

"Oh! Yes, I remember Bony."

"Of course you do," Dr. Scott assured her. "Now you can only see them one at a time. Who will you see first? Bony?"

"Yes."

The doctor's face withdrew into a wall, and the dark, smiling face of the man she had first seen in the lockup cell emerged from the vague background and became distinct. She essayed a weak smile.

"Well now, Rose Marie, you seem to be getting better already," the remembered voice was saying. "I am glad that you are well enough to see me because I have to go back to Sydney, and I wanted to tell you that I will be writing a letter to you soon."

"Will you be away for long, Bony?"

"Yes, perhaps for a long time. And you—why, you are going to get well quickly and go back to school. Will you promise always to remember me?"

Rose Marie nodded.

"Promise with your fingers crossed," he urged gently. And when she had crossed her fingers in the proper manner, and he had done the same, they both promised they would remember each other always.

"Never break a promise, Rose Marie," he whispered. "Always keep a promise no matter what happens, won't you?"

Again she nodded, and he saw that she was struggling to remember something.

"Don't worry your head about anything now," he urged her. "Later on will do, when you write to me after you receive my letter."

She persisted. Then she smiled, saying:

"I know. I heard young Mr. Jason tell the garage cat that you were a funny kind of man, like him, looked down on by everyone. But I don't look down on you, Bony. I love you . . . like young Mr. Jason."

"Oh, I forgot, Rose Marie. Young Mr. Jason is waiting to see you. Shall I tell him? Yes? Very well! Good-bye, and thank you for giving me the afternoon tea in the lockup with your beautiful tea set with the blue stripes round the edge."

She smiled at him, wonderfully, when he drew back and motioned young Jason forward. At the door he turned to see the young man on his knees beside the bed, on which he had laid the very large dolls, Thomas and Edith, brought from the station by Bony.

Out in the hall Bony shook hands with Mrs. Sutherland and Dr. Scott. On the veranda he shook hands with the Rev. Lawton-Stanley and Edith Leylan. On the sidewalk he shook hands with Mrs. James and asked after her husband. Mrs. James told him that the Rev. Llewellyn James was not at all well, that he had a violent headache following all the excitement of the preceding day. She herself was quite well, and she thanked him again for cutting the wood for her.

Straight as a ramrod, Constable Gleeson stood beside Marshall's car, in which the sergeant sat waiting at the wheel.

"Good-bye, Gleeson," Bony said, offering his hand. "I shall not forget you in my report. All the best."

"All the best to you too, sir," replied Gleeson.

"Thank you. And don't you ever forget that I am Bony to my friends."

Bony got in beside Marshall, who was to drive him to the railway at Ivanhoe. He had made his adieu to Mrs. Marshall, and now saw her hurrying toward them from the police station. Arriving a little breathlessly, she passed into his hands a box, saying in a whisper:

"Just a little snack for the road."

Like his namesake, he smiled at her and pinched her cheek. And then the car was moving down the street. Many of the people on the sidewalks waved to him. The car slid off the macadamized roadway onto the natural earth. Ahead of them lay the mighty Walls of China, grandly impervious to the schemes and the hopes, the hates and the loves of little human beings.

"There are some women who are utterly hopeless," remarked Bony.

"Referring to . . . ?" enquired Marshall.

"Mrs. Llewellyn James."

8:52
9:08

1 2 9
1 1 5
‾‾‾‾‾
1 · 4

10:52
10:48

1 4 8
1 3 7
‾‾‾‾‾
1 2

Drill — Mag 2
        561.2   649.9

Black   649.9